Nothing Beside Remains

Nothing Beside Remains

A. B. Dekkar

ISBN 978-0-557-09443-1

See how eagerly the lobsters and the turtles all advance!
They are waiting on the shingle – will you come and join the
dance?
  Will you, won't you, will you, won't you, will you join the
        dance?
  Will you, won't you, will you, won't you, won't you join the
        dance?
'You can really have no notion how delightful it will be,
When they take us up throw us, with the lobsters, out to see!'
But the snail replied 'Too far, too far!' and gave a look askance-
Said he thanked the whiting kindly, but he would not join the
dance.
  Would not, could not, would not, could not, would not join the
        dance.
  Would not, could not, would not, could not, could not join the
        dance.
'What matters it how far we go?' his scaly friend replied.
There is another shore, you know, upon the other side.
The further off from England the nearer is to France –
Then turn not pale, beloved snail, but come and join the dance.

~ Lewis Carroll

Contents

Part One 1

   I. Down the Rabbit Hole and the Pool of Tears................... 3

   II. Heaps of Men 13

   III. The Doctor 17

   IV. A Caucus-Race 23

Part Two 27

   V. The Usefulness of Things Learnt in School............................ 29

   VI. Wire Party.. 33

   VII. The World Exhales.. 37

   VIII. Let Me Tell You My History................................. 41

   IX. News 57

Part Three 63

   X. Jabberwocky 65

   XI. Advice from a Caterpillar 85

   XII. A Day at the Beach.. 99

   XIII. Gas 103

   XIV. The Memoirist 107

   XV. Wool and Water 113

   XVI. Walls and Lines 119

   XVII. Entertainment 125

Part Five..131

   XVIII. Friends...133

   XIX. Sappers...137

   XX. The Duchess's House.................................141

   XXI. Attics and Cellars.....................................147

   XXII. Lenora's Perspective on Things 161

Part Six...169

   XXIII. Mind the Gap 171

   XXIV. The Lioness...175

   XXV. Art and Insects...179

   XXVI. A Mad Tea Party....................................185

   XXVII. Schoolboy Soldiers................................193

   XXVIII. The Red Queen and the Final Party 199

   XXIX. Parrish and Lowe 205

   XXX. A Trial and Alex's Evidence.....................207

   XXXI. The King of Nothing................................213

   XXXII. The Potato Cellar...................................223

   XXXIII. Waking...229

   XXXIV. The King in Repose 233

   XXXV. The Return of the King or Which Dreamed It?............237

Part One

A boat, beneath a sunny sky

Lingering onward dreamily

In an evening of July –

I. Down the Rabbit Hole and the Pool of Tears

Finally, he tired of resting with Lenora in the warm grass as she read without enthusiasm stories he had selected for her. She was tired of seeing him here, at her feet, when so many others like him, young, able bodied men, had already gone. It was only a matter of time, they both knew, before he would be called up. Talk of conscription hung heavy in the air late in the spring of 1915, so that his reason and logic were polluted by fear of looking like a shirker. Events elsewhere seemed so dramatic and significant that it seemed inconceivable, at least in her view, for his life to go on in a common way.

He was not a coward, but he believed that if he were to voluntarily put his body in front of fast moving metal, he should feel more passionate about the reason. He was always the sober one, and his friends had relied on this and his maturity at a young age. But now the age was changed. The century was new, there was wholesale slaughter in the air, and appearances were everything.

So like the others, that is, without thinking, caught up in some tidal wave that at first transfixes with beauty then smashes and drowns with the indiscriminate force of nature, he drew his name on the line, won over by the curiosity that drove him to know what had happened to his friends, worn down by Lenora's concern that he was running out of time, and not giving a thought about how he would leave this new world once he entered it, as it is hard for even the most pessimistic of people to truly imagine their own deaths. Alex wasn't such a visionary, but he suspected such visionaries existed and that they saw doom for his generation if not for him personally.

In a flurry of activity, he was sucked away from the life he knew in Braintree, his home on Violet Street, his mother still mourning her war-dead husband, the job he had held since as a child he was forced to take on work to support his mother, the books he had turned to for support and company during the loneliest of times, his uncle who treated him like a son, and Lenora. She was the most complicated of the list, but she was the one he would say the least about at this time, as he didn't have full command of his feelings for her, did not understand her, and could not comprehend then how much she influenced the choices he made, which he preferred to believe were the result of rational thought and independence of will. And so if asked, Alex, why did you volunteer, if not guided by rationality and independent will? He would only withdraw and get angry at this because, I suspect, he knew that this act, this grandest of gestures, was the least like him of all the small gestures that when compiled made his life. This, this most consequential thing, which he rejected wholly, which he resisted with all his sense of self-preservation and all his suspicion that war was not as it was made to seem to those who must do the bloody work, this he agreed to with only minor objection and short-lived protest.

It angered him to betray himself so readily, to know that he had done so to satisfy Lenora. It bewildered him to know that everything that seemed constructed to make him feel safe and secure so that he could grow to lead a healthy, long life- his mother, his home, his friends, their parents, his schoolteachers, the church community, the community at large- seemed overnight to bend in unison toward a different end. It angered him to think that this end was meant to ensure their healthy, long life and the preservation of all they knew at the expense of his own. It was a curious feeling to think that he was the only one to feel this way about the war. But, apparently, it was so.

And so Alex went to the war already angry, bewildered, and perplexed at the situation. But that alone can't explain what happened to him there.

By 19, his life in a dull place had been extraordinary; he was about to enter a world that was extraordinary in every sense, but in which his experience would be quite average. He would do what millions of others did. Until then, he had been singular. His unusual circumstances required that he become used to playing the part of two different people, the child he was and the head of household he had been forced to become, and this plurality made him singular in the eyes of those who knew him. Now, when all the boys he had known disappeared in a blink to far off lands, he seemed to diminish in all those eyes until he hardly made one respectable person. When he joined the effort at last, his singularity would suffer another assault, as he would be swept up in the homogenizing wave that blended one into many.

He didn't know this yet, of course. He didn't know what to expect because the only things he knew of war were those he had learned from limited experience: that his father had not returned from it; and from lessons at school: that horses were involved, that war was the place where leaders were forged; that kings strode before their men; that, in war, legends were born. Yes, Alex was mature about many things but as a result of this extraordinary life mentioned earlier, he was quite childish about many things still.

If pushed on the matter, Alex would explain his behavior by saying things like: "It was inevitable." If pushed further, he would grow physically agitated and say, "Everyone had to do their part, whether they wanted to or not." I don't know why I pushed him. It was my job only to listen to him, to let him give voice to the things he'd seen and done. It was my job to determine if he were merely under a heavy strain or if he had been driven clinically insane. It was up to me to send him back to the war or leave him in peace. Perhaps I pushed him because I knew he would say, "Everyone had to do their part…it was inevitable;" I needed to hear him say this because I knew what I was about to decide in his case, and I wanted to be absolved of any personal guilt.

What I know of Alex I learned through nearly sixteen months of treatment and interviews at the convalescent hospital in Swansea, Wales. Some days he talked quite enthusiastically, so much so fast that I could not keep up in my notes and had to reread them and make corrections based on what I remembered him saying immediately after he had departed. Occasionally I would have to start anew, reconstructing entire interviews based on my memories of his words, vaguely aware that I should not use direct quotation marks when I couldn't possibly remember his words with precision. Though, rereading them now, I see that I used them often.

Eventually I talked to Lenora as well and even to his mother. Lenora would visit Alex several times a month, though sometimes he would not see her, and sometimes she did not really want to see him. She would see me instead, and sit where he sat, on the worn, brown leather chair across from my desk, in my cramped yellow office with no windows. She would talk to me because she could not talk to him, and sometimes she would write to me as well. She would include letters he had written to her. As an officer, he had been the censor of his unit, screening and shortening the messages his men sent home to wives, girlfriends, and children, a job he despised. His messages lacked the blacked out passages typical of other war correspondence. His were raw and short without outside influence. She shared them with me to absolve herself, too, I suspect. She wanted me to tell her that after considering all the evidence, there was certainly nothing she could have done differently. It was inevitable.

It strikes me as I write this that I call him always 'Alex'. I called the rest by their rank and last name, so he should have been Lt. Liddell to me, but he reminded me so much of my own son, that it was Alex from the first day to his last.

Alex described his entry into military life as a blur. There were no long goodbyes or wistful partings. He signed his name to the line and it was as if the pen he held became a weight that held him fast to the form, that the form expanded before him until it was an irregular rectangle five times its normal size, that his legs rose weightless into the air, and the large rectangle became a hole into which he plummeted, pulled by the weight of the pen and by the gravity of the situation. On the way down, his cotton clothes became wool, his longish, charcoal-dark hair grew short, and as he approached what he thought was the bottom, he could sense that he was receiving instruction of some kind, as many voices shouted things at him, objects- a pistol, grenades, a gas mask, a brown haversack- were thrust at him, and he grabbed them and held them close, afraid as he fell that he might drop a grenade and kill someone. He heard what sounded like men chanting, he remembered hearing loud counting, and words he only vaguely understood, like 'dropshort', 'accessory,' and 'brass hatter', sensed jabbing motions, and smelled shoe polish, until he landed feeling underprepared, overdressed, and confused in a communications trench in Belgium, not France as he expected, more than one year after the war had begun.

He thought that distance and the hectic nature of war would keep him altogether too engaged to trouble much about Lenora or anyone else he had left behind, but he was wrong. She dominated his thoughts from the start. In fact, he wrote this note to Lenora to describe the first moments: "Nothing could have prepared me for this. Stripped trees, verdant fields turned to mud, blighted and crumbling towns, skeletons of abandoned vehicles, hollowed eyes, stooped shoulders, lice, rats, stinking horse carcasses, ghastly wounds, rows of trenches like scars in the earth, shell craters transforming farmers' fields into lunar landscapes, the rank stench of mold, rot, and filth mixed with the cold freshness of morning. It is all real, but a reality so altered and foreign that to make sense of it, one has to believe it to be a surreality, as if I've entered a painting or a novel by some mad genius, or some mediocre talent so enraged by rejection that he is bent on destroying the world."

That was what he wrote to her. She enjoyed reading gothic romance, which he knew because most of their relationship was constructed around his recommendation of books to her and their brief discussions of the content, his desire that the themes expressed on the pages would express to her all which he could not. He was eager now to expose her to a new genre, and judging by the unrestrained nature of his further correspondence with her during the war, I can tell that he did not spare her any details or soften any blows, and I suspect that she despised and longed for this in equal measure, as it appears that, until the war, he rarely spoke to her from the heart and without constraint.

That first day upon arriving at the war, in the unit controlled by Colonel Flint and his Adjutant, Major Knight, Alex was pleased to find himself in Belgium, not France, and in a communications trench nearly one half of a mile from the front line trench. The pleasure was quick to dissipate when he realized that he would not be leaving this place for a barracks at the end of the day, that this trench looked nothing like the illustrations he had observed at school, and that these men filling it seemed to expect him to provide leadership when he felt he was the one most in need of guidance. The trench was not deep, requiring him to always bend at the knees to keep his shoulders and head from being exposed. This perpetual hunch made the creatures inhabiting the trench look like old men, hobbling and dirty, with sour breath and peculiar looks. Some observed him directly, with mixtures of humor and indifference; others only glanced in his general direction. He felt like a new exhibit at a zoo, a caged spectacle, or a shiny new piece of merchandise on display behind a store window as a significant portion of the men stared at him with hope, an expression that he found most disturbing. He could sense in their raised eyebrows and temporarily brightened visages the momentary belief that he was some divine messenger. That he would shout down the length of the trench: "Today's the day, mates! I've just got word from the Top Man himself. Your job is done here. You're free to go!"

The realization that this would not happen caused some to burst into tears, others to grumble loudly, and one to slip into a listless state marked by the steady beating of his helmeted head into the back wall of the trench as he stood, knees bent, for hours and rocked slightly back and forth, as much as the narrowness of the trench would allow. Alex did not want to meet these men yet, overwhelmed as he was by the circumstances themselves. He wanted only to familiarize himself with his new environment, to look at the trench and get a feel for living here day in and day out. He saw that some had gouged out shelves and carved stools into the walls when the long summer and copious rains softened them. Tin cups and bibles rested on these shelves, as well as packs of cards, journals, and photographs. This trench had a parapet that was only the height of two sandbags. Socks were strewn over it, meant to dry in the sun, though this day seemed only to promise clouds and falling temperatures.

Alex would see a great variety of trenches in his time. Some as deep as a basement, others so shallow one had to lie down and crawl like a snake or a rat. He learned soon that the size and comfort of the trench was only a psychological trick. The men felt safer in the deeper, roomier trenches, but grenades and gas and artillery shells would infiltrate them all the same. There was simply no telling when it would be your time, and the architecture of the trench hardly mattered at all. But they had to believe that some places were safer than others, didn't they? How else could they have stayed?

On this day, he was relieved to be in a communications trench and believed he was safe, even though the obliterated desolation of the land around him suggested otherwise. He held out a hope that, come nightfall, a whistle would blow, their shift would be over, and he and these hunched, smelly creatures around him would trudge out of the trench like mine workers leaving their daily drudgery. When night fell and there was no relief, though, he settled into the idea that this was it. He sat on one of those gouged out stools, the irregular sides of the trench wall lumpy and unyielding against his back, and he looked up, into the dark, starless sky, and he pictured Lenora's moon-bright face, her dark hair and her prodding, and he thought, "I wish you were down here with me!" Not so that he would be with her again, but so that she would know what she had done. He wrote her then.

That night, his eyes struggled to adjust to the shapes of the helmets silhouetted in the dark, the fast movements of rats in and around the trench, the sudden illuminations of harmless explosions high overhead, lighting the field between them and the other trench lines. He would learn the different sounds made by harmless explosions and life threatening ones soon enough, just as he would understand more clearly about the geography of the trench system in the morning. But tonight he could understand nothing and could make no sense of the sporadic sounds of battle that punctured the silent night or the sounds that escaped the men around him as they dreamed. He sat with his arms wrapped tight around himself, rubbing his hands up and down furiously not to ward off the chill but to prove to himself that he was actually here and experiencing this. That this was real and not a dream. In the dark, a heavy hand tapped his helmet. "Drink this," a slow and rough voice croaked. Alex looked up, seeing only a large shape looming near him, smelling of sourness and whiskey. He took the small bottle from his hand and took a sip commensurate with the amount that was left. He nodded his thanks and the hulking shape shuffled past him, settling into the shadows several yards beyond.

In the long hours of night, lightening developed over Belgium. To the men in the trench, who saw only a slice of sky from their vantage point, these natural flashes were indistinguishable from illumination shells. Alex sat into the night, face tilted toward these

flashes of light, as commands and rules he had heard in his journey from civilian to soldier roared in his head. Things like "Take utmost care to ward off infection through proper hygiene", and "Maintain superior grooming standards to mark yourself as an officer in the eyes of your men", and "At the sound of the whistle, charge forward without hesitation to engage the enemy." He thought of these things and about Lenora's face when he told her he had joined and how he had kissed her but should have done so much more, and he started to cry.

He was used to, in his extraordinary life, being two different people, a boy who had to act like a man, and a friend who had to disguise his desire to be more. Here, though, he felt wholly exposed. He was terrified and everyone knew it. He cursed himself for crying and shut his eyes tightly to hold in the tears, slipping into sleep as he did so. But it was with great alarm that he woke to find that the trench was flooding, and that his tears were still falling, covering the trench floor at least four inches deep. Yes, this sounds ridiculous, I know, but Alex had seen his best friends vanish, had enlisted himself, had been transported to a trench in Belgium, and had not been relieved at night despite the horrible living conditions~ in short, he was growing used to believing impossible things.

He scrambled to his feet, disoriented, embarrassed that not only could his fear be seen by all, but it literally touched them as well, seeping into their pant legs, sloshing against the sides of the trench, disintegrating the trench wall and swirling around them. He hardly registered the fact that it was raining or that the sky was the slightly lighter purple-gray of morning, as rounds whizzed by his ears, carefully aimed at his exposed torso. The hulking man, Lowe, reached up to pull him down and he sank like a stone against the slippery mud, relieved, not about the rounds, but about the rain.

In the distance, he heard a whistle blow.

II. Heaps of Men

The whistle sounded in the distance, a more fearsome sound to him than even the artillery shells that would come later, for the whistle demanded increased exposure. The men in the front line trench were advancing, and it would be their turn soon. All around him, purple-gray shadows rose in anticipation. He realized that he must, with all the rest, abandon the close comfort of the trench and run, without cover, across the field to engage the enemy who were, it was hoped, dazed and weakened by weeks of preparatory blasting from the artillery that had been launched by their side, starting well before Alex had even departed England and continuing until the very day of his arrival.

As often happened, the enemy was rested, not dazed, as the artillery had fallen far short, scattering across the barren fields as innocuously as shells dotting a beach, and they had waited out the blasting with calm minds.

Alex's men gathered in bunches at the various steps constructed inside the trench so that they could quickly climb out, nearly in single file, easy targets for machine guns. The trick was to scatter immediately upon reaching the ground, zig zagging across the gap in a desperate gamble for survival. They had several hundred yards just to reach their own front line trench system; then they must traverse the trench to reach the battleground proper and continue on to the enemy trenches several hundred yards distant.

Gathering near the firing steps, pushing close to each other, their breath mingling, the men stood with hands on the backs of the men in front of them to maintain their own stability in the crush of humanity about to surge forward and to give an encouraging shove to anyone who might find their courage lacking in the crucial moments. The large man, Lowe, rested his hand on Alex's shoulder, and he felt some comfort in this, as he had not been privy to any orders or previous knowledge of what was transpiring, and so he felt unsurprisingly ill-matched for the occasion. He felt, in fact, that perhaps he had, in the dark, transformed into someone else, one of his many countrymen who were properly trained for this. He examined his own hand, resting on the shoulder in front of him, to see if the rain had washed away his skin revealing someone entirely new underneath.

Lowe tapped him and gestured for him to look ahead. Alex could see the glint of metal on the collars of other officers down the line of the trench. The one closest to him was looking closely at his wrist.

Only the officers wore watches and new exactly when to expect the whistles to sound, but all sensed their imminent deployment and most stood quietly with their own thoughts in an effort to mediate between the two worlds that were violently juxtaposed around them and through which they were expected to transition seamlessly. Many men described to me the feelings that they had immediately before an advance, and I was always struck by the dread and excitement that seemed to take the place of fear, by how quickly their bodies transformed from cave-dwelling hunchbacks to vigorous athletes. They felt much like performers standing on a shrouded stage, waiting for the curtain to lift, revealing a packed house expecting instantaneous entertainment.

In the one world, behind the curtain or in the trenches, as it were, they sat or leaned for hours and days, waiting, waiting, waiting, breathing the heavy air that sank to the lowest parts of the earth, laden with dust, foul odors, their own exhalations, and lingering sweet traces of gas. Their eyes grew tired of gazing at the dirt brown walls of the trench and their own mud covered faces. Their necks strained for looking skyward at the narrow channel of light that reminded them that their graves were not entirely closed in. Even the sky offered only minor variations of color and light intensities throughout the day, as no birds flew overhead and there seemed to be an omnipresent, cloudy barrier that muted the sun.

Their bodies grew cramped and weak from inactivity, as did their minds. Some endeavored to keep their wits sharp through intellectual conversation, the writing of poems, or heated debates about sports teams and war plans, and endless speculation about the wars duration and the fate of their unit.

Those new to the front lost themselves in pining for their past life, telling listless fellow soldiers about their girlfriends and wives and school standings. They were still close enough to remember their lives and loved ones with some clarity, having only departed England within a month or so. Their lives were still moored to past conditions, situations, and people. They could not stomach the smell of the trench because they could still recall the smell of their favorite cigar, their beloved's hair, and roses in bloom. As time passed, these memories would become like a receding shore on their horizon until they would almost- almost- forget the details that made their life what it was and them who they were.

Until this happened, they could not function rightly as soldiers, and so most men, with the exception of Lowe, who had been in the trenches for too many months, stayed away from the new ones as much as possible.

Alex was surprised to find himself at this moment, with only seconds remaining, thinking of his sister. He wondered what she was doing and prayed, or rather wished intensely, that she was happy and living her life as a child should.

Before he could ponder the likelihood of this or the meaning of this reemerged awareness of his former existence, the shriek of whistles sounded and he felt himself involuntarily pushed forward by the masses desperate to get up and over the parapet in order to dodge the machine gun fire trained on their exit points, to get to the other side as fast as possible, running on legs weakened by constant dampness and lack of use, to finish their required business, to put on a show. The Big Show.

So from the claustrophobic, monotonous, body- and- mind- cramping environs of the trench, they exploded onto the open ground with its fresher air and full light, and ran like escapees from prison, hounds on their heels, yanked like fish who've taken the bait, pulled from the comfort of their murky depths, suspended for all to admire at the end of a line in the poisonous air. They felt less like aggressive warriors than like footballers charging a goal, or like children released from school, streaming out of the schoolyard, filling their lungs with freedom and allowing the momentum to carry their bodies faster than their minds thought prudent. They forgot they were holding rifles and some forgot to ever fire. Fear mixed with euphoria and compelled them to run on and on, even when those before them fell. And fall they did, until the ground in front of Alex was covered with heaps of men.

III. The Doctor

When I first saw Lt. Alex Liddell walk into my office, a space which had previously been an oversized pantry in Swansea Hospital, a country estate converted into a convalescent home for wounded soldiers, my heart cramped for just a moment as I thought I was seeing- just for a moment- just as he raised his head and the yellow light from the desk lamp cast a glow on a particular facet of his face, the fall of dark brown hair breaking the line of sharply sculpted eyebrows, dark eyes raising in cold slits like flashing fish rising from some deep murk, only to disappear again quickly, pale skin, and a smirk that carved a deep 'c' into the left side of his face- my own son.

I made this mistake often, surrounded as I was by young military men with strikingly similar features: short hair, athletic physiques, unsmiling faces, eyes so full of images yet to be processed that they seemed barely available for seeing anything in the present moment. Also, I made this mistake because I was always looking for him despite having been notified of his death.

Jack, my son, was taken to Australia by his mother when he was nine years old and I had not seen him since. In my mind, he was still a rambunctious, precocious, gap-toothed boy with lanky limbs, pale skin, and bowed legs. I have one picture left, but it is a blur. He was always moving too fast for the camera mechanisms to capture him well and hold him fast. It was a picture taken in my first office, a smallish space in a three story building on the outskirts of Cambridge. I took it. I can see my wife's arm as he reaches for him, but it's too late; he is already spinning and passing through the door, a ghost form even then.

When we were together, he chiefly enjoyed gaining my attention through physical achievements requiring increasing dexterity and not a little bit of luck: running a fixed path faster than a count of 10, joining a football team manned by older, rougher boys and fairing well, scrambling up rock faces only to jump into pools of water beneath. I suppose my attention was hard to gain, as I was engrossed in research and rarely had my head outside of books. My former wife would certainly agree to this point. I always was plagued by an inability to determine what I should do and what I ought to do as a father, as a husband and provider.

When they left, I was shocked; though I suppose in retrospect, I should have seen it coming. I understood my wife's motivations, but I could not fathom the loss of my son and chose, instead, to hardly acknowledge the both of them. I would often receive reports of his performances in distance races and with rugby teams once he moved to Brisbane. I shouldn't have been surprised when I received a letter announcing his commission as an ANZAC artillery battery officer shortly after receiving announcement of his successful matriculation at the University of Adelaide. His entire life was a list of achievement that I did not witness first hand. The details of the events and the numbers- scores, times, heights, grade point averages- took the place of conversation. Perhaps it was because of his desire to continue that pseudo-conversation that he pushed himself onward always, never pausing to enjoy his gains. 'I am the fastest middle distance runner on the West Coast; that is enough'. No, there always had to be more.

'Look at me, Dad! Look at what I can do.' I had not seen him since nine, and now he was dead somewhere in Turkey, and I could not picture his grown man face in its final repose. All of the details of his life, the smell of his skin, his favorite books, his love interests, his usual breakfast, all of these I had to imagine, looking around me at these other boys and men, trying to form some kind of composite that felt true.

If I saw a boy walking side by side with his father on a narrow walk, holding his dad's finger in his small hand or imitating his father's behavior by stuffing his balled fists deep into his pockets, or a young man gently guiding his father through a park with a hand to the shoulder blade, I would try out these behaviors on my Jack. Would Jack do this or that? My answers were informed only by intuition of course, projections, dreams. But these answers helped me to form an idea of my son, and though I often searched the faces and postures and habits of soldiers for some glimpse of Jack in his last days, it was in Alex Liddell that I thought I recognized him most.

So it was with great enthusiasm that I took his case at Swansea, though I kept my mood tempered in those somber surroundings, and it was with great consternation that I took his case as well, as I knew that I would have to let this boy go, too, to his early and violent death.

The walls of the office were a dull yellow, an ivory yellowed with age, with the millwork- even in the enlarged pantry there was millwork- the same dull yellow. I brought in a small oriental carpet with navy, red, and cream flowers and scrolls to make the men more comfortable. It was meant to remind them of their homes, where they had lived out their youth. Many of my colleagues in England and Wales believed at that time that the men we treated were traumatized only by their recent experiences at war. But I was swayed by the work coming out of Austria, that their reactions to wars' horrors were in part linked to earlier experiences, reaching back to childhood, infancy, or even latent memories from the womb. I did not have a couch or large reclining seat as some were popularizing, but I did have a comfortable, deep, brown leather chair with brass buttons, scavenged from a library that had been converted into a pantry deep in the sprawling home, for the men to relax in as we searched for the deeply buried roots of their problems. Of course, this work was frustratingly ridiculous.

As a peace-time psychiatrist, I would help patients, women mostly, cope with phobias or disturbances brought on by advancing age. We would explore memories to help them make connections and uncover explanations that empowered them to understand the why of their current situations and how to objectively and effectively cope with or accept life as it was for them presently.

For soldiers suffering mental collapse through exposure to unrelenting bombardment, death at its most grotesques, what could I do for them? Who would not go mad at being reduced to shoring up one's ramparts with the rotting remains of a friend unburied or unearthed by explosions? At following absurd orders written by leaders far away from the front, knowing that both obedience and defiance of these orders would cause real, flesh and blood death and agony to men depending on the wisdom of men with shiny bits of metal on their clothes?

I confess that I didn't have such sympathy for these soldiers always. Until I heard that my Jack had died in combat, I was against these men, I must confess. I was not on their side. I did not empathize with them, did not want to know or share their pain. I did not want to provide relief. I only wanted to make sure that any obvious problems were corrected, so that they could be sent back to finish their jobs. Some were rendered temporarily mute; some suffered debilitating nightmares or hallucination. All of these, I knew, could be treated. But treating them meant returning them fit for continued service to the Crown. I was not protecting them, but readying them to accept further exposure to life-threatening dangers, the very ones that had landed them in the hospital in the first place.

I was on the side of England, the Allies. Not these men who represented England on the battlefields of Europe. Then I got that notification, and my perception changed. It was as if a layer was peeled away that had separated me from them. A film that, in my view, had colored them with cowardice and weakness. That film was gone now, and I believe that I saw them for what they were: men who wanted peace in their lives.

Some, like Alex, wanted something more, that I was not able to grasp then.

Diligently, though, I listened to them all unburden themselves. Some could not talk at all; they would hold themselves tightly, rock gently in that brown chair, and stare at me imploringly, with eyes that seemed to beg for something. Others' eyes were distant- never empty- just seeing something or someone that wasn't present. Many had no words. Many used words that seemed to dissatisfy them with inadequacy. They told their stories matter of factly or in whispers. But they seemed distraught at their impact. As if they expected me to run screaming, but I could only sit. One man said it and I'll never forget it. He looked at me after telling his tale, a sordid affair involving his first encounter with flamethrowers, and he squinted, as if examining me clinically. He raised an eyebrow and pulled back from me, repulsed. "This should destroy you," he said, before falling into a long and troubled silence. I didn't know what it meant to be destroyed, but these men did. We weren't the same, and I couldn't forget that. In a life characterized by personal failings, I'd never felt so inadequate.

Again, my sense of what I should do and what I ought to do was tested; was I a doctor, fulfilling a role for the government or a bloody human being, with empathy, with common sense, with…

Thus my enthusiasm upon seeing Lt. Alex Liddell settle into that brown leather chair, exhaling deeply as he did so and rounding his shoulders in utter defeat, like a prodigal son returning to me, offering another chance for us both, was tempered by my knowledge of the future: I would not be able to help him. Indeed, I might not even be able to save his life and, in fact, my role was just the opposite: to ready him to return to war, where he would, in all likelihood, be killed. But in him, I found not only my son, but a kindred spirit who himself had struggled with knowing what he should do and what he ought to do…only for him, the matter was clear. It was people like me who stood in his way. I was drawn to his certainty and wanted to learn from it. So, I reveal some of my selfishness.

Alex Liddell was never ready, in my opinion, to return, even though he wanted to, desperately. He was ready, technically, but I was not willing to send him away. I did not want to lose him like I did my boy. The war ended with him tucked safely away in the cavernous upper levels of Swansea. I think he knew his readiness and he knew he missed his return, and this drove him further into despair. After the Armistice, Alex Liddell became himself to me, and not my son. Jack, I realized after the war, was truly dead. He was among those departed souls for whom Alex raged and for whom he drowned in shame, remorse, and despair for not having gone with them on their journey. I did not understand this component of wounded minds until after the war. In truth, I don't think anyone who has not shared their fate directly can ever understand the truth of their experience and their emotions. So while our relationship began with promise, Alex quickly exposed my inadequacies as well.

He, and all of them, really, could have benefitted from real psychological treatment. But I, completely out of the habit of doing any good for anyone, was not the man for the job. So, in the end, I washed my hands of them all and jettisoned their pain from my memory as best I could, and along with it, the desire to picture or know the truth of my son's life and death.

IV. A Caucus-Race

The men ran forward and it seemed exactly as a race, not a football match, as there was not another team running toward them but rather an open field. They were meant to carry with them bombs that required two parts: the bomb itself, which was not unlike a cricket ball and was meant to be thrown as such and the detonating handle, without which the bomb was as useful as a cricket ball. These two bits were packaged and delivered to the lines in separate containers, to be assembled before use. Today, though, only the handles had arrived, so the men ordered to carry with them three bombs carried instead three handles and hoped Col. Flint and Maj. Knight would not be too particular.

Alex did his best to determine the purpose of their advance as he went. He followed the others, though the men before him fell or broke off running in a different direction without advanced warning. When he reached the front line trench, rather than traversing it, he jumped in to catch his breath. Parrish, Lowe, and Mouse followed, as was their duty to their lieutenant.

They ducked down low so as not to be kicked in the head by the boots flying across the chasm. Parrish yelled above the din of battle, "What is it, sir!"

"What's going on here?" Alex yelled back, foolishly.

They looked at him quizzically, eager to get on with things. Alex outranked them all, Lowe was the largest and oldest, but Mouse was a Belgian on Belgian soil, so he felt the authority to apprise Lt. Liddell of the situation at hand.

"Let me tell you my history," he said in accented English, "and you'll understand why we hate the Germans here and what is going on today." He shifted his weight back on one leg as if settling in for a long tale. Parrish interrupted with a roll of his eyes and a vulgar

Liverpudlian curse that even Alex, his countryman, could hardly decipher.

"Speak English, why don't you, you tommy bastard," Mouse hissed good naturedly.

Lowe weighed in with his deliberate speech, heavy with experience and the natural inclination some men have to assess a situation quickly and accurately and determine the appropriate course of action.

"Sir, after the shells stop falling, we go. The shells cut the wire, so we can go all the way to their trenches and beyond. We just go until we are told to stop. We have to g-g-go *now*, sir" he said with an emphatic stutter, simplifying the situation as best he could.

Alex nodded and they all scrambled out of the trench. There was no one, two, three, go, just a furious activity to get out of the dugout and run like everyone else, zig zagging as if bullets could be fooled. Everything in front of them was uniformly denuded and ravaged, dried and brown, so it was difficult to tell if or when they had arrived at anything of significance.

By some luck, the first wave of troops, the ones who had charged forward from the front line trench, had overrun the German line to good effect. The Germans Alex saw in the first trench that he encountered were all dead, with bullets in their foreheads or blood on their coats where they had been run through with bayonets. Three or four tommies were still in the trench, making sure that the dead were dead. Alex continued on, sensing that some objective might be within reach, until he heard above the whizz of bullets the sound of whistles screaming again, furiously. Men stopped in their tracks or abruptly turned and began jogging back the way they had come. The Germans seemed content to stop firing, and the race ended.

"What just happened?" Alex ran alongside Mouse.

"We won't know for sure, but I have a guess," he leaned his head toward Alex conspiratorially. "The messenger who goes to tell Col. Flint that the advance has launched per his orders arrived at his headquarters and told him that the bombs were not bombs and not even cricket balls. So the good Colonel called it off. He really likes explosions."

"But we seemed to be doing alright!" Alex assessed.

"Do you like to read, sir?" Mouse asked unexpectedly.

"Yes," he responded, after a pause.

"When you settle down for a good read, and you open your book and someone has traded out your favorite Greek tragedy for a mystery… do you just read what you've got, or do you shelve it and get what you want?" Mouse didn't wait for a reply. "The Colonel likes bombs."

"So are we here to win or to please the Colonel?" he asked with a mounting anger. Parrish and Lowe had joined them by this time.

"We are alive still, aren't we?" Parrish asked, with a shrug. "Everybody wins." He nearly tripped over the body of a fallen man. "Well, nearly everyone."

"Front line trench, gents!" yelled Capt. Whitesell, the man Alex recognized as the man with the watch and the whistle from a few moments ago, and they dropped into place in their new home, deeper than their last, but as crowded and uncomfortable, with at least two inches of undetermined wetness along the floor.

They sat and cleaned their weapons as best they could and they tried not to think of the men on the ground just above and in front of them and behind them. There was no way to retrieve the bodies, as daylight provided no cover, so out they sat in the sun, like doomed creatures trapped in evaporated tide pools, waiting in vain for the tide to come in. A sergeant walked the length of the trench with a memorandum pad, taking a roll call of the living so as to determine the dead. Once their status was confirmed, men settled into routines that were meant to pass the time until the Colonel decided conditions were right to give it another go.

They didn't have to wait for the Colonel, as Fritz had other plans, and that night, a small party of them crossed No Man's Land and, quietly, with bayonets fixed, rushed over Alex's section of the trench, which was in a bend and somewhat isolated from the rest, a grouping of about twenty men in a row before another bend connected them with another fifteen. The infiltrating Germans jabbed with silent, quick motions toward the head and shoulders of the men below them who, though not asleep, were lulled into a drowsy state through boredom and darkness. Alex struggled to makes sense of the dark forms and the grunts that accompanied their movements. He heard a man close by shriek, and he reached up to grab a pair of boots braced on the parapet above him and yanked them hard. The attacker fell on his back, awkwardly splayed over the parapet, and Lowe set upon him savagely; having not fixed his bayonet to his rifle, he was able to wield the knife with the precise, quick brutality of someone skilled at gutting fish. Alex felt the legs still in his hands give a few jerks; then they stilled.

The momentum seemed to shift and the raiding party pulled back, having lost three of only a handful of men and inflicted only superficial wounds. The men in the trench mounted their rifles on the parapet and fired several rounds into the darkness. "Small party," Mouse noted. "Those men must have pissed somebody off, poor buggers."

They stared a few moments longer after the poor buggers, but they had disappeared into dead silence and darkness. The men stood down and returned to their previous occupations wordlessly, but Alex found himself wide awake dripping wet, cross, and uncomfortable, and wondering what they would do next. No sooner had the thoughts expressed themselves in his mind than he was nearly hit by something that had the impact of a cricket ball lobbed from a hundred yards. The men ducked their heads as they were pelted with an avalanche of harmless pebbles. They picked up the missing bombs from the floor of the trench where they settled, and Alex smiled, happy to have thrown all the handles away earlier in the day.

Part Two

Children three that nestle near,

Eager eye and willing ear,

Pleased a simple tale to hear—

V. The Usefulness of Things Learnt in School

A lex was open to suggestion. He was easy to hypnotize, and I found out much about his early days this way. For example, early in his time with me he was quite able to describe in detail this memory from his youth:

"I am twelve. The sun is shining and I am striding confidently through the exterior corridors of Briarside while my mother and uncle meet with the headmaster. My part of the entry interview is over and, having answered all questions with rehearsed restraint, I am free to explore the limited grounds while Uncle Clive helps my mother fill out the required forms.

Briarside is an ancient school, more than three hundred years, located on the outskirts of town. It looks like a church or a castle ruin, looming over the factories and houses. I often thought it housed a mad scientist who might unleash some monster on the townspeople any stormy night. Briarside doesn't have the prestige of one of the academies that required parents to send their children away to live with strangers. But it is a good choice for me, as I need to keep an eye on my mum and my sister.

The windows are large, leaded and dark. Peering through them I can barely make out the dark wooden features of the class and meeting rooms. I am reminded of the heavily lacquered wooden pews and solemnity of church. My eyes blink from the radiance of what I find in the third window of another dark room. Dominating the small space is a massive painting. Its white, gold and red colors glow as if illuminated. It is a battle scene. Chivalry, knights, gleaming armor and all that. Good and evil. Swords and lances, breast-plates and flags, radiant faces and noble deaths. Blood flows like scarlet ribbon and faces shine like porcelain dolls or ivory statues. The portrait hangs high and centered in the dark room like an object of worship. I wonder if this is a history classroom or perhaps a place where we learn to be

English gentlemen. As I'm wondering, I hear what sounds like a row. Naturally, I investigate.

Around the corner is an enclosed courtyard, in the center of which is a group of older boys, or taller boys, roughing up a short, hunch-shouldered boy with dark hair and a pile of books at his feet. Despite the shoves and some unpleasant vocal provocations referring to his apparent Jewish ancestry, this boy is desperately attempting to gather his books as if the knowledge they contain will ward of the ignorant and unsporting bullies. Clearly he needs my help.

I trot into the courtyard, pushing up my starched sleeves as I go and yelling: 'If you pick a fight with my mate, you pick a fight with me!' The bullies turn. Roman Foster. There are two others I don't recognize, but they are thin and dim and no worry. I go right for Foster, who is grinning. If he falls, they all will."

"I thought he was your best friend?"

"I've known him as long as I can remember; he was there when my father died. About a year later, he began spending most of his time with Henry Crowne and other boys. We've grown apart and I no longer see him regularly; in fact, I haven't seen him all summer. Physically and mentally, he is nearly a different person when I encounter him on the yard that day. He is a sportsman, a leader of the other kids. But he is something of a jerk. Friend or not…sometimes you have to act."

"Go on."

"Roman is at least a foot taller and eight months older than I, a monumental span when you are twelve. I don't even know if I can reach his face with my fist, an uncertainty that compels me to charge and dive at his waist. He falls to the ground, flat on his back. He laughs a full-throated, high pitched laugh that I tell myself is forced. He easily grabs my thin arms and tosses me to the side, but he takes his time getting up. I am ready to go again, but Foster is chuckling to his friends and directing them off the courtyard with a face-saving good natured 'Come on gents; let the boys have their fun while we go find some real adventure.' I watch them till they've disappeared down a long corridor. Only then do I remember the boy I defended. I turn to him. He is inspecting his books for damage and doesn't make a move to wipe a clod of dirt and grass from his ear. I extend my hand.

'Alex Liddell, first year.'

He looks up with a directness that surprises me and firmly shakes my hand. He is more formidable than I took him for. I suppose he just doesn't wish to fight.

'Bernard. Bernard Merrick, first year.'

'Well, I guess I'll see you around,' I say as if I have somewhere important to go. I walk off the courtyard in the opposite direction of Foster, leaving Bernard to his books.

Moments later I am striding through the corridors of Briarside as if I've lived here all my life when a door opens not twenty feet away and my mother, uncle, and the headmaster step out. Heat creeps into my face as I become aware of my pushed-up sleeves, barely tucked in shirt, and grass stained trousers. Wisely, my uncle ascertains the situation and uses his immense size to block the headmaster's view of me. The headmaster is engrossed in conversation with my mother, so I'm not in much danger. My uncle twists my right ear anyway, though not very hard."

"And Bernard and Foster…you patch things up?"

"Yes, of course. Boys fight, naturally. It doesn't mean anything. Within the year we are all of us close: Bernard, Foster, Henry and I."

"And Lenora?"

"Well, yes, of course. She is always there. Always close, to all of us."

"And you all stay close?"

"Yes, until we aren't close anymore."

"What do you mean?"

"We stay close until the war separates us. Bernard goes first."

"I'm surprised by that. I thought that Foster would lead the way, being more of a natural leader…"

"I don't want to talk about Foster."

"Fine…Henry?" "No."

"Bernard?"

"Not really."

"Lenora?"

He was finished. I had not released him from his hypnosis, but he folded up like a telescope in front of me, collapsing in on himself, reaching his head down toward his knees and wrapping his hands around his ankles. Silence took him then, and the session ended.

VI. Wire Party

Alex, like everyone else, reported to me that the incessant oscillation between days that felt like years elongated by boredom and moments that felt like hours elongated by terror soon took a toll on his nerves. Often, he found himself with plenty of time on his hands, as he realized quite quickly that men seemed to keep themselves occupied with nearly senseless tasks or to belabor a chore so that a simple activity, like rinsing out one's tin cup and cleaning one's area, stretched from morning to noon. Picking off and squeezing lice fit into the 'senseless' category, as it became clear to Alex that they would never be alone here, overrun as they were by bugs and rodents. Still, Alex was jarred by the inactivity, as he had been taught to expect battle to be an aggressive and offensive campaign requiring extreme physical and mental fitness to endure. He found his mental fitness to be tested quickly, as boredom took its place with the lice and rats as a condition of the battlefield that would only be alleviated by short bursts of terrifying activity, as sudden and powerful as lightening strikes illuminating clear, blue, still skies. His men helped to relieve some of the more agonizingly slow days, a distraction he valued so much that he often voluntarily shared with them moments of terror that were not meant for him.

He met Parrish and Lowe first, a pair of Liverpudlians who bantered like brothers and were seldom to be found more than a few feet distant of the other, though they had not known each other before entering this New Model Army. They had enlisted in 1914 in a 'buddy' program, though they were strangers who coincidentally showed up at the recruitment office on the same day and liked the sound of the program and the idea of having a buddy. At 20 and 23, they were salty veterans of the unit, with a history longer and more storied than any other soldier present, even the commanders, whose long careers featured little by way of story, consumed as they were by training and battle scholarship.

Lowe was a dockworker and whisky enthusiast whose fear of water was a source of constant teasing by Parrish, himself a gifted swimmer, rower and illiterate. Lowe had a stammer and the burley physique of a rugby stand-out, reddish hair and a flush to his square face that made him always appear to have just thrown back a shot. His size and strength and battlefield résumé were enough to make the stuttering and blush not matter to most people, with the exception of Col. Flint and Maj. Knight, who knew next to nothing about their men and seemed to think that the less they knew of them personally, the easier was their job to design and deliver assignments that would ultimately decide their fates. They suspected Lowe to be a coward and Alex soon observed that they took pleasure in testing his bravery with tasks that would imperil them all nightly.

Lowe, and so Parrish as well, was an infantryman. Routinely, they, along with the Belgian wireman called Mouse who matched Lowe's height though his bones carried half the weight, and now Alex, their new lieutenant, were sent on wiring parties at the darkest hours of the night. Alex did not have to go; rather, he was only to be sure that the party took place, but he felt an obligation that some did not understand, so he went as well.

They departed silently from their trenches and inched forward on bellies like worms or low-crawled on their knees to repair damaged communication wire. When they rotated to the front line trench, the party looked to repair damage to their barbed wire defenses inflicted by German wire parties or weaponry, or to inflict damage of their own by cutting German wire so their advancing men would not be ensnared and entangled.

Alex soon learned that there never was a sound as loud as the crack of a barbed wire coil rent in two by heavy wire cutters in the dark of night on a silent battlefield only a few hundred yards wide. He felt a bit like a thief who, entering a yard guarded by a ferocious, sleeping dog upsets the rubbish bins with a loud clang. He found that he nearly stopped breathing during these outings which seemed to last for hours but were really only twenty minutes or so due to the closeness of the enemy line. He had to remind himself to breathe when he caught himself closing his eyes and resting his head on the ground for long moments.

The stakes were much higher at the front line parties, where enemy snipers might sit in the darkness just meters away, firing randomly into the black before them, or an illumination grenade might brighten the sky like a white hot sun, casting its deadly glow on all of them below. Here, what was in the communication trench a slow nightly evolution transformed into an intense internal battle. Once they were exposed on the level, cleared ground, out of the confines of the trench, the internal dialogue began. Alex's brain urged him with increasing volume to go slow when his body wanted to run and get it over with, to sip the air when he wanted to gulp, and to lead his men when he wanted this least of all.

All the men thought the same thing: please don't let me be hit out here in the dark. It was a plea to God that revealed not their fear of death but their concern that they might cry out in pain or surprise, thus exposing the presence of the party to the enemy guns and drawing a storm of rounds upon them all.

So they didn't pray for relief from the parties or relief from death, but only so that they would not be responsible for the deaths of their friends. Never mind that it was friends who had gotten them involved in this mess in the first place. These parties broke the boredom, and for that, no one complained.

That was what it was like near the beginning. Here is what it was like more than a year later, near the end. Somewhere in the middle all his old friends and some of his new ones died, but I'll tell you more about that later, when I've reviewed my notes.

VII. The World Exhales

Sunrise. Stand-to. He breathed deep the cool morning air and from the presumed safety of the trench, stretched his face toward a sky just stained with the faintest red, one that might inspire the musings of a poet lying on his back to admire it in another age. In this one, the clouds were drifting smoke and the sky lifted and swelled, a great balloon eager to sever its tethers to this exhaling world. Beauty, his momentary comfort, left him and all those like him to their own devices.

Ypres, September, 1917. It may well have been taken for the surface of Mars, the ground cratered and stripped of life, mysterious pools of stinking liquid glinting ominously. But when he considered the flames, the skies, the bloated horses, and the bodies shoveled into sand bags to contain the rising waters when the artillery smashed the drainage system in this godforsaken field, he thought only of some distant planet. Surely this couldn't be Earth. That would be too devastating.

He wrote often in and around the Ypres Salient. Several of his shorter letters came from the first year of his time in the war, but after mid-1916, Alex wrote copious, sometimes illegible entries in his personal journal, which he carried on his person. He also continued to write to his sister and to Lenora, of course. There was something about this place, in particular, that produced in him a strong response, even before what happened. It was on this same ground that Foster died, just weeks before his own unit had arrived. Two battles had already been fought for this same acreage, lives lost for no gain. Here he was in the third, and there would be a fourth yet, and he suspected many, many more. He had come to the war to join his friends, and, I believe, here he felt closest to achieving this. Foster had died just a few weeks before, so all three boys were gone. Though they were here, somehow. Not in England, but still here, in the ground.

October. His writing revealed that a nearly relentless German barrage had resumed. The first lasted for hours and temporarily destroyed his hearing. Numbness overtook his body and the thunderous shell blasts were reduced to a dull roar that surrounded him as if he were underwater and hearing voices from a distant shore competing with the incessant rumble of the tide. This barrage lasted several days. The continuous sound lulled him to sleep and greeted him when he rose. He didn't record the exact time that he lost his mind, but then, no one ever does.

I saw many, many men driven mad by barrages. The noise, the duration, the endurance required to sit passively while roaring trains dropped out of the sky and all around you for hours on end...usually these men recovered after a time. Shell shock, as we called it, was a condition that was temporary, usually relieved through rest and quiet far away from the front. Some men never lost a certain look of nervous anticipation. One man I had seen briefly before sending back to the front, a sergeant from Leeds, appeared quite recovered after a long rest, only to throw himself in front of a subway car in December of 1919 when the roar of the approaching train resonated in the station as he waited to commute to a new job. His wife informed me of his passing by letter shortly after.

Alex was certainly maddened by this barrage that precipitated his arrival at Swansea. But after talking to him for only a short time, it was clear to me that his mind was compromised before it, infiltrated by senses and experiences that combined to betray his reason.

Early in his time with me, believing him to be a common shell shock victim, I hypnotized Alex in my windowless office. He went under well, willing to succumb to the power of suggestion, as in their exhausted state, most soldiers were. His words enlivened the description of the early moments of the barrage that I had read about already in the journal that was found in his coat pocket. He had written:

> The streaming scream of the first shell as it traversed the distance between them and us announced the earth-heaving crash that would inevitably follow. A momentary sense of euphoria washed over me the first time I sat helplessly under an artillery barrage and found myself still in one piece, spared by god knows what luck. But that euphoric sense only dared

make itself known once. The successive screams and crashes kept it in check. My luck will surely run out soon enough.

And he when he spoke under hypnosis:

"Scream and crash. Scream and crash. First, one at a time, then overlapping, a cacophony. An hour; I'm numb, can't feel a thing; can't focus. Night, sleep, I'm in the ocean, waves washing over the beach, new breakers crash then wash out again. Sea birds calling. Blackpool, spray on my face…"

"What is it?"

"Water, blowing sand, I don't know."

"Go on."

"She is there, too."

"Who?"

"Lenora. She grabs my arm; she's telling me something."

"What is it? Listen."

"Go. Go, with urgency. That's all. I'm looking at the black water, back to her eyes. It's dark, but when her mouth moves I see her teeth. She is screaming, RUN."

"Run where?"

"I don't know. To the sea or to the train? There's a train leaving the station beyond the beach. I can't tell what direction is the dangerous one, so I don't know what she wants from me."

"Ask h…" (I didn't finish as he yelled out voluntarily).

"Tell me! I don't know what you want from me!"

"What does she say?"

"She doesn't hear me; my voice is drowned out by crashing waves, the people on the beach."

"Is this a dream? You were telling me about an artillery barrage..." His face distorted into a cruel grimace, his fists clenched, his voice harsh and raspy.

"Screamandcrash. Inandout. Knee deep in muck, water, mud, and piss, and still they come. Shells sailing in the air. Black pools. Lenora."

And then, after an anguished pause in which he seemed to wrestle with himself: "What did you think would happen?" An accusation, not a question.

I don't remember what I said to bring him back or how I ended our appointment that day. I remember a nurse escort appearing quickly at the door in response to my call. Alex rose and shuffled with slumped shoulders out of my office, toward his room on the second floor. I had turned away from him and hid my face in paperwork and files. I felt my cheeks reddened from his words as if from a physical slap, and I was thankful for my full beard, but feared he might see me still, and lose professional respect. In his wake I could hear my very own son yelling his words to me: What did you think would happen? Why were you surprised to get my death telegram? Why, when I sent you letter after letter showing you all I had done to make you believe I was becoming a fine man, why did you never write me back: that's enough. Why didn't you tell me I could stop? You don't even know what became of me. Listen to him, he will tell you.

VIII. Let Me Tell You My History

He was a boy when his father died in the Boer War, and overnight he became a man and his young, nervous mother transformed into an old woman who failed to hear anything clearly, though her ears worked fine. The last words she heard with clarity were those of her son, Alex, reading aloud a recently arrived telegram dispassionately announcing the death of Alex's father, her husband of eight years.

It had arrived in the morning, as she cleared breakfast dishes from the table, her own coffee and spoon, and two plates with eggs, the orange yolks punctured and bleeding into the gelatinous whites. The toast had been eaten, though, and its crumbs sprinkled over the plates like brown sugar. The oval table at the rear of the house, directly across from the open living area and the front entry, was small but nicely appointed, with a century old lace table covering from Ireland, and a happy view of the verdant back yard, whose generous willows and flowery overgrowth obscured the neighboring homes and provided a sense of privacy. The baby would often sit with the cat, on the floor here at the back of the house behind the table, staring at the colors swirling in the gentle breezes for many quiet minutes. But this morning, the baby waited noisily for her breakfast, rolling around on a soft quilt on the floor in front of the table and crying out when she remembered to.

The knock at the door was a surprising burst of three sharp raps delivered in quick succession, unlike the rhythmic, excited sounds generated by Alex's friends coming to call him out for a day of play.

She knew it was different, and so she steeled herself instantly, as if she had rehearsed this moment, though she had not. Alex was at the door before she could move from her spot at the sink. She heard low voices, and then a higher pitched one, her son. Then the door closed.

She could sense the boy in the doorway to the kitchen, standing in the frame, unsure of how to approach, but she refused to turn from her chores. She set the scraped plates in the white porcelain basin gently and tried hard to listen to any sounds coming in through the window: birds, children playing, rain, anything that would anchor her shifting world with its familiarity. But she heard only a voice, tentative for just a moment, then loud and forceful.

"Mum, a telegram's arrived." His voice betrayed that he didn't know the contents. Perhaps he hoped that it was a message announcing his father's unexpected return. But she knew better, and she suspected he did as well.

"Read it," she commanded softly, pressing the backs of her hands against the cool porcelain for support and to counter the rising heat she felt surging around her.

He read it all through without a pause till the end. Then silence.

"Read it again." She had sensed a question in his voice, and she couldn't answer him. Repetition, she hoped, would provide needed clarity.

This time his voice rose as the words fell from his mouth until he was nearly shouting the last of it, something about thanks and glory and dedication to God and country. Silence for a moment. His eyes searched her back imploringly, desperately, and then around him, at the tops of end tables and buffets weighed down with heavy silver frames encasing photographs of relatives smiling in their wedding best and frowning in their military uniforms, eyes solemn and certain. A tradition of men clothed in wool and trained for battle with sabers, on horseback, in shining black boots. Most had died before Alex had known them, though he realized vaguely that they were a part of his genealogy. He didn't quite ascertain that these men affected his life in ways other than- stronger than- DNA alone. That their absence made them somehow more influential, not less. That, in their absence, their stories attained a life of their own that communicated to the living ones in ways their silent, frozen mouths could not. Perhaps this explained the sad resignation in their faces. He didn't understand this, then. He saw only the blank faces of dead relatives who had gone to war, just like his dad. These eyes offered no consolations now, the frowning mouths no explanation.

"What did you think would happen?" he nearly screamed at her back. The dead had been around them all along, a warning unheeded. "You should have known!"

His mother stood still save her left arm, which traced a slow, graceful arc back and forth against the porcelain sink, till the sound of the scratch of her golden wedding band against the smooth surface was the only sound in the room. Alex stood for a long moment, trembling, though he didn't know if it were anger, fear, or sadness that caused it. He waited there, in the middle of the narrow kitchen, for his mother to turn and embrace him, but she did not. The cat walked across his feet and rubbed her soft cheeks against his ankles. The hungry baby cried. He couldn't take it any longer and fled the house through the front entry. Maybe he thought that if he could catch up with the messenger, he could sort out the mistake or convince him to change the content of the telegram, rewriting his family history and so his future. As the door slammed behind him, the cat watched the telegram float and fall through the air like the first snowflake heralding a blizzard.

How do I know this, what the cat saw? Alex told me he fled the room, that he did not take the telegram with him nor did he set it down. I could not recall exactly what I had done with the telegram when it came for me, but I found it later, on the floor…so he must have let it fall through the air. And later, he described to me that his world felt like a snow globe, so from a storytelling perspective, the simile of the snowflake seems to work nicely. And of course also because I know that what came after was a blizzard of sorts, and I know well the initial calm, stillness, and normalcy that preceded these storms.

In his mind, his world was like the contents of a snow globe being shaken relentlessly. His father was no longer. He would no longer sit perched on the stairs watching card games where cigar smoke burned his eyes until the wee hours of morning. No more coming downstairs to see Dad handing Mum her coffee as they sat at the table by the large window overlooking their garden, softly lit by morning light filtered through ever present clouds. Questions swirled. Would his mother stay the same? Would she marry some new man? Would they change their name? Who would he be if not his father's son? Would they have to leave their house? And then, Did it hurt?

How did he die? Where is his body? As he ran down the gravel road called Violet Street, following the river Brain as it rushed toward the Blackwater, he wished desperately for God to set the globe down so everything would settle into position. So he could be reassured by knowing with certainty just what would become of his life.

He had run nearly a mile and though his nerves fired rapidly and fueled his legs and his will to move on, his lungs burned in the cool air and he had to fling himself to the ground to recover. He came to rest, on his back, on the wet grass of a home on the same side of the road as his own, near where it branched off from the main road. He didn't know the owners, as he believed they had only recently arrived, but he didn't care. It was still early, anyway, and most people would stay in on a morning like this. Feeling the dew seep into his clothes and smelling grass and earth, he wondered if his father was lying in the ground right now, and if he could smell it. Was the South African ground just like England's, rich and dark and sodden? He imagined the soil in Africa to be light and full of sand, and he hoped that at least there might be a coast, and his father might be resting in earshot of crashing waves. Every other weekend in the summer season, when his dad was home, he would take him by train to the resort town of Blackpool, just the two of them, and they'd spend the day or sometimes overnight at a hotel, playing on the beach together. He would pick Alex up as if he weighed no more than a feather and throw him again and again into the relentless, cold, dark waves. Dad could get great height and trajectory with his tosses, and Alex would yelp and shriek with delight at every turn, never once fearing for his safety or thinking that anything would change.

As soon as he could, he would go to the sea himself and when he smelled the salt air he would know (though he would be wrong) that his father smelled the same air forever.

His world stopped spinning. It was confusing to him how still and normal everything looked and seemed that morning while inside his body the world still swayed and the pieces of his life threatened to settle out of place and upended. He could see wet morning glories hanging limply from vines that choked the white painted posts alongside the gate of the house at No.7, Violet.

He heard the sound of bicycle tires moving slowly over wet, gravel road, popping and crunching, and the low grunts of a boy's effort as he climbed the gradual hill from town toward Alex's house.

"That you, Alex?" A voice called quizzically. "Watcha doin here? Are you hurt?" Roman Foster was older than Alex by 8 months, but looked about a year taller, more muscular and coordinated.

"Dad's dead, just heard," Alex's voice came steady and casually between panting breaths as he fixed his gaze on the leaden sky and watched the burning air in his lungs burst white from his mouth and then fade into the air like a cooled firework.

Roman stopped the bike by hopping off the seat and left it there in the street before dropping his body next to Alex's in the wet grass. They were boys even when no one else looked on. They didn't embrace or cry. But they sat on the lawn for an hour, twisting blades of grass idly in their fingers and sitting close enough for their shoulders and bare forearms to touch, on occasion, witnessed only by a young girl in her bedroom window, intrigued by the site of two strange boys in her yard who made no attempts to call her out to play. She longed to go to them, but something in their quiet manner told her that she should keep her distance. For now.

Alex would often plea to God to shake up his world again, like a snow globe, to see if the prominent features that made up his young life- mum, dad, friends, school, the house, the cat, the baby, the town- would settle in a better version, But in this version, his Dad was never to return from a far-off war he knew nothing about, his mum spent hours standing at the sink or sitting by the large window, wordlessly, and he rarely saw his friends anymore, as he had been swept into the world of work by his well-intentioned uncle.

He was too young to work officially, of course, but Uncle Clive felt it necessary to keep the boy busy and away from his mother's grief. Clive was his father's only brother, too young to see action in the Boer War and with bad eyes as well. He had never been close to his brother, John, but his death in war had changed all that. Pictures of John in uniform adorned most walls in his 4 room flat, and he would quickly bring up the story of his earlier, successful campaigns and his early, tragic death at social functions, as if he had discovered some significant contribution he could make to the war effort which might help ease the sense that his own living seemed so shameful in the face of his brother's sacrifice. Of course, constantly reminding everyone of his brother's death perpetuated and magnified his brother's legacy and highlighted the divide between their fates...but in Clive's view, amplifying the heroic deeds and focusing attention on the bereft wife and children championed both his brother's name and military service as well.

Alex recounted this with irritation: "He told anyone who would listen, 'Look, this is what military life can get you: accolades, endless reminiscence about a life lived well and cut too short, pictures of your handsome self on every mantel, the thanks of the King himself.' Not, look at what military life can get you~ death at 31. Some people suspected he might be on the payroll of the Royal Marines, his word of mouth was so flattering, unceasing, and unsolicited."

Clive worked at the National Bank, Braintree Branch, a small building with an elevated ceiling to give the illusion of height and elegance, gray marbled columns at the entrance, and a gray stone façade that gave way to brown brick sides and back. The bank was jammed into the center of a row of storefronts, newsstands, and small businesses that made this the most bustling area of a town divided by textile factories and housing areas. Braintree was a suburb of London, and the younger adults gazed longingly toward London and imagined the life there to be filled with opportunity and excitement, just an hour away by car and connected by train. Parents and elderly residents of the town enjoyed its quiet lack of character and predictable pace of life, and the children played often on the banks of the rivers that defined the town, as Pod's Brook became the River Brain under the Roman Road, merging with the River Blackwater before reaching the sea.

Alex's uncle had toiled a few mostly satisfying years at the National Bank, the occupation of those members of his family somehow unqualified for military service. According to Mrs. Liddell, John Liddell, had not been a banker at heart nor a soldier, despite appearances. He was an artist; he had even taken private artistic study while away at the military academy at Landhurst from an older man living with his sister and her two children about forty minutes walk from his dormitory. This man, Edward Burroughs, supported his extended family through pottery production, creating the blue and white vases, urns, platters, and bowls that had become associated with the region and were prized even in Scotland and Wales. Burroughs was a painter, but his pottery put food on the table, and so his canvasses and brushes were slowly sold off until John Liddell discovered his small home on a walk and stopped in for a glass of water.

John Liddell, though, soon became the one abandoning his art for the reality of fulfilling the promises he had made, to his parents, to the military, and to his wife and children, even the unspoken ones. He slipped into the skin of a cavalryman, and the twenty or so canvasses he had brought home with him from the academy were packed in suitcases or stacked to line the back of his closet, buried under white shirts and creased woolen pants, where they stayed, waiting to be discovered.

As Edward Burroughs had done for John, Clive instructed John's son in the only way he could. He showed Alex how to alphabetize files by last name and how to code and classify the files for different loan categories. Alex learned to use a calculator to verify interest and how to fetch drinks and late lunches for the staff on his way to the bank after school. At closing time, Alex would sweep the floor, polish marble counters, and shine brass ornaments. He liked the quiet grandness of the place after hours. The building had been a private home previously, and the ornate millwork, scarlet ceiling, and plaster ornamentation made him feel like a prince in his palace, albeit one who did his own straightening up.

At the end of the week, his reward would be a few coins that he would give to his mother. On weekends, he would catch up on schoolwork, but he had lost his interest in schooling. He felt like a real working person now, and he knew that his future at the bank was secure. He gave no thought to what he wanted to do with his life. Childish fantasies of heroic employment as pirates, explorers, and aviation pioneers had been replaced by his early entry into the workforce, and he was too eager to keep his life settled to look upon this determined path with skepticism. Of course, he was too young to know about love, as well, and love has a way of changing plans, altering perspectives, and awakening dormant dreams.

When he was ten, he stopped giving his mother all the money he earned weekly and instead set up an account in his own name at the bank. He took over his family's finances completely, with a bit of initial oversight provided by his uncle. His mother did not notice and never said a word about this arrangement or gave a thought that her young son had transformed into the man of the house and was shouldering all the traditional responsibilities of that role.

When Alex's father died, his mother began calling for him late at night, awakening him after he had fallen asleep, to sleep in bed with her. Lying in her empty bed with her husband's pillow still in place on the left side of the small, thick mattress was too much for her to bear, though she couldn't imagine removing the pillow and reconfiguring her own space on it. Her husband's military service had meant many nights alone in this very bed, but without the promise of a return, this situation was entirely different. Unlike a drop of water that could conform to the shape of any container, his mother was icy and rigid in maintaining her old life as much as possible, even when a ten year old could see that it clearly was not working in her best interests.

She lay on the right side of the bed, staring at the empty pillow and knowing it would never smell of his aftershave and would never cradle his head again. His absence was seldom made more permanent than when she looked on the pillow, and this deceptively small, feather-stuffed rectangle enrobed in white cotton became a constant reminder of the deprivation of love she would experience for the rest of her life. Only Alex's warm, small body beside her could convince her of her attachment to this world and connection to another human. Her young daughter, Elizabeth, was like a doll to her, left half-dressed for hours on the floor, unfed. Only this boy who looked so much like his father could provide the comfort she craved. She would lose herself in dreams only when he was beside her in the bed. Her body curled around his made him claustrophobic. He longed for her to free him from this nightly prison, and soon began luring the cat into bed with them with a well-timed pat on the blankets when she sauntered past the doorway. The cat was hugely obese and as warm as bread out of the oven. Slowly, over the course of two weeks, Alex trained the cat to sleep the night through next to his mother. Soon enough, he was free to return to his own bed, after checking on his little sister.

At about the time that Alex reclaimed his sleep with the help of a cat, he noticed that his friend Roman never came by on Sundays after church services anymore, or during the week, as had been the long custom of their short lives. Walking, biking, climbing rocky hills, buying candy in town, or gathering friends for games of dodge ball or football had filled their afternoons and weekends for years, but since starting at the bank, Alex was rarely at home. Roman disliked knocking on Alex's door for fear that his mother would answer and he knew his mother wasn't well. He didn't need to worry, as Alex's mum never answered the door anymore.

Nonetheless, Roman would ride slowly by the house at the end of Violet Street hoping Alex would see him through a window and come running out the door to join him. On this day, someone did come out, but it wasn't Alex or his mother. Indeed, it wasn't even Alex's house at all. As he rode slowly back and forth, up and down Violet Street, he had attracted the attention of someone in the house at No. 7, with the morning glory vines.

A girl stood impatiently at her front gate, arms crossed, waiting for him to pass for the fifth time.

"If you want to know who I am" she called out to him, "all you had to do was ring the bell." Her tone puzzled him, as it was much like an owner addressing a dog who has scratched a doorframe: If you wanted to come in, all you had to do was bark.

No one had ever spoken to him like that before, certainly not a girl. He took a moment to size up this rather tall, thin person with pale skin and shiny hair the color of melted milk chocolate. Still astride his bike, he steered directly toward her, coasting to a stop. She possessed a dramatic series of expressions courtesy of darkly arching eyebrows and a propensity to suck in her cheeks, bite her lips, and stretch her neck like an ostrich. Roman pulled alongside her, his front tire touching her booted foot, which remained firmly planted on her front walk.

"I'm Roman." He said simply.

"And I'm English. Is this a game?" she replied quickly, squinting in irritation.

"No, that's my name. Roman Foster. I live in town, on Cabot" he responded quickly and defensively, as if he were being interviewed by a truant officer.

"What are you doing on my street?" she emphasized the 'my'.

"My friend Alex lives here too, you know" he countered.

"Bully for Alex. Where is he?"

"I don't know; he doesn't come out often."

"What's the matter with him? Is he sick or something?"

"No, he's not sick."

Roman turned his handlebars toward the street and placed his feet to push off on the pedals.

"I'm Lenora," she rushed, sensing she was losing her audience.

"Couple of my mates is tossing a ball around Tenley Park. Gotta bike?" he asked. She was wearing a long navy dress, but it was plain enough for a game of toss, he figured.

"No," she said. "I'll sit on your handlebars. Can you ride me all the way?"

He nodded, not noticing her bike parked on the side of the house, obscured by yellow rose bushes. She hopped up without so much as a word to her parents, and off they went slowly, meanderingly to the park. Roman had forgotten about Alex, but Lenora, remembering one morning a small boy running nearly to her doorstep and collapsing from exhaustion on the grass, where he lay for an hour impervious to the wet ground and the cold morning, could think of little else.

Foster was dead when Lenora told me about this day; she talked often to me of Foster and Bernard, but she refused to discuss her brother and what became of him. After hearing the details from Alex, I doubt that she ever knew what had happened to him, or at least I hoped she didn't. Then again, knowing Alex, perhaps she knew everything and that was why she couldn't speak about it.

Christmas, 1907. When Alex was 13, he gave his mother small cubes of lavender soap that he knew she liked, bought with one day's earnings at the bank, along with a stuffed duck for Lizzie. He had the soaps tucked under his socks in the top drawer of his dresser for nearly two weeks, and the smell had permeated his clothing so much that he had not worn socks for 2 weeks in the cold, wet winter for fear of revealing his gift and ruining his mother's small pleasure.

On that morning, she opened the carefully wrapped package in her trembling hands; she couldn't speak when she saw the contents, the perfectly formed cubes her husband would often surprise her with after work for no reason at all other than he passed by a small grocer's shop where they were offered for a good price on his way home. Even though she preferred the smell of tea roses, she loved his thoughtful gesture enough not to correct him. As she had done every Christmas since his passing, Mum smiled through tears and grabbed her son in an embrace tighter than he could understand. He thought she must be happy and made a mental note to get the soaps again next year.

As for Alex, books and new trousers revealed themselves every Christmas morning, the trousers in the long rectangular boxes, the books in the small rectangular parcels. Friends and relatives were in implicit agreement that books would offer the boy an imaginative outlet for his life, which surely must have been pure drudgery for one his age. And, I suspect, they believed that books would teach the boy lessons about life that his absent father could not provide.

That Christmas, Clive gave Alex a volume of Tennyson that included "Charge of the Light Brigade"; his mother gave him a slim volume entitled "Alice's Adventures in Wonderland." He always smiled brightly and kissed her cheeks no matter what the title, and this time was no exception. Though he put the "light brigade" on top of "Alice" when he set them on his nightstand, he revealed to me that he longed to read about Wonderland and began that very night. He couldn't wait to spend time alone with another child about his age, in a place unlike any he'd encountered before. He was charmed that like him, Alice was a child who was on her own, and was expected to take the lead in difficult circumstances. When he read about Alice crying a pool of tears that turned into a lake, he cried himself for the first time in ages and made a silent promise to slip into Lizzie's room and read it to her, too.

It was a Christmas filled with unexpected surprises for Alex. He had already given himself the best present that year when he discovered his father's untouched oils and canvasses while cleaning the house earlier in the week. He had marveled that he had never seen fit to look in his father's wardrobe before that day, fearing that he might be invading his mother's privacy.

But Christmas would mean guests (he hoped), and he wanted the entire house to look and smell as if the residents therein were perfectly sane. The wardrobe's contents were untouched, and so not dirty, but not fresh. He lightly fingered his father's hanging shirts before shifting his gaze down over the black shiny shoes and then toward the back, where he saw something large and solid. Expecting golf clubs or a grouping of hunting rifles, Alex pulled out the first canvas. At first he stared at the unfinished painting, vivid red paint applied thickly to stretched fabric; this first one he placed on the bed. Dropping to his knees, he removed each of 13 canvasses, large and small, one by one, and a bundle of red handled brushes with stiff yellow bristles wrapped in green silk cloth bound with a leather strap. A case of well-used oils, pigmented and clear, emerged from the darkness as well. After taking in these mostly incomplete works, and after a few days of wondering what to do with his find, he took up an unfinished canvas himself with the intention of painting. The potential that he felt when he held his father's brushes and stood over the empty wheat colored rectangle filled him with more expectation and excitement than any wrapped present under a tree could ever give. He could not wait to see what he would create. But after standing in nervous expectation for twenty minutes or so, he carefully, methodically, returned the paints to their leather satchel and the canvasses to the wardrobe, as he found he had no subject.

His hesitancy was due in part to an utter lack of training with the materials or in artistic technique and theory, partly due to lack of subject, and partly due to his puzzlement over his father's own canvasses and sketchbooks. Early drawings seemed to be studies of sculptures, faces with aquiline noses, wormy hair, and stony eyes with detailed lids but no pupils or iris. They were remarkably realistic, but they looked dead and Alex found himself staring into the blank eyes hoping to find some element of life, a twitch or blink, a reflection, some depth of soul or character revealed in the gaze. But he found none; his father must have been dissatisfied with these efforts as well, as pages later Alex could see him experimenting with the faces, turning the noses upside down, scrambling one into a puzzle with eyeballs on opposite ends of the page, giving one decidedly Greek torso a contemporary moustache and bowler. Most of the paintings resembled these later drawings, but few were finished and many canvases were blank.

The last work in the stack was a self-portrait so like his father that Alex felt as if he were standing before him again. The image was from the waist up, his father as he remembered him- dark suit, earnest expression, slight smile- except that there was a large chunk missing from the top left portion of the skull, just above the left eye. His head was open like a meat tin, brain exposed. Beams of light emitted from this gaping hole, lavender against a purplish gray background. The brain itself was a bulging mass of color and shine, thick entangled strands of possibility and potential which reminded him of a handful of pearl necklaces from a pirate's treasure chest, or a cluster of roads going everywhere. He wondered if this were a painting of his father's death, a premonition of his soul leaving his body after sustaining an irrecoverable head wound. He didn't know how his father died and would never know, but this he accepted as the truth. He stood staring in awe at the prophetic power of his father's art.

He looked away from the brain and into the eyes again and again. They were rich brown and dimensional, unlike the flat, empty sockets of the statuesque drawings. But these eyes seemed just as dead, as if all the light was escaping out of the hole in the head instead of illuminating them. He didn't know if it was this lifeless quality that bothered him or the fact that in his memory, his father's eyes were as blue as the sea.

IX. News

Alex was naturally curious about the Colonel who craved explosive advances, decided where his unit moved and how fast, and had his hand deep in other matters of grave consequence for them all. His curiosity was soon satisfied by a face to face introduction on the occasion of a formal inspection of the unit's temporary residence, another slit of dirt in the ground.

Alex had much to say to this man, as people newly arrived on a scene tend to have questions and ideas for improvement, unaware that they are not there to question or improve. Fortunately, Alex's bravado was tempered by the appearance of a rumor, in the form of a messenger through the communication trench lines, who carried with him a listing of the recent dead. When he arrived, as nondescript as nearly everyone around him, wearing the same grimy uniform and the same exhausted look, people parted and gave him room to pass as if he were the reaper himself, with the power to choose whose names he transported. Alex had never seen him or the list of the dead before, so naturally he was immune to this foreboding. It didn't take long for him to find Henry Crowne's name, as it was near the top of the alphabetical listing.

"Are you sure? This is unquestionably accurate?" Alex implored.

"No arguing the list," the messenger said with disinterest.

"How do I know if it's him, maybe there's someone else with the same name?"

The messenger proceeded to dispel his doubts, as he too was from Essex, about 20 miles from Braintree and had been previously asked in idle conversation if he knew a Henry Crowne, dead from trench fever. He told the speaker, no, but the speaker continued to provide the details of how the fever escalated into crippling pain so that near the end, the Crowne boy was driven near to madness, chewing on his hand until it was nothing more than a mangled lump. The messenger shrugged and repeated that he did not know him, but he was glad to find someone who did so that he could lighten the load that the story had placed on his mind by passing it along to someone else.

Alex didn't remember if he thanked the messenger for the information or not, as his previous clarity and enthusiasm for meeting the Colonel was replaced by the haze of loss. Those near him- Mouse, Parrish, Lowe- moved away under various pretexts, as words of sympathy or encouragement never seemed to matter much in these situations.

The quiet that surrounded him was interrupted as Captain Whitesell gave loud notice of the impending inspection with exaggerated flourish, and the enlisted men greeted the news with sighs and set to work, happy enough that they had been given something to do that, while arbitrary, at least had a foreseeable endpoint. From the

looks and words exchanged by the other lieutenants that Alex observed, it seemed that fear of punishment and desire for praise were equally effective motivators.

Lieutenants tripped over themselves in their efforts to be the hand responsible for repairing the crumbling dirt wall just so, or to be the one whose stashing of loose bibles under the sandbags propped up and leveled the parapet in a manner to rival any textbook description of proper fortifications. He noted with distaste how quick they all were to snap at each other or place blame for anticipated failings on the man to their left or right.

It seemed to Alex to be a baffling effort at deception; he thought it counterproductive to put on a show to this man, to demonstrate that all was well and tidy and as it should be when in fact everything was crumbling around them. If he only knew the true state of affairs, perhaps he could help to right things? Alex had been determined to illuminate the Colonel, but the recently gained knowledge of Henry's demise pained his soul and shocked his senses, even though, as he tried to remind himself, he had told Lenora that it would happen.

Alex listlessly gathered loose papers and other personal writings- letters, journals, postcards-from the men, as he had been instructed to hide away any evidence that the men here employed had their minds anywhere else.

He was sorting through these items, mostly letters he'd already censored and a few new messages that he would soon have to violate with his black marker, a job he found both interesting and despicable, when he came to be aware of the presence of a large, dark form beside him and knew, from the shape and mass and the peculiar vacuum that seemed to exist in the space between himself and it, that this presence was not Lowe but some other being entirely.

The Colonel was not a large man, actually. In fact he was short, with a large head, light hair, and long lips wrapped tightly around gently smiling jaws. The Colonel's entourage consisted of his Adjutant, Major Knight, whose pale, fleshy cheeks reminded Alex of a freshwater fish whose name he couldn't recall, and Capt. Whitesell, whose normally earnest face seemed to Alex frozen and grim.

As Alex was blocking the group's progress further through the trench, there was an unavoidable moment of introduction that became an awkwardly long moment of complete silence. Alex was sure he was meant to speak first, but couldn't think of the words. Slowly removing a cigarette from his mouth, the Colonel parted his lips and oozed out a question whose words fell as if dropped from a height.

"Who. Are. You?"

"I…I…I…" Alex stammered. There was so much he had planned to say to this man, about the Mills bombs, the lost opportunities, the absurdity of inspections, the character of Lowe, the loss of his friend, his unshakable sense that his life was changing more and more every day in ways that he anticipated but had not prepared for, until he felt entirely out of control…but the only response that pulsed in his mind strongly enough to coalesce into words and leave his mouth was:

"I don't know, sir."

"Explain yourself!" shrieked the Adjutant with such unexpected violence that even the Colonel jumped.

Alex, his words sounding too simple to convey the complexity of his feelings and the pressure to do so in the briefest amount of time possible, murmured only: "I'm sorry, gentlemen. It's just that I'm not myself, you see. But I think…"

"You. You are not paid to think, Lieutenant, only to execute orders I've thought of for you," the Colonel sneered contemptuously.

"This is Lt. Alexander Liddell, sir, recently arrived from Essex. He's just getting settled in," Whitesell leaned into the conversation from behind Maj. Knight in an effort to get the party moving on in a positive direction.

"Liddell," the Colonel said, curling his tongue slowly over the L's and nodding curtly to the Adjutant, who wrote something down in his book.

"Yes, that's right, Lt. Liddell, sir," Alex repeated, scrambling to find his voice in time, "and I still have a right to think, as an

Englishman." He meant to say as a human, but his actions and his thoughts were increasingly at odds.

The Colonel, stepping closer as he made to pass by, stared at Alex coolly. "Naturally you retain your rights to freedom of thought, Lieutenant, but do remember that I have the right and the duty (and he stressed this last word to show that duty trumped rights) to not be concerned with the contents of every individual brain crammed into these trench lines, as I have a war to run." And then the three pushed past.

In a moment, though, they stopped and turned as if they shared a body, "Come back here," the Colonel said in afterthought, even though it was they who had moved onward.

Alex dutifully approached with his hands at his sides in some form of attention.

Another awkward pause followed as the Colonel seemed to consider his words. They looked at him closely, as if examining him, until Alex became alarmed that something might be happening to him presently, before their eyes. Finally, the Colonel spoke evenly: "Keep your temper," he said, "and you might keep your head, Lieutenant."

And then he was gone and Alex felt his body fall limp in shame.

I asked him, "It didn't turn out to be a rumor then?"

He replied, with his head hung low, that no, Henry was certainly dead and as to the fever and the hand chewing, he would never know and what did it matter anyway, the details?

I stammered something about not knowing what even the smallest detail might illuminate in a situation, and then I changed the subject. I asked him whether he thought he might have been searching for a father figure in these older men- Capt. Whitesell, Col. Flint, his Uncle Clive- as I often wondered if Jack had sought to replace me in his life or even if I had left a void in his life so gaping and traumatic that it needed filling.

Alex shook his head. "Of course I needed advice sometimes, information based on experiences that only older men would have ...but no one replaced my father for me, not even close, ever. He's a space in my soul that will always be reserved for him and those memories…even as forgetting threatens to erase them. Even if in the end there is just a hole the shape of him, I'll never try to put anything there that doesn't fit just so."

His eyes were watery, as talking about Henry and his father in the same conversation was too painful. He had pleased me though, so I didn't press him on it and instead, let him go.

Part Three

Long has paled that sunny sky:

Echoes fade and memories die:

Autumn frosts have slain July.

X. Jabberwocky

Despite his reluctance to talk, Alex was with me twice the time that a regular patient, that is one who does not remind me of my son, would have stayed in the hospital for his condition, which I can best describe as shell shock. So though we had short sessions of near or complete silence, we often had some long talks and of course there were the journals and letters from which I could cobble together the story of his war life quite thoroughly. As I sit at my desk, in the early hours of evening, I am compelled to go think back to his more routine experiences in 1916, before he was wounded and sent home on a two week respite.

After days manning the front line trenches, a unit would rotate back to the communications trench or even further back to a rest area before beginning the evolution again. Their life was dominated by unpredictable routines. That is, they knew they would move from one trench to the next and so on, but they had no idea how long they would be forced to spend at any one location, or whether the war would end in one week or in a decade. They were not enlisted for a specific period. Their service to the Crown, their absence from their families and the lives they had planned, would only end when the fighting ended or when their lives ended, whichever came first. So they stumbled listlessly from one trench to the next, from one town to the next, engaged, retreated, advanced, waited for orders or attack.

Often, when the orders came, they seemed so baffling to the men that they competed with ever-present rumors for truth and action. When told to cross uncrossable terrain, they would shake their heads and curse the Colonel and the messenger who had delivered his words, suspecting he misunderstood the message or brought it to the wrong unit. Then they would step out into the swamps and lakes that were meant to be fields and promptly sink, many of them never to be extricated from the sucking mud. The messengers arrived at the units after racing from the Colonel's headquarters area, sometimes miles from the front. As they gasped for breath, they would spit out numbers, times, units, and dates in random order to Capt. Whitesell, Alex's immediate superior officer, who would try his best to make sense of it all. The messenger would wilt under cross examination from the lieutenants bent on clarifying the situation at hand. After a number of failures, the Adjutant, Maj. Knight, began transcribing the orders Col. Flint devised, informed by the desires of the generals, whose locations were typically even more remote. These notes were given to the runners and delivered to the captain, who read and interpreted them to the lieutenants. None knew which orders to rightly execute with confidence and which orders would execute them, which were legitimate directions and which were confused speculation, but without exception, they did what they were told by anyone who seemed to have the authority to do the telling. When failures occurred, it was difficult to trace the origins of the orders or at what point a critical deviation might have entered the communication chain, until the men lost faith in the authenticity of the orders themselves and began to doubt the existence of a higher authority.

Winter in Belgium, 1916, was excruciatingly cold for men forced to sit, often wet, in trenches day after day without relief from exposure. Alex could hardly believe that Col. Flint would desire for them to leave the relative comfort of the trench on the coldest nights to conduct another wire mission. He found himself enjoying the phenomenon of warmth on his face that he could generate by exhaling hard against the trench wall. If the air forced out was from deep enough in his belly, the breath reflected from the hard dirt wall seemed warmer than the air around him, and so it was a miraculous luxury he was sick to abandon.

But abandon it he must. They would drag their bodies across the winter-hardened ground, passed the bodies littering the expanse, most preserved in the cold in their death grimaces. When a star cluster grenade would light the sky, Alex and his men would freeze in their position on the ground, indistinguishable from the frozen corpses. Still, a smattering of machine gun fire would spray the field, just to be sure that all on it were unquestionably dead.

And when he was not crawling with Lowe, Parrish, and Mouse, across the frozen ground, he was peering at the same ground for hours on end through small dugouts in the parapet, wormholes, really, the size of the single finger that spiraled through the packed mud to make it. Moonlight swept the field before him with cold white light when not obscured by black clouds, darker than the night sky.

One night, staring into the flood of darkness, Alex's throat closed as he recognized movement. There were figures out there, in the field, and he was sure they were moving toward him, crawling stealthily over the frozen ground, freezing still like statues when light broke through the clouds and then lurching forward again under cover of darkness, as slow and deliberate as glacial floe.

So certain he was of this advance that he slept not a wink but stood rigid at his post, blinking furiously to try to pierce the dark with a finer concentration of sight. He did not initiate firing on the forms, as he was nearly transfixed by their slow progress and wished to see if they would make any threatening maneuver before sunrise doomed them.

When dawn came, he and his men, who watched alongside him, provoked by his keen attention and believing because he did that the forms were coming toward them, saw in their exhaustion that the bodies in the field were their own men, wounded in earlier fighting, who had managed to turn back toward the safety of the trench. They had frozen where they fell or as they travelled in vain, their bodies rigid, necks raised, some arms reaching upward, propped up on elbows welded to the frozen ground by mud and ice.

The darkness and light had merely deceived their eyes, giving these figures life they no longer had. Alex was certain, though, that they were not long dead, and that at least a few had moved toward them in the night, without the strength or ability to call out to their comrades before succumbing to the silent cold.

Rotating back to the communication trench was meant to be a relief, but Alex found the cramped conditions of the dugouts there to be nearly unbearable. For days on end he could not stand upright. When he tried to sleep, he could not stretch his body, and it was not long before he looked like the others, or rather until they all looked alike, which is to say that it was not long before they resembled a long row of turtles, humped, slow, and awkwardly out of their element, collected and assembled, upended and overturned and flailing.

When the shells came, as they seemed to do nightly as spring approached, Alex felt not only uncomfortable, but trapped, like a bug waiting, drugged and helpless, to be pinned forever into a display. He felt always exposed and soon realized how much he valued and longed for his private spaces. More than privacy, though, he longed for room to stand erect, move forward and back freely, to run. He had always envisioned his father at war riding his horse over great swathes of desert, his gaze scanning miles of sand interrupted only by waves of heat rising from ground to air. When he thought of war and his father, he saw men and horses and dogs riding as if they were on the hunt. He saw sport. But here, crouched in a hole in the ground hoping that the shells flying overhead would fall long or short, his misconceptions were dispelled.

As the shells continued, hour after hour, as heaps of cold, wet dirt dropped on them as if it were being thrown, and other things, unearthed by the explosions, rained on them as well, new ideas about war began to form in his mind. These ideas were cold and conspiratorial, and they hardened him against the screeching of the bombs, and when matter flew from the battlefield over the parapet and onto his head, even when it smelled like rotten meat, he remained still and calm, staring at the trench wall in front of him. It was this night when he noticed for the first time that the whitish color in the mud walls of the trench were bone, and that, indeed, bone stuck out from the irregular surface in some spots. Knobby bones like elbows. When he observed their smooth whiteness, he often thought of Lenora and how she had felt, hard and soft, when he had pressed against her. He thought of chess pieces, carved from bone, and how this was not at all like a game to him, and he thought of how whole they were when this all started.

On August 4, 1914, war was declared, after an Austrian archduke and his wife were shot by a Serb gunman in Sarajevo, a place Alex had never been. Based on a series of treaties and agreements, nearly every country in Europe was pulled in like fish gathered up in a net cinched tightly around them. Plans for school, work, vacations were put on hold. The word spread on the day following, which was a day like any other until Uncle Clive burst through the Alex's door in the late afternoon, red-faced from the heat and exertion, breathless, to announce to his nephew and young niece, it is official; we are at war.

Alex sat on the couch with his sister, listening to her recommend a Bronte book for his next reading session with Lenora while his mother roamed the upstairs of their home, looking for something he knew she wouldn't find. He stared at his uncle and tried to absorb the gravity of his words, but they seemed strangely powerless to seep into his core.

Leaving Lizzie with her books, he stepped outside to get a sense of what being at war felt like. The sun shone on his face; Mrs. Morris swept her stoop just down Violet lane; the smell of pungent grass and fresh flowers permeated the air; three young boys, the Kellogg brothers and their new Polish neighbor, strolled toward him with hand-fashioned fishing poles and rolled up knickers. Despite the normalcy, or perhaps because of it, a chill rose in him, forcing a hunch in his shoulders; he retreated into the confines of the house, unable to wrap his mind around the delayed significance of such an outbreak of hostility.

Later that week, in the evening, he walked to the Crowne's house because he felt a nervous energy that he suspected might delay sleep. There was much activity there as always. He could hear Henry's voice engaged in heated debate with his lower-toned father. As he approached the door, Alex hesitated before knocking, enjoying for a moment the sounds of a father and son. He knocked softly, not wanting to interrupt the moment. Lenora flung the heavy walnut door open in a flash, as if she had been expecting him.

"Oh, it's you!" she squealed, not without some disappointment.

"Were you expecting someone else?" he asked dryly, glancing left and right dramatically for any sign of Foster before stepping forcefully inside.

"Maybe," she responded, closing the door and following him to the sitting room. Her excitement was barely contained. He saw her through his periphery moving from one side to the other in the narrow passageway, looking for her chance to dart past. He slowed his step and blocked her entirely.

"What has you so wound up?" he asked over his shoulder.

"The war! Don't tell me you haven't heard." She is shocked.

"Of course I've heard. There's a war. Again I ask, what has you so wound up?"

"Alex Liddell, this will be the defining moment of our generation!" She chided him with an arched brow and a haughty sigh. They arrived at the sitting room where Henry, on the floor before an unlit fireplace and a century old chess set he is arranging for the start of a match, addressed his father, sitting in his chair, an overstuffed, green eyesore whose matching ottoman was claimed as a resting place by Lenora.

Mr. Crowne had the latest paper spread across his lap; it was open to the advertisements. As Alex entered, both men looked up and flashed a winning smile in an identical fashion, immediately assimilating him into the conversation.

"Tell him, Alex," Henry urged tacit agreement with his views: "England has no duty whatsoever to intervene on the Continent. Germany is one misbehaving county that will be contained eventually by Russia and France. Let them handle their own affairs."

"Ahh!" Mr. Crowne waved his son's reasoning away and made his appeal to Alex directly. "Europe must stand strong and united. England must assert herself as the major European power. We can't hide across the Channel isolated and irrelevant as the future of Europe is decided without us."

"The future of Europe!" Henry scoffed, placing the last ivory pawn in place on its square.

Alex had little authority or conviction about either side. His narrow world of work and home had absorbed so much of his focus that the events of the past weeks had ambushed him completely. His father's loss caused him to resist the notion of war and voluntary death at the hands of national interests, but he had never voiced these feelings to anyone and doubted that doing so now would make him sound like anything other than a simpleton or a child. Fortunately, a knock at the door and Lenora's rush to welcome Foster to the group relieved the pressure on him to weigh in on the matter immediately.

"Look at what the Germans have done to poor Belgium! The monsters- formidable or not- they must be dealt with swiftly." Lenora announced brightly, smacking her fist into her hand as she resettled on the ottoman, in a more glamorous pose than before, back arched, legs stretched to the side, ankles crossed.

"Yes," Foster chimed in with a nod to all in the room. "Germany isn't playing by the old rules, certainly." He accepted a glass of port from Henry.

Alex felt compelled to assert himself and heard his own words tentatively lurching forward: "Germany…isn't like England or France, not at all. They have different ideas, a different mindset. To consider them from within the framework of our traditions, our values, is foolish. They won't do what is expected of them because they aren't bound to our expectations of how one is meant to live and act."

"To be hesitant about moral relativism is a mistake we cannot afford to make. Germans are not Brits, for sure, but that does not mean we should stand by while they lay waste to the Continent, violate neutrality agreements and borders, kill innocent people..." Foster's argument crushed his own, but he delivered it with gentleness that belied its power, not wishing to humiliate his friend with bombast.

Henry jumped in at this point, easing the subtle tension between his two friends. He rubbed his bare right foot against the worn carpet in his unconsciously thoughtful way and admitted his quiet resignation, black knight in hand: "I suppose that I agree with you both on some level. I don't believe that England should jump to the aid of France and Belgium, though I know a treaty exists that says we will."

And Alex: "Of course we will stand by our word and adhere to the treaty, but the ones who drafted it, they aren't the ones expected to back it up, which is complete horse shit."

And Foster: "I do think that Germany should be challenged for changing the rules of the game without telling anyone. That's just not sporting. I don't want to be the one to remind Fritz how we conduct ourselves in this part of the world, but if the King is going to assemble a team to send over, I suppose that it would be quite unlike me not to join."

And Alex, silently to himself, as Lenora beamed at her man: That's what they are counting on, Roman.

"Well said," Mr. Crowne nodded decisively. He rearranged his paper as if to change the subject. "Germany has moved a pawn across the board of Europe, but he will be met with all the might of a coordinated and steadfast advance. It is our duty to keep each other in check."

"But it's not like a chess match at all!" Foster was quick to counter with a nuanced view. "You move, I move. That's chess. But now, the Germans have moved and we've stood still. And still they move!"

"I wish we could stop talking about war in terms of gamesmanship" Alex said, throwing his hands up in frustration. He may have missed out on games as a younger boy, but as a young man, he was growing tired of them.

"What and spoil the fun?" Foster smiled, sipping from his glass. "Anyway, I leave for Surrey on Friday next. Signed up at school with Bernard. How about you lot?"

There was silence all around, though all stared at Foster with a mixture of admiration, shock, and dread.

Henry's voice was first to venture forth with tentative enthusiasm, a tip of the head and a raise of his glass toward his friend: "You move, I move."

Alex remained silent; Lenora fumed.

At evening's end, she walked him to the door to show him out, a courtesy she always extended guests in her home, but tonight she marched a bit ahead of him, with added pomp, as if she were escorting out one who had crashed a party.

"Mind the gap," she said with coldness as she placed her hand on the dull brass knob.

"Pardon?" he stopped too close for her to be able to swing the door inward, so it remained closed.

"The gap. Between you and them" she nodded to the sitting room where the others still spoke softly.

"You mean between me and those who are willing to die for ideas they can barely articulate and others who support them in that effort, knowing they are themselves safe from harm?" She heard his words as anger and irritation, but he meant to convey confusion. Perhaps she mistook anger for desperation? She could hardly see her face in the unlighted entryway, but he could imagine her disdain. He put his hand over hers on the knob and pulled the door open himself.

He was the only one in the house privy to the warm bath of summer evening air, as Lenora was wedged between the door and the wall, and the others were engaged in matters beyond the weather and the time and the moment. He moved his right hand from the knob to the door itself, holding it ajar so that she could release her own hand and reposition herself. He pushed the door fully open so that she could feel and smell the air with him, though she was more interested in following him out so that she could continue to blast him with her sudden fear over Foster's imminent departure, which she translated into anger over Alex's own lack of desire to depart. He knew her game, even if she did not, and tonight, he had no interest in playing along.

So before she could open her mouth again, he turned back to her and pressed her against the door, kissing her slowly and heavily, with little movement, paying close attention to the taste and feel of her lips, memorizing them, because he knew, even on that day, that he would be leaving with the rest of them. He knew, too, that this kiss would change nothing between them. But he wanted there to be no artifice between them, not now. For a minute, Lenora stood silently and kissed him back, barely hearing the soft civilities inside and the century exploding around them.

Yes, that sounds about right. Jack would be thoughtful about the future, so he would grab the opportunity to kiss his girl then, and she would kiss him back. Certainly. I can almost see him there, at the door.

As the bombing intensified, Alex suspected that this phase was coming to a close, and that the Germans would send the infantry next, to flush them out of their hole in the ground. He hoped their wire had withstood the shelling. He crouched down deeper into the trench and tried to squeeze his muscles in isolation, to get blood flowing through his body and to make sure that everything would work when the moment of action arrived. He started at his toes, which were deadened due to wetness and cold, concentrating on squeezing first the right toes and then the left. He rotated his ankles, first the left, then the right. Then he moved on to his calves, thighs, etc. As the ground vibrated around him and the explosions rang in his ears, he squeezed his eyes and clenched his jaw out of turn, unable to wait for the process to move from his legs to his head. As it did often at times like this, his mind began to travel.

He told me of these well visited memories with loving detail. The smells and warmth, the feelings. They did more than pass the time. They created a barrier between him and his present reality; they tricked his mind into believing that he was still a member of a species of animal that distinguished itself through advanced thought, creation and appreciation of art, compassion, and love. He knew men who seemed only to think of the present moment; they viewed the memory as a dangerous device intent on sabotaging their soldiering. They were as they appeared and nothing more. No mothers, fathers, pets, favorite teachers or best friends colored their shadows. They seemed dead to Alex, or as flat and one-dimensional as a profile on a playing card. Lowe and Parrish were of this persuasion. They may well have never had a friend beside the other. They complained the least. They seemed professional and efficient; but this attitude was not enough to spare even them from the randomness of death on the Western Front. And if death was to get him as well, Alex refused to live the last of his days like a portrait of himself instead of as himself.

I had patients like these men Alex described. They turned their back on their former selves so abruptly and decisively that they could not recognize and reclaim their abandoned selves again. I struggled with this notion when it came to Jack. Would he have held fast to his memories of his school life, his friends, his mother, and perhaps even me? Would he have withstood the assault on his sense of decency and defended his sense of self, bearing all the strain that an emotional soul bears in conflict? Or would he have transformed into a soldier through and through? Lost to the fight. Nothing felt right to me. Perhaps I didn't have enough information from Alex to fill up the well from which Jack would have drawn his conclusions and made his decisions. Or perhaps nothing felt right because as proud as I was that he had joined up, as accepting as I was of the fact that he would either live or die, I had scarce given a thought to what might happen in the middle.

When Alex's mind traveled, one of his mind's favorite events to recall during the worst times was this:

"Bernard and Lenora sit in the grass talking. They have come to support our team in the first rugby match of the 1914 season, but they aren't paying attention to the game at all. I can hear Lenora's laughter occasionally and it is driving me to distraction. When I run out of position to their side of the field, I can detect the low tones of Bernard urgently explaining something to her, but I can't stay in one spot long enough to properly eavesdrop. I am sure they are talking of books. Bernard has a tan canvas bag filled with them, and Lenora is holding an emerald green volume in her hands while arguing lightheartedly with Bernard, who does nothing lightheartedly.

When the whistle blows, I forego the opportunity to get a drink of water with the team and trot over to Bernard and Lenora. I throw myself on the blanket beside them nonchalantly.

'What have you got there?' I address Bernard, although clearly I'm talking of the book in Lenora's hands.

Bernard begins to reply 'Lewis Carroll. It's...'

'Ridiculous!' she interrupts. 'Listen to this, Alex.' She clears her throat and holds the book in her outstretched hand and begins reading in a horribly theatrical way. ''Twas brillig and the slithy toves did gyre and gimble in the wabe. All mimsy were the borogoves and the mome raths outgrabe...'

I rise to my knees and continue with intensity: 'Beware the Jabberwock, my son! The jaws that bite, the claws that catch! Beware the Jujub bird, and shun the frumious Bandersnatch!'

I am leaning strangely close to her. Her eyes flicker and her mouth is open.

'I can't believe you know this nonsense,' she says, closing the book with a snap.

Bernard jumps in to continue his defense of the work. 'It's genius, really. Carroll anticipates your linguistic sensibility. He changes words only enough so that they are simultaneously incomprehensible and lucid.'

She isn't convinced.

'It's an old tale,' I tell her, 'told in a new way.' It's hard not to look at her mouth.

'Why not just tell it the old way?' she is asking me.

'Repetition becomes mindlessness,' I shrug. 'The slaying of the creature happens over and over in history and literature, but it is never routine to the creature or to the slayer. Lewis Carroll doesn't think it should be routine to you, either. He creates a new language because the old one is dead. It fails to move you.'

'Yes, and..." Bernard jumps in to pick up on his argument, but Lenora stops him by unexpectedly grabbing the back of my head with her free hand.

'Come to my arms, my beamish boy!' She demands with a confident smile. I stiffen. She dissolves into laughter as Foster and Henry arrive dripping sweat and water on us all. Releasing me, Lenora returns the green book to Bernard and turns her attention to Foster's bloody knee. It's not lost to me that she knew that line by heart. I think about that and smile even when there is no reason on earth why I should have a smile on my lips."

Lenora remembered reading Alice too, of course. She told me often of how they read together, sometimes outside, often in her home near the fireplace. Never at his home. She talked to me of the book and Alex wrote about it often, in his journals and in letters to her. An image from their discussions emerges:

The hillside, the pale blue and white striped blanket, the moment squandered. Alex lying on his back near her feet, absorbing the sun and her words, assaulting him with similar intensity while he handled them with similar indifference.

Roman and the boys engaged in a lively rugby match so close that her words were often interrupted by her shrieks and smiling criticisms as stampeding feet trampled the edges of the blanket or a ball threatened to take her head off before being intercepted. She was the queen here, and she would have it no other way, even if the price for her singular adoration was near trampling.

Alex breathed in deeply, hoping to smell her perfume but instead inhaling the pungent smells of grass, fresh, moist earth, and laundered linen. The mingling of these quintessentially clean and dirty odors transfixed him and he breathed with greater purpose, losing the sound of her voice altogether as sensory awareness and physical weariness began to overtake him.

"Alex!" her voice reached through his slumber and pulled him back to her. "I can't imagine if I should be offended or not. This ….book is for children!" She snapped the slim, green volume closed on her lap and tossed it to him, hitting his chin and chest. He often selected reading for her and some of their most intimate conversations took place in her drawing room discussing the passions of Austen's heroines, the questionable virtuosity of Penelope. She wanted more of this, but she never asked him for a selection of a particular kind. She gauged their relationship on his choices. She took some thrill in thinking that if the novel featured a feisty, remarkable girl, that things were going well. In the end, the girl always ended up with the man of her dreams, whether she had to suffer through gothic horror or the internalized turmoil of polite times wherein society seemed less like an exciting maze of possibilities but a preordained grid of relationships closely connected and as rigid and binding as a corset. He always chose novels for her, perhaps thinking that ladies only read novels, which bothered her; but in truth, she did prefer novels to other readings, and preferred nearly every novel to the reading at hand.

Here was a feisty female heroine in Alice, clearly. But she was a child and there was no romantic interest, no love at all. A child engaged in ridiculous relationships and meaningless conversations that seemed important but ultimately dissolved into gibberish with hints of sub-text that stayed so far below the surface that nearly every interaction ended in frustration, screaming, or tears.

She had begun her reading hungrily, thirsty for some indication of the standing of their relationship. But somewhere between the pool of tears and the lobster quadrille, she began to puzzle over whether or not he was telling her she was a ridiculous child.

"Again," she said, this time her voice steady and low, as if she had decided that surely she was meant to be offended, "I can't imagine why I'm reading this."

He rolled over slowly to his stomach, looking up at her with a slow stare that she met unblinkingly. His hair was tousled and his shirt nearly pulled from its formerly securely belted position, and she was distracted by all this, though she fought through and kept her eyes level.

"No, I don't suppose you can imagine it," he said after staring at her face for some time. She was thankful that his response allowed her to express anger, for this would explain away her certain redness.

"But I wish you would try," he continued with a sad urgency.

It took her a moment to realize that his carefully considered words were devoid of the sarcasm she had come to expect of him and which he used to keep a safe distance between them.

This he had said to her plainly.

Because it was such an unexpected departure from form, for a long moment she forgot the aggressive play of the young men on the grass, the sun, the promise of summer and its impending separations. For an instant there was only him with his clear blue eyes like a melting glacier, glistening with anticipation and even hope that she would reciprocate with an honesty and plainness completely unlike her. Then he blinked, and it was gone.

JABBERWOCKY

`Twas brillig, and the slithy toves
Did gyre and gimble in the wabe:
All mimsy were the borogoves,
And the mome raths outgrabe.

"Beware the Jabberwock, my son!
The jaws that bite, the claws that catch!
Beware the Jubjub bird, and shun
The frumious Bandersnatch!"

He took his vorpal sword in hand:
Long time the manxome foe he sought –
So rested he by the Tumtum tree,
And stood awhile in thought.

And, as in uffish thought he stood,
The Jabberwock, with eyes of flame,
Came whiffling through the tulgey wood,
And burbled as it came!

One, two! One, two! And through and through
The vorpal blade went snicker-snack!
He left it dead, and with its head
He went galumphing back.

"And, has thou slain the Jabberwock?
Come to my arms, my beamish boy!
O frabjous day! Callooh! Callay!'
He chortled in his joy.

`Twas brillig, and the slithy toves
Did gyre and gimble in the wabe;
All mimsy were the borogoves,
And the mome raths outgrabe.

On the days that Alex crouched and huddled in freezing trenches trying to remember past times (not so he would be reminded of why he came and feel rededicated, but so he could remember that he was still a human with a particular life that he wished to return to), Lenora wandered around her quiet house, unable to sleep. Never had her home seemed more empty and cavernous. The streets of the city, even in the middle of day, seemed lighter and airier. Trains and subway seats were emptied. She was used to crowds and admiring glances and conversation. Now she could go anywhere and do anything, work in nearly any capacity she chose, attend any elite school desperate to fill its empty classrooms, jump any train to any destination in the country. She was more free than she had ever been before, but still she rubbed her throat as she paced the long hallway from the foyer, where Alex had kissed her, and the living room, where her brother and Roman had debated the war so hotly, feeling stifled and unsatisfied.

She could remember (as she would tell me later), the opposite sensation, the sublime comfort and freedom of floating on gently pulsing waves on warm days with him. His mind, too, seemed to crave the memory of spreading his body out fully, extending his limbs over the water, his entire front exposed to the light of full sun. They both spoke or wrote to me often of the shore.

Many times they found themselves alone in the ocean, floating side by side, the two stronger swimmers among their friends and her family. Floating like starfish, arms and legs out wide, they could stay on their backs at the surface of the undulating waters for hours. Sometimes the push and pull of the current would cause their finger tips to touch. Occasionally their heads would knock together gently or their hair would entangle like seaweed.

Sometimes they enjoyed the silent closeness of these moments, but this day, she wanted to talk more about Alice, as he seemed to like the topic and it was a harmless subject.

She asked him about suitcase words. He corrected her, as she knew he would:

"Portmanteau words: French for a kind of suitcase, something that carries two things together in one space. Carroll describes this himself, a little bit after the Jabberwocky poem. You read it all, right? He talks about slithy being both slimy and lithe at the same time…"

His voice trailed into the sleepy sea, and in few minutes, she voiced her thoughts to him again.

"What am I? Describe me in a portmanteau word."

He was inscrutably silent for a long time and she smiled contentedly while he gave the matter great thought.

"I've got it," he said after a few minutes of bobbing on the gentle waves. "Prossy."

She didn't like the sound of it and folded inward, ending her back float abruptly. She touched her toes to the unseen sand below them and stood as steadily as she could while she took his proclamation apart.

"Prossy." She repeated.

"Yes. Pretty and bossy."

Her lips twisted and her eyebrows seemed to consider whether this was good news or bad.

"What about me? Come up with one for me." He thought it best to deflect her rumination with a challenge of his own.

He dove under the water and swam around her for what seemed a full minute before breaking the surface, inches from her. She pushed off the bottom and circled her arms to launch herself once more into the current and to create a more comfortable distance between them.

Even though the knit of her brows suggested otherwise, after a few moments she said: "I can't think of anything!" She swam off so that he would know that the conversation was ended.

He wished he knew what was in her head, but then he thought it only fair that he did not. After all, she was not 'prossy' to him. She was more than pretty and she wasn't really bossy, just good at knowing what had to be done.

In fact, after challenging himself, he found that he could not think of a portmanteau word for her, either. The only two words that appeared in his mind when he thought of her were her name: Lenora Crowne. And the word that remained in his mind when he had dismissed everything else was not a combination of anything at all, but expressed his feelings for her in the purest way he could summon: "mine."

He wrote her a letter about this day and revealed to her what he had been thinking. She wrote one back, revealing her surprise. That had been the word that had resonated in her own head, pulsing like an alarm while her brain sifted through a thousand other possibilities that she would have been more comfortable expressing. She couldn't tell him "mine," and she couldn't even write 'mine' to him later, not even when life breathed down their necks like a hovering beast. She wrote it, in a letter, but she did not send it to him to read. She kept it, with all the other letters she wrote but did not send, in a large cloth bag with wooden handles, the day bag that she often took on their outings to the shore.

Even though revelers had returned to the beaches in the summer of 1918, before the war had even ended, she believed that no one paid any particular attention to her when she swam out with the bag in tow into the cold ocean, walking out until the water reached her neck and the bag was submerged, filled like a balloon with opaque water, the ink on the pages within loosening and lifting until words disappeared, entangling like seaweed and floating away into the infinite sea. She dived into the murky depths to fill the bag as best she could with sand, ensuring that her words to him would remain, unread and unreadable. When her task was complete, she dragged herself through the water and to the dry sand, where she lay on her back, feeling the sun on her face, breathing hard, and wondering if the pain in her chest was her heart sinking like a stone or struggling to redefine itself.

It saddened me that their love had failed to take flight, that it was sunk and abandoned. I wanted to tell them both to try harder, to not give up! It made me morose to think of Jack at the end, without even love to accompany him through the most difficult times. I cast my glance glumly around the lives I knew, some only remotely, some more intimately, and I surprised myself at the amount of people who seemed to be living without love and companionship. I wondered if the war was a symptom or a cause of this sad state, and then I considered that perhaps love seemed underrepresented in the lives of those I knew because I was on the search for an image of love that belonged to another age, an idealized, romanticized, novelized notion of love that had grown older and adopted modern clothes and a face I simply could not recognize.

XI. Advice from a Caterpillar

"I went to the Tocqueville House about six months after arriving in Belgium," Alex told me. I had been questioning him routinely and he was growing exasperated at my requests for simple information He seemed irritated as if he suspected I was wasting his time or stalling in his treatment. I wanted to know who he was, not his name, but who he was really. It was important that I understand how he considered himself. Some men are unable to separate the soldier from the self and so can't reconcile the ethics of soldiering, the ever present violence and death, with the normal life of a young man residing in Britain.

He told me with a sigh, "You know my name; you know why I'm here," he frowned. And then after crossing his arms tightly and glaring at me from across my oriental rug: "You remind me of Tubby Clayton."

Clayton was an apparently large man, if monikers are to be believed, a reverend, who had converted a house at Tocqueville into a place of solace and relaxation for men of all ranks, aptly named an "Everyman's Club."

The first floor was for socialization, but the second was a chapel, a simple white room adorned with black and red striped curtains and cushions on otherwise spare pews. It was here, in the chapel, that Alex had talked with Clayton, shortly after finding out about Henry. Alex's men were completing their march along the southern border of Belgium to new positions on another battlefields outside of Ypres, and the Everyman was on the way.

Clayton had heard many, many men unburden themselves, and so when Alex talked of Henry, he was patient and only mildly inquisitive.

Henry had died of trench fever during the Battle of Loos, near Lens, in the fall of 1915. This was an extremely painful condition that we suspected was brought on through exposure to the many rodents and insects populating the dugouts. You know already of the hand.

Alex did not believe this last detail at first. Not Henry. He wouldn't come to that. How was it possible? But the messenger was sure of the veracity of his information. How could he mistake such a thing? His disbelief led Alex, who had stopped attending mass quite young, to seek out the comfort of the upper level of the Everyman. Clayton himself was there, taking long drags from a cigarette and exhaling languid clouds of smoke into the room. As he told me about their meeting, I suspected that his detailed recollection was in part obfuscation, a way to avoid addressing the fate of his friend, Lenora's brother, Henry.

"'I don't know what's real anymore. Surely these things can't all be real,' I exhaled despairingly, taking a seat by the rotund man on the striped cushions, leaning close to him as one would a confessor.

'Do you think you are real?' he responded slowly, after a long pause.

'Of course.' I suppose I hesitated. Tubby let me explain without interruption: 'Sometimes I feel like I'm a figment of his imagination,' I whispered low.

'God's?'

'Lewis Carroll's,' I ventured. Clayton's expression never changed; his voice bore the same languidness that at once provoked and consoled me.

'I feel as if I've read this story already. All of this: the trenches, the crowding, the pressure, the animals, the executions, the arbitrariness of everything. He saw all of this. He wrote about it years ago. In a children's book. As if to get to us young, before we were told what it was to be a man, what was expected,' I left off there, hoping that my listener would understand. I didn't mention my father and his paintings. Clayton took a long, slow breath.

'Artists can be visionaries, certainly, but only God's light can illuminate that vision. Artists' minds are open to seeing what others cannot…artists cannot understand what it is they see of God's plan. They only do their best to record it and share it with us. Interpretation and true understanding are other matters entirely.'

'Then I'm a figment of God's imagination?' I wasn't convinced.

'Why a figment? Aren't you one of his creatures, flesh and blood?'

'Maybe God is asleep, dreaming all this mess. Wondering what would happen if he stepped out for a moment and let mankind take the wheel, so to speak. Maybe I'm still back in England, helping my mother, and this is not reality at all, but just God's dream vision.'

'Many men feel as you do, that God is somehow absent from this place. Yet you do not doubt his existence; you only doubt your own,' Clayton seemed to weigh this situation in his mind, staring at the blankness of the white walls beyond the altar. 'So God is asleep, dreaming you are a soldier on the Western Front. When he awakens, what will happen to you?'

I shrugged. 'Maybe it's not God's dream, but mine,' I was growing irritated, my voice thick and breaking, "and when I awaken, you'll disappear and I will rejoin my life in Braintree. But I know this isn't true. I could never have imagined what I've seen here. I'm not an artist or a visionary. If I were, I could never have let this happen.'

Clayton seemed amused. 'You're not an artist, not a visionary, not a dreamer…who are you, then?' 'I don't know,' I responded honestly. 'I'm not myself, certainly.'

Clayton prompted me: 'You are a soldier fighting a foe that needs to be vanquished if order and justice is to be restored on the Continent and those at home protected from the devastation you see around you every day.' From his tone, I could not decide if I was being admonished.

'Well, that's how one story goes, anyway. We've killed as many innocents as the Germans, no doubt. I'm sick of anyone creating a story out of this war. None of it is true. Everything anyone at home thinks they know of it is imagined. We don't know the truth of why we are here, when it will end, what the logic is behind our orders. Our leaders don't know a thing about the conditions here and how their strategies affect the men carrying them out. No one sees the thing clearly. Those at home, their imaginations are so limited that they can't guess at the truth, so they absorb anything that seems plausible and palatable, that fits what they know of battle from poems and paintings.'

'And you know the truth?'

'I know nothing except that our leaders keep generating plans of attack, but I don't trust that my survival matters much to them. And

I know that when we die, those at home will look in the Mirror and believe lies, lies, lies about it."

Even behind my desk in a pleasant country manor house I could hear the venom in his voice and for a moment I was afraid he might leap up from his chair, lunge across the desk and throttle me for being one of those at home who believed the lies.

Recounting this story animated Alex in a way that I hadn't seen him before. I wanted to exploit the anger he had conjured up to explore his relationships further. Lewis Carroll could wait for another day.

"Are you angry at the people at home, or just the newspapers?" I asked him. He seemed to relax, unclenching his fists and sinking back into the chair.

"Tell me something about them," I requested as gently as I could, eager to hear more of the details of his life, to picture the people he saw every day. He shifted in his chair and cleared his throat. I had no water to offer him, and I didn't want the session to end just yet, so I declined to excuse him to fill his glass down the hall.

He said: "I walked through town on a drizzling morning. Since plans for school were scrapped, I had taken to helping my uncle at the bank again. Some of our customers were too elderly or infirm to come to the bank offices to sign needed paperwork in a timely way, so I would transport papers or money directly to them.

Bernard, Foster, and Henry were gone. Bernard had signed up with Foster but had finished training first, his family knowledge of engineering being highly prized by the expeditionary forces. Henry and Foster had completed their officer training together and had shipped out the Sunday prior. I did not go to their graduation or their send-off. The pageantry and uniformity of it all made my stomach turn. I could still remember sending off my dad the last time. The uniforms, the feelings, the palpable feelings in the crowds watching military parades, reminded me of peering into the dark windows of Briarside Academy, into the solemn classroom housing an arcane, profane portrait of duty and glorified death. It was a timeless rendering of young, keen men who sacrifice free will, logic, common sense, and all their future plans to an ideal determined by, and meant only to perpetuate, empire. I would have none of it.

Up ahead, on the corner of Fairfax and Lucy Street, Lenora stood with two other women I didn't know dressed in pale gray. They spoke animatedly to a middle-aged businessman whose face was fixed in a smile, flattered by the attention of attractive ladies. I heard Lenora's strong voice rising above the rest.

'Take this, sir, as a reminder of the sacrifices being made on the Continent not just on your behalf, but in your place.'

It took the poor sod a moment to decipher and contextualize her rhetoric and, even then, he didn't throw down the white feather that Lenora has pressed into his hand. He merely flushed, bowed his head, and moved on with haste.

I, too, had smiled when I saw her, but I could feel my mouth drying and hardening as I approached. She was Ophelia and Hamlet's ghost at once, beckoning me, summoning me to kill, to fulfill my duty, summoning me, ultimately, to my death. She waited for me with a feather in her hand.

'Save it,' I warned as she opened her mouth.

She shrugged, 'You didn't say goodbye to Henry.'

'I hope you did,' I countered harshly.

'He'll be home on leave in two months,' she said with certainty, 'and he'll be received as a hero. Really, Alex, I don't know how you can walk the streets so brazenly when so many men are…'

'You like brazen men,' I charged, hoping to disarm her annoying militancy.

'I like men who do what's right, what's expected of them, even when they don't want to. This war is right. The Germans are barbarians with no grasp of civility, no respect for laws or human decency. If we don't defend Belgium and France, England will be next. The Huns will creep onto our shores and life as we know it will end.'

I smiled at her conviction. 'Your life as you know it has already ended.' I didn't hesitate to continue. 'Do you really think that Henry is coming home? You are already no longer a sister or a girlfriend. How will you identify yourself? Who will you become? Who is Lenora if not Henry's sister and Foster's girl? Will I know you when I see you again?'

'Shut up,' she hissed. 'You are always so damn pessimistic. Don't speak to me like that again. Don't speak of Henry or Roman or Bernard either. Henry will be back in two months; Roman before the New Year or sooner if the war ends.'

I couldn't take it anymore. 'Your beliefs…they are so pathetically received. Who is stuffing your head full of such rubbish? You are a challenging girl, Lenora. I've always liked that about you. Why on earth do you not challenge these ridiculous ideas? They are like a religion for you, believed beyond reason, believed because the absence of belief would force the acknowledgment of cruelty, malice, stupidity, and nothingness. Mark my words, dear. People you love will die and it will all be for nothing.' People were looking at us, and it humiliated her.

Her face flushed with anger and she broke eye contact with me, turning her body away from me all together. The other ladies huddled together, several paces away, showering us with disdainful looks. I frowned at the situation: Lenora's involvement with the feather girls and our inability to communicate about important ideas without a fight. I turned away from it all, unsatisfied, and continued my delivery to Mr. Charles Halston, #26 Fountain.

When I arrived, Mr. Halston was in his small side garden, mostly chrysanthemums and greens. He was pleased to see me. I noticed that he was wearing house slippers that were now muddied.

He thanked me for the delivery and took the envelope from me.

'Enjoy your garden. It's quite lovely,' I nodded to him and turned back down his short walk. In my mind I was debating whether I should avoid Lenora's corner or insist on going any way I chose. My thoughts were interrupted.

'What's this, my boy?' I turned to Halston. He had removed a long white feather from the envelope and squinted at it with confusion.

'Ahh…I found it on the sill this morning and thought Mrs. Halston might like to wear it in her hair,' I replied stupidly.

He beamed and shook the feather at me, 'Good thinking, boy. A right romantic you are.'

He tucked the envelope under his arm, and went inside to see the missus. A romantic! Are we all blind to each other, or do we simply see only what we want to see, a grand hallucination? I decided to avoid Lenora.

She was right. Henry did make it back in two months for a short leave. He didn't die until September. But I was gone by then and didn't hear of it for months. Not even from her."

"And what of the others....your mother, your uncle, tell me more about them," I wanted to redirect him toward his home life again.

"Uncle Clive didn't talk much about the war. He was usually the chatty sort, but had recently taken up humming. He rarely spoke to me anymore, though he always wanted to be around. I suppose it was because so many topics seemed off limits. Everything, suddenly, revolved in the uneasy space surrounding the war, and the smallest of conversations took on monumental tones and significance.

At dinner that same night, Clive was drawn into the subject because I asked mum what she thought of Lenora and the white feathers. I had to ask three times before she talked as if she heard me correctly. She considered her response as she cleared dishes from the table.

'I don't know. I can't say I remember anything like it before. Or maybe I never noticed. Women are different now, I suppose. Suffrage is coming; women are gaining power and a voice. They want to be heard; they want to be a part of the big issues.'

'They want the power to send all the men away, to certain death?' I ask incredulously, but as gently as I could manage.

'Well, you can't really say that it's certain, can you?' she countered. 'The Germans could surrender any day. They've got the Russians on one side and our boys on the other; they can't hold out for long.'

'Perhaps not,' I conceded, though I suspected otherwise, 'but I suppose that I mean that war is not just an issue. It's murder, death. Children robbed of their parents and families robbed of their homes. It's easy to call it an "issue" when it's happening far away.' Clive kicked me under the table.

'What do you know of war?' she turned on me with unexpected sharpness, setting the dishes down in the kitchen with a rattle. I didn't answer her. I wanted to tell her: I know it took my father. But something in her voice restrained me.

'What would you have me do, Mum?' I asked her quietly. She breathed deeply and wrung her hands on a dish towel.

'Alex,' she began, 'I've always taken a sort of pride in your willingness to fight over the smallest thing, to argue just for the sake of a challenge. I'm surprised that you haven't joined this fight. I'm just surprised.' She disappeared into the kitchen, and I sat in the high-backed, rigid chair quite stunned. I hadn't joined the fight! I seemed to be the only one willing to fight for anything that mattered!

Clive cleared his throat and stirred his tea loudly.

'Take it from me,' he started. 'If you don't go, you will be plagued by your decision for the rest of your long life.'

I looked at him and saw the years of guilt and regret in the creases around his sensitive eyes. Without a word, I pushed my chair from the table and retired to my room, my last refuge in this world gone mad.

The next day I joined up. There would be no fanfare, no trumpets blaring. Just my name on a line, a few papers to read, an oath to mumble, and a date for training.

I don't remember training, I told you that before. It was all a blur, it happened so fast and seemed so foreign to me, like I was living someone else's life and couldn't quite figure what had happened to mine.

It was inevitable. Everyone was involved, even though motivations and justifications were wildly variable. Bernard desired to prove his loyalty and physical ability; Foster believed that military experience was the right thing to add luster to his future in politics; Henry asserted that the war was his generation's calling and would always join just about any team that would have him. Lenora, my mother, my uncle. The means hardly mattered; the end was common. Men were going to the war; I was a man; away I went. I was alone in England. I was missing something, clearly. Even if I disagreed with the generals and the politicians, even if I disbelieved every bit of news I read or heard, even if every fiber of my being wanted nothing more than to survive to old age, it all came down to one thing for me: My friends were going. The ones who had been there for me.

When I told my uncle of my decision, he was visibly relieved. His shoulders sagged, his mouth smiled, and he embraced me warmly.

'God be with you, Alex,' he said with touching emotion. 'You've made the right decision.' He clapped my arm lightly and sent me home from the bank early to get my affairs in order.

When I told my mother, she was hard to read. She placed her tea cup back in its saucer and her mouth contorted into a half-smile, but her eyes registered something like panic.

'I'll be alright, Mum. It'll be over soon,' I heard myself saying and couldn't believe I was consoling her. I was doing her bidding! Perhaps there was a transformation that began to take place once you'd given in.

I didn't tell Lenora, but somehow she knew. She saw me at Kippers in the morning, my regular place for morning tea when school was out of session. She caught me outside the door before I could enter, approaching from the opposite direction. I got to the threshold first and stopped to wait. She halted a few paces away. Her brows were knit and her face wore a peculiar look as if she was examining a captured insect never before seen in these parts. Merely to break the awkward silence, I began:

'Well, you have your wish. The last male holdout will soon be gone and your women's club can secure the vote, take over the business world, and install yourselves in all the top posts. I suspect it won't be long before we are all singing God Save the Queen.'

I smiled, but it was not reflected. She reached out quickly and grabbed my coat sleeve, just above his wrist, giving it a slight tug. Her fingers tightened, just for a moment; then she disappeared.

Quite dumbfounded, I stood for a moment alone outside of Kippers. When I entered at last I ordered my regular, Earl Grey. It was tasteless and forgettable.

And my sister, my sister…..''

His voice was ragged. A face came to me: heart shaped and pale, with thick lips and large, serious eyes. Alex sketched in his journals sometimes, and a face that belonged to his sister, Elizabeth, appeared more than once. He continued:

"I came to tell Lizzie about enlisting because she was the only one who didn't know. I was abandoning her, the only person in my life who seemed to want me to stay. She had the same aversion to war that I had. She'd lost the same father, although she couldn't rightly remember him, being only a baby when he'd gone. I think she imagined me as some shadow of him, as some vessel that carried him around inside it and protected the idea of him and of the kind of normal family life that she wanted.

She was in bed with her lamp on. She liked to read before dreaming and liked it even more if I read to her, as I had since she was little. Tonight, though, she sat upright, waiting for me, eyes wide open, alert and angry.

'Don't go,' she said before I could tell her I was going. 'You don't have to.'

I shook my head, sitting down beside her. 'It's too late. I already signed the papers.'

'Change your name then! People do it all the time. When they get married, when they get a new position, or just when they find a name that better suits them!' She was crackling with energy.

I wanted to smile but I just looked at her.

'Do it, please! You could be Michael Clayton, or Owen Graves… no Meadows. They won't be able to find you to honor your contract. They'll come looking for Alexander Liddell, but we'll say in all honesty: sorry! No one by that name lives here.'

I put a hand on her shoulder to weigh her ideas down, as the opportunities she saw seemed to give her real buoyancy.

'It's done. I'm going. Don't waste the short time with this nonsense,' I said as gently as I could.

Two fat tears rolled down her cheeks and splashed onto my hands. Her swimming eyes met mine.

'You are my brother. I don't want you to kill people. I don't want you deformed or dead. What if you come back and you are not yourself anymore? What will we do? What if you are gone so long that we don't recognize each other?'

'The face is what one goes by, generally,' I said, knowing that she would recognize this line from *Through the Looking Glass.*

She smiled, but it was a sad smile, attempted only for my benefit. I wanted to plant this memory in her before leaving. When I thought of my father, it was always the times we spent in the ocean together. I wanted Lizzie to remember me reading to her, so many nights, from before she could rightly think or make sense of the words. Whispering in the evening so we didn't wake our mother, talking about Alice's shifting size and laughing, late in the night, about the melodramatic turtle and his beautiful soup. When she grew old and thought of her childhood and her family, I knew she would not think of her raving mother, and she could not think of her missing father. She must only think of this.

I read to her again that night, hoping she would drift off into pleasant dreams, but it was not to be. When I closed the book, she turned onto her side and faced the wall and said, 'I wish you would change your name, still. Don't tell me what it is. When I read the lists in the papers, I won't know if I'm reading about you. I'll be able to believe you're alive, which is almost the same as truly being alive…and I won't be able to tell the difference. Not until the war ends.' And just like that, I knew my little sister had transformed already into someone I hardly knew. She was grown."

He was finished; his voice dissolved into a detached whisper. His words had unearthed a memory in my own mind, of sitting in my reading chair, case studies filling my head with ideas, when Jack scrambled onto my lap, his own book in hand, eager for me to discard my work to read aloud from his own tales. He had no sense that the books I was so devoted to would help secure his future. He wanted to read with me, to do something that he thought we might enjoy together. In my memory, I imagine him having this awareness even as a child: the sense that he did not care at all about the story and its words, wanting instead only the few shared moments stolen from the day. I imagine we enjoyed this time together, father and son, close and safe together in a moment that was both outside of life and life most significant. But imagination is a kind schoolmaster. It allows you to erase memory and make infinite corrections.

There was a long silence after he finished before I realized that I should speak. Jack did not have a sister to miss him but did have a mother who, I am certain, loved him very much. How difficult was the decision to join for him? Would he have gone willingly or felt pressured? He would have, like Henry, joined out of a sense of duty and for the sport of it all. Then the mangled hand... no not like Henry at all.

I looked hard at the boy in front of me who was not Jack, I reminded myself. The look on his face was clouded. His eyes, which had shined briefly as he spoke, slipped away again, into the depths of his memories. His stories were something I needed; they helped me to see my son more clearly than I ever had before, an illusion, I know, but a deception I couldn't resist! What kind of father would not know these kinds of details of his son's life? As the interviews, not just of Alex but of Lt. Oster and all the rest, as they continued and the war dragged on, filling the haunted halls with more haunted souls every day, I became overwhelmed with my inability to help these men. I could accept being a professional failure, but I could fix my failings as a father! I could know my son again and somehow do honor to his memory. If only Alex would keep talking...But for him, I could see that talking was not enough.

There was something really wrong with Alex Liddell, and I hardly needed the reports detailing the condition he was in when they dragged him out of the trenches that last time to know this. I had been working with him long enough for him to be ready to return to the battlefield. Ready or not, it was time for him to go back. I needed another opinion to prolong his stay. Of course, I could not have known then that keeping him longer would be more dangerous than returning him to the fields of Europe. I can't know the future! But I knew that I would have to talk with Dr. Hack about him.

XII. A Day at the Beach

Lenora and Alex returned to the shore once more before he departed. It was her idea; in his mind, he did not owe her anything, but he could not quite explain his agreement to accompany her. He was angry at himself for forfeiting his free will to decide how he spent his time, but he figured this was just a dry run for the time ahead, when his free will would be all but lost.

Both of them liked to speak about the time they spent at the beach together, though this visit was not as enjoyable as most. It gave them pleasure to recall floating weightless on their backs in the water together, just the two of them, feeling all the entanglements of their relationship and the choking strands of the words they never spoke to each other floating loose from their fingertips like seaweed while they closed their eyes and basked in the warmth of their physical closeness and the otherworldliness of the sea. He would write to her about these memories at times, and in his letters he was able to tell her how much they meant to him, though he seemed incapable of telling her, precisely, what she had meant to him.

It was a warm June day in 1915; his departure loomed in his mind and so a day at the beach was not his preference, but this day he felt an intensification of life and fatalism in the air that was far too interesting to ignore. They took the train. It was crowded with beach goers, but they were not pleasure seekers. A strange quiet hung over most and those that did speak were far too loud, as if they could deny some inevitability with the sheer power of their voices.

They were couples mostly, some families. The families were impossible for Alex to watch for long. Wives with frozen smiles and trembling eyes clung to their husbands' arms while children wiped their noses and squabbled unaware that their daddies would soon be gone, probably for good. And the men? Most were somber, taking the family on an obligatory last fling before their obligatory tour of duty and their obligatory death. Those who talked reassured their wives that all would be fine. It turned Alex's stomach. These were the very same women who stood on street corners in skirted gangs passing out white feathers and shaming men not yet gone to Flanders to defend the raped and ravaged Belgium. Now as their men prepared to go, they thought of life without them and began to crumble. Alex tasted acid rising in his mouth. The poor sod about to do his part, at her bidding, must spend his last days and hours of freedom comforting his forlorn wife who will spend the duration safe and warm at home in her bed, he wrote later that day.

Lost in a peculiar and fast-growing hatred, Alex did not notice his face souring, but Lenora did, and she tugged at his arm as the train slowed and raised her lovely eyebrows at the mood displayed so prominently on his countenance. He took her hand and pulled her to the front of the car, pushing past other passengers rudely, but he didn't care. He couldn't stand to be in the car another minute.

Disembarking, he gripped Lenora's hand tighter and marched off to the sand and the sea, the whole point of this disastrous outing. Fixing his eyes on the shimmering water, he imagined that beyond the horizon was a continent at war and here England safely sat, isolated. Of course, the continent was not across the sea from Blackpool. The water here lead only to more of the same, ever deepening and darkening, and finally to Ireland. He was struck by a mad desire to grab her arm and pull her into the water, to see if they could make it to the Irish coast or die trying. She was a good swimmer, but not as good as he was. They would always go out deeper than the others, who often stayed in waist high waters, engaged in horseplay, rugby-like games. She and Alex would swim out, sometimes over her head, but she never felt fearful with him. They would float, sometimes silently for long moments, feeling the gentle push and pull of the current, watching the water slip through their fingers, swimming in slow, strong strokes that made them revel in the sensual experience of their bodies moving through the water like fish.

She had hoped for that again on this day, but she knew it was not to be, and even on the train she had wished the car would transform into just about anything else, a department store, a café, her sitting room. Now she struggled to keep up as he stalked off the train and pulled her with him across the sand.

It was slightly overcast. He could not pinpoint the sun, but the sky and sand glowed the same shade of white and a land breeze blew them toward the dark water. Lenora had been talking, he realized as his breathing began to regain normalcy.

"Alex!" He turned. Her face was stricken with alarm. They were alone; the other bathers were just reaching the wide beach from the station while he had dragged Lenora at a fast clip across the sand to the water's edge. Her yellow dress was askew and she yanked her hand from his and straightened herself. She was annoyed; he was glad for that.

"Well, here we are, my dear." He swept his arms outward to the sea dramatically and dropped to the sand like a spoiled child. She hesitated but sat beside him. She was angry; he was being stupid.

She let out her breath in a controlled exhale. Though he looked at the ocean, he couldn't help but see her lightly freckled forearms dusted with sand, her feet, still in their white boots, dug into the ground. A sea gull, invisible against the white sky, swooped down to the water twenty feet away and left with a fish. His cry startled Alex and his white feathers reminded him of how he had let her win. She, whom he had depended on for advice and a better perspective when he wanted to quit all he was doing to keep his family afloat, when he wanted to beat up another boy out of a sense of injustice. She was like a sister to him, and now she was asking for something he didn't want to give, but she knew he would give it. He was furious, though, that she would ask, knowing that he would.

He reminded himself (after I prompted him to explain what he meant about 'letting her win'...after all, did he really enlist just because Lenora had challenged him?) that she was not a clear victor. He was going for many reasons: to support his friends, to do what his family expected of him, to do what his country thought was the right thing for young men to do. He hated all of these reasons and resisted them for as long as he could. But her....he lied; she was not just a sister to him. His sister, alone, wanted more than anything for him to stay. Lenora was more than a sister, and though his head and his heart were at odds over doing her bidding, his heart won out, even though he knew there was nothing romantic about the notion of war. No matter what she'd read in the novels they shared. He knew with certainty that the victory would soon enough be tarnished with the same devastation that had so altered his mother's life. And so to prepare her for the emotional wasteland that lay ahead of her, to rob her of any sense of accomplishment, he punished her with his lack of affection and indulgence. She had to know that if he died, it would not be doing something he loved. If he died, there would be unfinished business. She must know that he loved his life and would not give it up to her without a struggle. She must know that telegrams describing his gallant death would be lies and she must not have bittersweet memories of a willing victim to comfort herself.

She removed her boots and buried her feet in the sand. He wanted her to tell him there was another train coming. One that goes straight to Edinburgh; he could take a ferry to Ireland and she would meet him there; they could wait out the war together in a cottage on the rocky green fields of Connemara, staring at the sea. She said nothing, disturbing the sand with her twisting feet until her legs appeared truncated at mid-calf.

"Why don't you go for a swim," she urged coldly. Go. She would deny him as well. But if he died, oh….god, she said to the sky as she watched his lean frame walk with slumped shoulders toward the water, please, don't make him die. We have unfinished business.

But of course, as both spoke mostly into their own heads, neither heard any of the words destined for the other, and their ears, quite accustomed to not hearing, went about their business quite unaware of the missed opportunities.

XIII. Gas

As he stared at the hard, brown trench wall for days on end, his mind traveled as far as he could allow it with his limited experience of the world. Sometimes as his eyes fixed on the walls chipped and carved with picks and shovels, imprinted with desperate fingers, the browns earth and cream flecks reminded him of his the wallpaper in his home in Braintree, which was the reverse, cream flecked with small brownish red flowers, like tea-stained cabbage roses. His memory-eye would scan an unbroken expanse of the wallpaper pattern until there was a disruption in his real vision. If a rat ran across the section of trench wall that had him so transfixed, he might actually see the back window overlooking the overgrown yard. If he something such as dirt was flung over the top, his eyes might come to rest on the doorway to the kitchen where she stood at the sink. Mud unearthed from artillery explosions flecked his face and caused him to see just that.

As the bombardment continued, the men cowered where they sat in the trench, unable to comfort each other with words, as yells and even screams dissipated into air too full of violence to conduct speech. They grasped the indifferent walls with their hands and pressed their faces against the mud as if the wall could embrace them back and extend its protection. Most just sat and, like Alex, thought of other things, waiting for the shelling to end and hoping that today might not be their day to die, but if it were their day, at least they'd be done with all this noise and dirt.

The whistle blew on that day unexpectedly, even before the barrage had ended. They could hardly hear it at first, numbed as their ears had become to the blasting. But Capt. Whitesell blew it furiously, repeatedly, and jumped up from his crouched position, waving his arms frantically. This caught their attention.

Gas shells were being used, and Alex could see the cloud moving toward them, threatening to suffocate them all where they stood. They scrambled to don the cumbersome masks and hoods; with so much gear and so much crowding, it was no easy task. Whitesell hoped that the men could run past the cloud before it settled too low in among them like a fog. But the men weren't ready for it, and they burst out of the trench as the cloud descended, running half covered, some forgetting their rifles, as they desperately tried to protect their lungs and their skin. They flopped on the ground like fish and writhed like snakes; they grabbed each other and clawed each other. Lowe, mask in hand and red face blazing, reached for Parrish, whose mask was nearly ready to be donned, the hood folded over the goggles in the most expeditious way. Parrish dropped to his knees while Lowe used Parrish's hair as a filter of sorts. Parrish was a good swimmer and could hold his breath longer than most. Today, it was long enough for him to fix Lowe's mask and pull it over his head before his own.

Alex ran past them, tapping the back of Parrish's head as he did, in thanks. It was the last thing he remembered doing before the bullets hit.

Part Four

Still she haunts me, phantomwise,

Alice moving under skies

Never seen by waking eyes.

XIV. The Memoirist

All the men who came to Swansea travelled first through a field hospital in Belgium or France. It didn't matter the country; the conditions they described to me were the same: the field hospital was another level of hell. The absence of the sounds of combat made the groans of the suffering more unbearable to the ears still able to hear them. Too many wounded men- at least eighty- were crowded together on stretchers or beds under three interconnected tents meant to accommodate not more than half the current residency. The canvas floor was permeable to the dirt beneath, leaving most wounded thinly coated with dust as if the earth were eager to claim them.

Several glaring lamps hung in the corners of the hospital, but they barely penetrated the overwhelming gloom. Shockingly white partitions separated the dying or dead from the injured, and Alex wondered if that separation was for the benefit of the men like him, fully awake and aware, or for the sake of the poor sod who was breathing his last in this dirty, depersonalized mob scene. The men were meant to be arranged in order of severity of wounds, but clearly, in his case, Alex was certain there had been some mistake. The shrapnel in his shoulder was a scrape compared to the man to his left whose face and neck were bubbling. He breathed through a damp cloth marked with blood, smelling of vomit and chlorine. A mixture of guilt and fear conjured up a voice in Alex's head that accused and comforted him simultaneously: *I don't belong here.*

After what seemed like hours with no doctor visit, Alex propped on his good arm and turned to this neighbor, who appeared mercifully unconscious. Cheerily he said to him, "Fine day for a lay-about, 'eh, mate?"

He was startled to hear a haggard reply: "I've seen better, mate."

Alex was sure that it pained the man to speak. His lungs and throat had been burned with gas. He cringed and felt ridiculous for having started this conversation but couldn't back out now.

"Alex Liddell, Lieutenant," he mumbled self-consciously. The body in the cot barely moved in response.

"David…," pause, "Thomas, sir." Alex nodded slowly and turned for some relief to the neighbor to his right, whose back was toward him. Propped up on one arm, the man mumbled and agitated his head and arm in an exaggerated fashion, encumbered by bandages and pain, no doubt. Alex could hear the shuffling of paper and the work of a pen.

"What are you writing over there?" He spoke to the back, which still bore the dirty undershirt of the required uniform. The man seemed too banged up to be working so furiously.

"I'm writing my memoirs," came the distracted reply in a rapid clip.

Then the writer stopped as though struck by a brilliant idea. He grasped the dirty paper propped on a bible in his left hand, crumpling it a bit, and turned toward Alex, hopefully.

"Maybe you can write them for me?"

Half his face, the right half, was melted and fused into a nearly smooth sheet of flesh, broken by two small holes where his nostril and ear weren't entirely sealed off. Then the mouth, which looked damaged to Alex, but was near perfect in comparison, continued to speak, while one eye blinked and fluttered, desperate for moisture.

"Here you go, take this, will you?"

"How can I write your memoirs? I don't know what's happened to you," Alex replied, though he had taken the paper out of a desire to render some favor.

"Neither do I, I'm afraid," he admitted. "One of the nurses, the young one with the glossed lips, you've seen her? What I wouldn't give to see her with two eyes" he sighed before continuing: "She has been kind enough to read me my service book that has some narrative about who I am and what I've been up to since arriving on the Continent. I might as well have been born the day my feet touched this soil, because I've got nothing in here before that" he said with a shrug and a stiff tap to his head with a bandaged, blackened hand.

"Now," he said, extending his hand to take the paper back from Alex, "if you aren't going to help me write my story, let me get back to it before I completely forget who I am."

Alex looked at the paper for a long moment and then handed it back, reluctantly. He sunk back into his bed, pressing his head firmly against the pillow. After a pause, he asked his companion, "Well, if your service book is all you know, then your service book is your memoir. Why go to the trouble of writing down what is already there?"

"Because it's a service book. It's not a memoir. A memoir should be written by a memoirist!" he sounded like a professor sharply correcting a slow pupil with whom he had become exasperated.

"But you asked me to write it for you, and I'm not a memoirist" he furthered, hoping to keep this tenuous connection open for a little longer before he was lost again to himself alone.

This last challenge seemed too much for the writer, who stopped what he was doing and turned as best as he could toward Alex, which caused several grunts and raspy breaths to escape from his nearly perfect mouth.

"But you are a human being and you are here! I won't have my life story coming out of a file. I want a person who sees me, knows my name, knows how this place smells, and how the days have passed here to be a witness to my life, not some fucking bureaucrat or secretary sitting back in a leather chair in an office in England."

Alex nodded without looking at him.

"I want my kids- they're just babies now- to know something about me, to know how I lived and died. They can't just have a telegram and pictures, and my wife's memories. She knows nothing about the last part of my life, this most incredible part. And she'll never know if she only reads it out of a file, and neither will my boys."

"I got it, mate" Alex glanced back to him. He understood his desire perfectly. But when he had looked at the sheet upon which his neighbor was working so furiously, it was filled not with dates and details, but with drawings of fish and with lines from half remembered rhymes.

Alex burrowed his head deeper into the mattress, feeling the sides of the pillow fold up around his ears, muffling the sound of the memoirist's mumbles and paper turning. He closed his eyes and welcomed the darkness until a voice pulled him out of slumber's welcomed grasp.

"Hey, mate, if you aren't going to write for him, maybe you won't mind reading for me? Just one letter. One page is all. My girl never writes anything too long. Or maybe it's the censors that make them so short."

The raspy, slow voice came from the man to his left and Alex instantly deplored the gentle persuasion and the apology he heard in the man's voice. He was tired of guilt and he was tired of meekness in the face of mortality. Some might have viewed this humbleness as grace, but he thought it a foolish waste of time and effort. They had, all of them, gotten there through the demands of others, mostly unreasonable demands. Barked commands, overt instructions, implicit expectations. But this, the reading of one letter, was the most reasonable of requests, and he wished the man would shout his desire like a spoiled child until a nurse came running in response.

But this was not to be.

David Thomas continued, "I've a letter in my right hand…could you read it for me, sir? If you aren't in too bad a way." His right hand lifted about an inch off the stretcher. Alex could tell by his face that this small movement was a tremendous exertion.

"Right, let's see it then," Alex rallied with false enthusiasm, forgetting about his blasted shoulder as he leant over the body of David Thomas to remove the letter from his stiff fingers. He sat facing him and unfolded the small, dirty sheet and read the large, flowery script which had not been blacked out at all and really was short and simple.

" 'Davy- I know that soon you'll come back to me. When I'm lonely I think of my birthday and look at the awful portrait you painted. It hangs in a place of honor. I wish I had a picture of you. I can barely remember your face, only your sandy hair. Stephen Clayton came home last week. He lost both legs. If you are injured, Davy, I won't care one bit, as long as you aren't much changed. Stay the boy I know and loved before the war, and I will love you always- Fanny.'"

Alex looked up at David Thomas and noted that his hair was still sandy, but Fanny might be surprised at the rest. David made a sound that might have been a laugh, but it quickly evolved into a bloody cough that pained him to hear.

"Not much changed…She's changed. I've changed. War, time…. changes everyone, everything. 'Before the war' is gone. It never happened. It's lost to us like a dream," David's voice was a harsh whisper.

"If that was a dream, this is surely a nightmare," Alex looked around wearily.

"Fair enough; this is a nightmare," Thomas agreed.

"But what do we find when we wake up? Is there a reality, then?" Alex asked this boy because he thought at that moment that Thomas might be closer to God and so might be able to shed some light.

"Some day, I suspect, something will happen that will force you, unexpectedly, to open your eyes…sir," Thomas said after a pause, turning his head and shoulders to Alex in one lurching movement. Alex could barely discern his eye sockets amid the bubbling skin and purple wetness that seemed to modify all the expected contours and textures of the human face.

He returned the letter to his burned hand and went to sleep thinking about Fanny looking every day at her badly executed portrait, hoping to see some image of her beloved through his rendition of her own visage. He imagined how her own life must be changed, if she were anything like Lenora, which he imagined she was. He remembered staring at his father's own self-portrait, believing that if he looked carefully, intently enough, he might penetrate the medium and find some actual connection to the artist. He wished he had a portrait or a photograph of Lenora, because he found he could not conjure up a detailed image of her face at all. He could think of parts at a time: a certain shape of her mouth, the color of her hair, the physical space she occupied, which he always noticed when he stood close behind her, as in a line for tickets at the train station, and sensed that her entire body could fit into his own frame with room to spare. He had always liked this physical dominance, but now he had a grotesque vision of himself like a Russian nesting doll, crudely split in two, with her inside of him, comfortable and protected, and his sleep was disturbed by the angry realization that physical strength was the reason men like him were sent to this war, but human bodies, no matter how strong, were no match for flamethrowers, flying metal, and gas, gas, gas.

When he opened his eyes, Alex saw white all around him, surrounded as he was by white partitions. His heart stopped. Maybe his wound had become infected and spread in his slumber…then he realized that the partitions were around the memoirist and also around David Thomas. He was relieved.

He was awake and he had no further understanding to help him reclaim his life or make sense of the war, but when he had awoken, for just a moment, surrounded by a white glow, he had thought he was in heaven. The notion that he still had some faith left made him smile in disbelief. Then something even stranger happened. A doctor came to his bedside and told him, in somber tones, that he would be going home for a two week respite. Home. As he turned the idea over and over in his mind, two words kept ringing in his ears: Lenora and respite.

XV. Wool and Water

Alex could not seek Lenora out right away, of course. His mother and uncle met him at the train station and delivered him safely home. He was happy for this buffer, as England felt so strange to him and his feelings for her oscillated so wildly, that he did not trust himself to see her that first day or even the fourth.

On the fourth day, his mother, eager to prove how well she was managing the household in his absence, planned a dinner with Uncle Clive and a guest. Alex sat at the table near the large window overlooking the garden while finishing his tea. His sister lay on the floor, writing in an oversized journal, stealing long glances at her long-lost brother. His mother ran wildly through the house ensuring all was in order. There was a manic quality to her efforts. She'd arrange and rearrange items on shelves so quickly that Alex could not focus on the contents, almost as if she were playing some shell game, switching and shifting objects in order to hide something. For a second, the middle shelf of her china cabinet displayed, in this order: figurine, sugar bowl, vase, picture frame. A moment later: vase, figurine, clock. Then: sugar bowl, figurine, egg decorated with colored paper.

"Mother," he said sharply to gain her attention and stop her movement, "please sit down for a moment." He pulled out the chair beside him at the table.

Her guests would be arriving within the hour, and ham was resting near the kitchen window filling the air with the pungent smells of cooked meat, an odor that Alex thought he missed, but now he found that it turned his stomach. Instead of activating his salivary glands, it seemed to activate his gag reflex, as he thought of all the bloated, screaming, groaning horses he'd seen scattered on roadways, victims of bombs and bullets and gas, just like the men.

Ham is pig, he reminded himself in a mantra to repress his nausea.

His mother was crying, loudly. Startled, he rose to her. "What is it?"

"Oh, John, not again. I can't have you die on me again," she said through tears. She reached her arms out and placed her hands over his ears, keeping her face and his locked in a gaze.

"Mother!" he grabbed her wrists to silence her. "It's me, Alex, in front of you now. Alive."

"Ah, yes," she smiled, tears evaporating as quickly as they'd come. "So you are. Sometimes I can't tell my dreams from reality. What's going to happen from what's already happened or what is never going to happen at all. I feel like there are ideas and images echoing all around me in this house, till I don't know what's real and what's remembered."

She walked into the kitchen and returned in a moment, a porcelain rectangle holding red jam and a spreading knife in her hand. "Here you are, my love," she handed it to him.

"Ham, mother," he said to her quietly. "You asked if I wanted you to bring me the ham. Not the jam."

She looked confused for a moment, staring at the dish in her hand and at her son's unwillingness to take it from her. Anger rushed into the space that embarrassment sought to occupy. She slammed the dish onto the table, blobs of red jelly jumping from the tray onto the white cloth.

"Don't you think I know what is best for you!" she asked, but it sounded more like a command. He looked away from the quivering red mess. He didn't know if she wanted comfort, rationality or understanding.

"Well, you can't possibly know the future, Mum. That much is impossible," he deftly picked the spreading knife from the floor and took it to the kitchen, choosing to ignore this incident and eliminate the evidence of her mistake. She picked up the strands of their earlier conversation as if nothing had happened.

"But you said yourself; you told me that I should have known what would happen to your father...." Her eyes started to wander around the room again, and she was lost to him. "I should have known he would die just as you will. And when I think of that morning the telegram came, I DID know, already. You read the words aloud, but I knew the truth even before it was spoken."

She was back to rearranging, this time the silver and napkins on the table.

"Soon, I will be the Virgin Queen, giving up family, love, everything for England. I should paint my face white so everyone recognizes my sacrifice."

"Don't dare, mother. They'll recognize you've lost your marbles and cart you off to the loony bin" he said, impatiently, trying humor as a tactic to calm her.

"I am Mary, giving her only son…"

"That would make me Christ, mum, thanks for the high praise." The guests would be here soon, and the pressure was mounting to get this situation contained.

"Fine, not Mary then" she thought for a moment. "I am Sarah, sacrificing her son on the altar of…"

"Excellent. Sarah's son got a last minute reprieve from God. Let's stick with that metaphor. Now, please, let me bring the ham to the table." He rose.

"Sit," she commanded. Ideas and emotions collided in her mind and competed for primacy, and his movement was something she could control. She tried to quell the pangs of guilt that assailed her stomach and filled her with the uneasy sense that she had allowed her loved ones to die. She had interrupted their otherwise happy existence and insisted that they answer the call and follow another, incomprehensibly dangerous path, all while she stayed at home, missed them, and reveled in her status as a woman alone, making do.

She held the back of the chair and steadied herself by grasping the walnut cabinet with her other hand, hearing her wedding band strike against the wood edge. She could feel sweat oozing through her pores and to stop swooning she closed her eyes and thought of water, a scene that always calmed her. She thought of the sea and her vision subtly shifted to a dream she had forgotten from the previous night.

Only her dream memory was also changed by the events of this day, as she was certain her face wasn't painted white in her dream. Here she was, in thick paste makeup and a heavily encrusted gown, waist deep in churning water. She looked to the beach and could see her children running from the grassy edge to the thin ribbon of sand and towards her. Smiling, beautiful children, all boys. Alex was there, she knew, and he would be the most beautiful of all, but seeing them all coming at her, dozens of children, all smiling, all in identical white trunks and white cotton sleeveless shirts, she could not differentiate Alex from the others. These were all hers, dozens, no, a hundred tiny children stumbling at first, knocking each other over, standing and lurching forward on unsteady legs toward her oblivious of the dangers of the sea.

Waves came with relentless inevitability. Foam surrounded her like gathered tulle. She knew she couldn't catch all these boys as they ran to her, but she tried. Her arms stretched out impossibly long and caught them as they came, shrieking in the waves. Ten, twenty, where was Alex? She was doing it, gathering them all up safely to her, throwing them on top of her head, her shoulders, onto her back. But the one she yearned most to see, she could not. She plucked children out of the foam like flowers, throwing them onto her back, oblivious that they used her body like a diving platform and simply jumped right back into the sea. She gathered them as best she could and moved slowly toward the beach, the weight of the babies and the sodden gown making her trudge slowly, slowly. Still the children splashed and floated face down in the water while others ran toward her from the beach, trusting her above all else, never sensing danger would surround her, never suspecting that she had limitations.

Alex knew his mother was elsewhere. She had turned into herself again and clutched the furniture tightly as she stared out the picture window, immobilized by her thoughts. He needed air. Grabbing the decorated egg his father had brought home from a trip to Ireland long ago, he wordlessly left the house, the walls of which seemed to be collapsing in on them, crushing them both. He didn't know if it was an illusion or if the house simply seemed smaller than he remembered it being, but the place actually seemed to shrink by the day, until he believed that when he returned from this outing he might find a dollhouse on the plot of ground where his house once stood, and his mother would be lying inside it, a doll with serious lips, a fixed expression, and unseeing eyes.

XVI. Walls and Lines

He shoved the egg in the pocket of the wool trousers when he saw her stop ahead of him on Violet Lane. There she stood, waiting, unwilling to meet him halfway. She wouldn't budge. When Lenora drew her line, there was no sand, no room for corrections or negotiations. She drew her lines into marble, stone. And directly on them she stood, unwilling to move an inch, guarding her certainty with a ferocious vigilance. She had risen in the ranks of the Women's Home Front League and had been noticed by Lillian Mackay, the prematurely gray-haired regional director-general West London and environs. Mackay had admired Lenora's passion, commitment, and attractive appearance at several rallies, informational meetings and fundraisers over the winter and spring of 1915. Being attractive was good for the image of the League and also was an asset when it came to the League's primary mission: encouraging other women to follow suit and work tirelessly for the war effort, and reminding the men who had not yet gone to fight that the women of England, embodied by Lenora's creamy skin and chocolate hair, certainly expected them to.

Lenora was dedicated. She would speak and argue the mission of the League to individuals and large gatherings alike with a shrill but lovely insistence that was matched only by her desire to avoid tedious factory work or disgusting medical duties and her assumption that keeping the cause alive kept those she helped send abroad alive as well. As long as she generated support for the war, no matter what the technique, the soldiers would soldier on. If she stopped and went about her normal life, the war might come to a grinding halt, and all those involved would be trapped in some inaccessible purgatory.

So she talked and yelled and distributed pamphlets as if her energy alone was powering the machinations of war that would eventually drive her friends toward success and England toward the future. After nearly eight months on the job, she was promoted to recruiter.

Recruiters went to schools to stoke the patriotic flame barely alight in the hearts and minds of boys too young to enlist for political, moral, psychological, or financial reasons. These boys were not ready to die for a cause and did not expect their country to expect this of them. They were, however, of the age to be quite taken with the idea that they could star in their own hero-myth. Especially when the person selling them this fantasy was a long-haired beauty in a beautiful dress, with clean skin and encouraging eyes.

These were boys who would enlist to get out of further school obligations and to stay close to their friends. In that respect, they weren't unlike the first who joined Kitchener's New Army. But these boys were children still, a sign that the war machine had eaten clean through the generation meant for such sacrifice.

To keep their minds off this unpleasantness, Lenora spoke breathily of Arthurian legends and harkened back even further to Beowulf. It's not that Lenora wanted death brought down on the heads of young England, or anywhere else for that matter. But for once in her life, Lenora felt that she had a cause, a purpose, and a duty that was clear. She was drunk on the freedoms that wartime bestowed on her, bleeding as it did the workforce of its saturation by men and traditional ideas. With the war around, she had choices she never fathomed as a young woman. She was on the edge of a truly modern era, and the sleek appeal attracted her like a magnet. Women drank in the bars after working all day and into the night. Women ran the shops and policed the streets. It was a world of women made possible only by war.

With men away, it was easy to idealize them and remember relationships as being stronger or more romantic than they were. When communications were reduced to heavily censored notes scrawled on tiny fragments of paper once a month, only love, adoration and support made it through. Petty annoyances, day-to-day irritations, imperfections were all forgotten. Marriages once rocky seemed solid, and everyone's love became true again.

Until the man in question came home on leave or to recuperate on home service. Then established routines were disrupted, the idealized love made achingly real by his earthy smell and changed eyes. Some women would slip happily, some begrudgingly, into their old roles as the men returned to occupy their positions as heads of household. For others, this return to normalcy simply would not do. The women watched with curiosity when a man did return to see the dynamic in play. It became a game to guess which of their friends and co-workers would acquiesce and return to the home and which would fight to keep her independence. Lenora was certain, as were those who looked upon her dedication and hard work with such admiration, that she would never give back any of the ground she had gained in these long months of struggle.

But when she heard that Alex Liddell had returned for two weeks of respite, her heart danced. When she heard, from a neighbor who baked cookies for the recruiters to bring to the schools, that he had been in town for days and not sought her out, her cheeks burned. Rather than preparing her notes for the following day's presentation, Lenora uncharacteristically left the recruitment office at 2 pm, blaming a headache, an excuse so flimsy that no one believed her, but no one objected.

The day was blustery and gray; strong winds moved heavy clouds briskly across the sky, trying to make way for glimpses of blue. The weather had been more changeable than ever that week, as the spring resisted succumbing to summer, 1916. She felt a chill in the air, tightened her black knit wrap around her shoulders, and breathed deep the rich smell of leaves not fully grown. When she focused her attention back on the gravel road that stretched from the center of town to her house, and beyond it to his, she saw him coming toward her from the opposite direction.

He was in his dress uniform, but the dullness of it all made him appear more forlorn than gallant. His gate was stiff and measured, not his usual nonchalant posture that seemed to challenge her at every step. Rather, he moved toward her with swift, steady determination, clenching and unclenching his fists with increasing intensity as the divide between them lessened. Startled by this, she stopped walking and moved slightly out of the road, her back against the low stone wall lining the left side, once a boundary for a farmer's sheep field. The mossy dampness of the cool stone assured her that what she was seeing was real. And then he was two feet away. He stopped sharply, feet firmly planted slightly apart, hands clenched tightly. His eyes were level and unblinking as they scanned her face, stopping at her eyes. For the first time in their lives, Lenora could think of no teasing words, no frustratingly flirtatious gesture. She could not even meet his gaze, though she did not understand why. Instead, she looked at his lapel, at his bandaged shoulder adding bulk to one side, at the drab, pilled wool of this coat and the wrinkles caused by the slight bend of his elbow as his forearms angled slightly toward her.

"You arrived a few days ago?" she heard her voice ask with some cheer, the same way she would have initiated pleasantries with any unknown soldier passing through town.

"Yes," he answered quietly, not breaking his gaze. He stepped forward and put both hands on her waste, lifting her like a little girl and setting her on the wall. Her eyes could avoid his no longer, and the unexpected contact seemed to break some invisible barrier that had held her back from him. She looked at him carefully and directly now, feeling restored to her commanding, admired self. His eyes were different. They had a fixed quality and a shallowness that disturbed her. Instead of pools into his soul, they seemed like mirrors, revealing nothing but reflecting everything. She looked down at her gray dress, but its plainness offered no real distraction. She looked, instead, as his coat, and the few bursts of color that were the ribbons adorning the drab wool, over the left breast.

"Aren't those lovely," she tried weakly.

In dazement he stood, marveling that she would see these colorful scraps of silk as an accessory when they were, to him, indicators. Indicators of injury or participation in campaigns that yielded nothing lovely. He faltered, unsure if he could talk openly with anyone who looked at a military ribbon and saw decoration. He parted his lips, but nothing escaped. All the terror, the sights, smells, sounds, boredom, exhaustion, disgust, surprise, frustration and thrill stayed where it was, firmly locked into the fibers of his muscles, into the unreachably cavernous expanse of memory, out of the reach of the process that transformed thoughts into recognizable language. He could not give this to her in a language she would understand, so he said nothing.

Unsure of this silence, she rushed to fill in the space between them. "You wouldn't recognize this place," she nodded toward the town and the city beyond it. "So much activity. Everyone is working and doing whatever we can to support…"

He put two fingers from his right hand on her lips to quiet her. They left a fragrant, soapy taste in her mouth.

"Who are you? I don't recognize you at all," he searched her face with curiosity, fatigue straining his voice. She was herself exhausted by these intrusive questions from him, not understanding their basis, though she pitied his absentmindedness and wanted to help him. So she humored him with a response delivered in a measured, upbeat tone, as one talking to a child or a deaf grandparent.

"I'm Lenora. I lived down the street from your mother. I took care of you when you needed me…I thought we might love each other once, don't you remember?"

"Love? Is that what you call it?" He found his voice.

"I say what I mean," she reddened. "When I use a word, it means just what I choose it to mean, neither more or less."

"You make words mean so many things," he said to her mouth softly.

"This from a boy who talked to me of Jab…"

But he wasn't thinking about boys or love. He was thinking about minds, hers and his, and he was thinking about gaps. His mind traveled but came back to her lips, still moving. He put his hands on her face and with his thumbs he gently pressed the corners of her mouth outwardly toward her ears so that her lips straightened and elongated and she stopped speaking in rising alarm.

"Of course, of course," he said with urgency. "But who are you? I don't understand. Are you a tradition bound romantic, or are you a progressive? You argued always for women's rights, you embraced modern life and fashion, the city….but you've shown yourself to rely on tradition to make your life what it is. Marriage to the right man, the boy slaying the dragon for you, you love all this, too. You've staged your own gothic romance, haven't you? You sent me to a war, for fuck's sake…and when I come back to you, this fabulous new world of yours, Lenora… I wish I could drag you by your hair through the mud so you could see and smell and feel the old fashioned cost, what we paid for it…the acridness of …" he stopped when he realized his hands had moved from her face and were resting on her shoulders, close to the base of her neck, squeezing her too tightly. She stiffened and her eyes were large and fearful, but she didn't pull away from him. She was searching for the boy she knew in those accusing eyes. He was there: serious, scared, desperate for someone to make him feel normal. The war had not changed him, really, she thought. He was so precious to her now that she wondered how she could have let him go. How could she have let any of them go? But she had; and only he had returned to her.

Now, though, it was he who released her. He turned and walked back down the lane with the same measured step toward his house, without looking back. She called back to him in her own defense, but even to her ears the voice rang with desperation: "Who am I, Alex Liddell? Who are you?" And to herself: Who are you to me?

XVII. Entertainment

They tried again before he left. Lenora wore a mint green dress. She never appeared lovelier to him, and he never felt more uncomfortable around her. She came to his mother's house and rescued him from another unbearable gathering there, a morning tea with ladies from church. Her entrance was like a breeze through a dusty attic or a belly laugh in church. The cloud of war temporarily lifted and he was a young man with promise once again. He marveled at her ability to do this to him. In their private moments, she was a harpie, but then she could enter a crowded room looking only for him and she was a raft for a drowning man.

They took an afternoon train to the city. She was spending an increasing amount of time there, more than he ever had, so he was content to let her set the agenda and lead the way. They walked on a crooked sidewalk leading to tea at a place called Monroe's. It was a long walk, but the day was pleasant enough and Lenora had plenty to talk about. Although her conversation seemed to smother his own ideas before they could even be voiced, he tried to control himself and let her talk.

She talked about her suffrage work and whether she would start at university the following fall. She talked about the latest fashions, a friend whose wedding had been postponed on account of a fiancé missing somewhere in France. She talked about the watercress sandwiches her mother made for a ladies' luncheon last week at the Women's Society of Essex. She talked about Foster's last visit and the banal contents of her last letter to him. She talked about shortages in flour and sugar. She talked about a new show playing in London. She bought tickets for them to attend. She did not talk about Henry or Bernard. She did not ask him about the war.

She finally asked, "What is it?" when she noticed that Alex was not looking at her and had ceased making the appropriate gestures and responses to her peculiar, hollow language. They were passing a ragged petting zoo at Covent Garden. There were a few goats, two peacocks, some gray sheep, and a tired miniature pony. They trod through their pens dejectedly with no place to hide from the gawking, reaching children and no way to realize their full mobility. Lenora shifted her gaze to follow his. She was delighted. She walked to the fence and stretched her arm across. None of the animals approached; she was disappointed.

"Well, those beasts certainly aren't up to the standard I remember. Pathetic!"

"Pathetic is right," he echoed her, aiming his criticism at the people who created these barbaric displays and the public who supported them. He looked at the sad, rusty-colored pony and thought of those horses, numbering in the thousands, bloated with gas or dismembered by shelling, littering the fields of Belgium and France, the air filled with the heavy stench of their rotting carcasses. No choice in the matter; no dignity.

"Someone should put them out of their misery and bring in a fresher batch," she said. "I've heard there's a farm in Dorset run by a cousin of Michael Felton- do you remember him? He was a third year at Briarside when he enlisted- they have magnificent peacocks there. I've heard that peacocks actually dance when it rains. I wish it would rain now," she looked hopefully to the clouding sky. "It would be a good laugh to see these old things dance a jig."

He couldn't tell, I suppose, that she was just nervous. That she spoke these inanities in place of all the things that she wanted to say, all the questions she wanted to ask, but could not.

"Lenora," Alex began tiredly.

"What? It's not as if they can hear me."

"No, but they're living things, you know. God's creatures like any other and all that. They deserve some respect, some common decency." She was unconvinced. He continued. "Imagine if you were a peacock. People would pick your feathers to create ridiculous ornaments, mark you so that you couldn't flee, breed you whenever and with whomever they chose, and when you were old and useless they'd…"

"Stop it," she said with a sudden firmness, her brow creased in disapproval.

"No," he pressed on, "imagine you are something or someone other than yourself for just a moment."

She folded her arms defensively across her chest and shook her head firmly, frowning, "No, I will not."

He pushed, "Come on; imagine you are a goat, or a donkey, or Henry."

"What?" Her voice went cold. "I don't know what you mean. I won't play your stupid game. I can't imagine such things. If you still want tea, I suggest we head to Monroe's presently before we both change our minds."

He was amused and relieved to have broken through her cheerful façade, but he was unsure if he had the strength or interest to confront what lie beneath. She walked ahead of him with purpose to the itinerary of her choosing. He followed her like a dog on a lead.

At Monroe's they drank tea with milk, no sugar, and ate small cucumber sandwiches despite their lack of hunger. The interior was bright lavender with white plaster adornments and lace curtains. Lenora spoke crisply to Alex when she felt she must. All the tables in the place were full, many of them with visiting soldiers in uniform. Alex noted that even without the identifying garments it would be easy enough to tell the soldiers from the other men in the room. They looked somehow dirty, as if all the baths in the world wouldn't clean away the filth that had worn into their skin. Many sported bandages. Most stared vacantly away from their companions. He wondered if he looked like this as well, and determined that he did. And he was glad that they stood apart from the others and that he stood with them.

Lenora tried hard not to even look at these men. Her deliberateness in avoiding eye contact with those in uniform was incomprehensible to Alex, almost hostile. As he set his cup in its saucer, he silently marveled that only a day or two ago, most were knee deep in mud and muck, trying not to be killed. Now here they sat, sipping tea in London with their loved ones, wishing they were back at the front with their men.

He later wrote of this day:

The war is a huge misunderstanding. A vast breach is forming between us and them, and soon we will have only the war. Home will mean nothing to us because everyone here seems to disregard or ignore this most fantastic event in our lives. It is no longer about us and the Germans. It is us and them- our mothers, and sisters, and lovers. It is about whether or not they will let us survive and acknowledge our existence, or if we are all already ghosts to them that they wish would vanish.

"Are you up for the show tonight, then?" Lenora asked him, speaking with the false freshness and slow tones of one speaking to a child. "I think it's a comedy."

"Yes," he said as heartily as he could muster, "I'm up for a good laugh."

The tea burned his throat and boiled in his stomach. He followed Lenora out of Monroe's and into the darkening streets crowded with entertainment seekers. There were couples of all ages, pairs and groups of women friends, a few soldiers, and a surprising number of young clear-eyed men who must be on home service.

There was laughter and flirting and hands squeezing elbows. He realized that he was neither touching nor speaking with Lenora and he had no desire to change that. As they approached the theater, they saw a crowd at the box office. Lenora broke their silence with a commanding voice: "I have our tickets; let's pass by."

No one paid them any attention as they walked by the queue and entered the brightly lit theater. He wrote, continuing his idea about ghosts haunting London:

It strikes me that no one notices anyone else. A man mistakenly elbows another and neither turn to investigate or apologize. A patron has dropped a ticket onto the walk. No one picks it up. The patron searches the ground on her own, without enlisting aid. They have erected invisible barricades around themselves, and they will not be disturbed; their worlds will not be corrupted by the sadness, worry, fear, or despair of another. I sit in my red velvet chair next to a fortified woman and as the lights go down and the theater fills, I want nothing more than to bring the war to these people who live with levity while just a few hundred miles away, tonight, a hundred Lowes bury their faces in the hair of their friends just so they can breathe.

Attention is drawn to the stage. As the curtains open, I close my eyes. There is a huge screen , as big as the theater wall, and before us plays, in real time, the scenes that are the subject of such speculation, misrepresentation and denial. Whizz-bangs cause the ladies to screech and cover their ears. Close-up on lice covered soldiers waiting in a rat infested trench for the bombardment to end. Wide-view of the battlefield. Explosions unearth long-buried bodies, flinging rotten limbs indiscriminately. I wish they could smell it. Men cover their faces with handkerchiefs. Lenora blanches. I smile cruelly at their inability to watch what has become their favorite spectacle- the longest running show in London! A sound escapes me that feels like a laugh. It is roaringly loud, amplified by laughs escaping from all those seated with me: a collective guffaw. No one has fled. It is only a modern comedy after all.

He wrote of this experience in the theater as if it was a dream vision, but I call this one of his first recorded hallucinations. Only in retrospect, though, after having confirmed with Lenora that they did, in fact, see a comedy. Theaters actually were showing clips and even lengthy films of war footage, created by the War Propaganda Bureau. Alex liked to call them the War Propagation Bureau, of course. I saw one such film myself, showing the opening moments of the Somme offensive. The initial explosions and charge of British troops was breathtaking, mesmerizing. No matter that this engagement resulted in a prolonged, nearly year long struggle that cost us more than 19,000 dead on the first day. When it showed in London in late summer 1916, though, there was no indication of this tragic outcome. It played to packed houses, quite the hit of the summer season.

Perhaps we went to these showings for reassurance that our boys were doing well, that we were the winning team. Perhaps we at home went out of a sense of guilt and duty, hoping to expose ourselves to the grime and violence of war, even if packaged as entertainment and viewed from an unthreatening distance.

Whatever the reason for the success of such films, Alex did not view anything like this the night Lenora took him to the theater. He didn't have to. He had already determined through the course of the day that the relationship between those at home and those sent away was incomprehensibly and irrevocably changed. He spent the last days of his respite home recuperating his injury in his bed, having given strict orders to his mother not to allow any disturbance. He wanted, more than anything, to get back to Belgium posthaste. His friends were still there, not to mention Parrish, Lowe, Mouse, Capt. Whitesell and the others. If he'd ventured out of his room to go downstairs and read the paper though, he might have learned that his dear friend, Bernard, was among the many, many recently departed.

Part Five

Children yet, the tale to hear,

Eager eye and willing ear,

Lovingly shall nestle near.

XVIII. Friends

Even though he did not yet know of Bernard's fate, I imagine that he must have sensed something significant was happening in his friend's life, as Alex's journals from his medical leave contain strange blank pages, pages with only trailing lines, and then floods of words about his friends, how they met, what they meant to him, and how he longed for those lost days, those irrecoverable connections.

After his father died, his friends, the true ones, never tired of trying to draw him out, much as they disliked encountering his strange mother whose grief was so removed from their lives as to be indistinguishable from madness wrought by some foreign affliction that might be contagious. In their eyes, she had slowly taken the form of a witch-like creature from fairy tales, imbued with special powers to appear both attractive and repulsive simultaneously.

They feared her, as did others; they pitied her, as did others, and they avoided her lest her misfortune touch their lives.

Lenora revealed that his friends saw her as a gatekeeper, a tormentor of their friend, Alex, who was unfairly imprisoned and sent to toil, a boy Cinderella who longed for freedom and frivolity. Until Briarside gave them a safe place to reunite with their friend, Alex often had to fend for himself in his strange new world. In truth, Alex adapted to things as children do. His uncle brought him to work one morning and showed him around the place, taking him into the public areas where Alex was already familiar, and then into the private ones- employee lounges, water closets, coat rooms, and small offices with heavy doors, where the real work was done behind the scenes and where private discussions were held between clients and lenders.

He was naturally interested to see the inner workings of the bank. There was some sense of privilege and importance to be let in on this adult world secret. So many others had no idea what happened after they handed their money or their applications to the tellers. They knew the system worked, because when they needed their money, it was there, returned to them over the same counter by the same smiling face and smooth hand. The labor upon which the system was built, the laws of history and economics and geopolitics, the nature of societies…none of this seemed to cross the mind of the average client, mostly factory workers, educators, clergymen, and career soldiers. Alex took some pleasure in knowing he was a child in the world of adults. He was singular, and soon enough he ceased to see himself as a child at all.

This was an easy mistake; barring his stature, messy hair, teeth that were too large for his mouth, and an occasional skinned knee from bike falls as he pedaled home in the dark, he seemed very much an old man. He had become the sole wage earner in his household, handled all the bills as best he could, listened patiently while grown co-workers confided troubles about their marriages, and took on the responsibilities of his house and family, tucking in mother and sister at night, feeding the cat, and keeping the home to the cleaning standards of a young boy.

His school work slipped, but Bernard was there to help.

His body weakened through lack of exercise, poor diet, and irregular sleep, but Foster dragged him from his bed to climb trees and hike in the woods at least once on the weekends and long holidays.

He would go a week without laughing or talking to anyone about childish things, and Henry would show up with a candy bar and a story to tell to entertain him on the short journey between home and school or work.

And then there was Henry's sister, Lenora. She would always remind them to be sure to check on Alex. Who had seen him last? When was the last time he played ball? How is he for exams? She would sometimes bring dinner for him at the bank, though she wouldn't stay to eat with him. She would talk to her father about his situation and, without knowing how, Alex would find his small yard neatly trimmed and minor repairs completed before he'd had a chance to report the problem to any tradesman. He also found that he was not kept from repeating grades at school even when his studies suffered from preoccupation and distraction and daydreams of Lenora, to whom he felt increasingly grateful, even though he could see that she and Foster were growing closer and closer as his place in their lives diminished.

Alex became to them like a relative invalided in the country, far removed. Everyone tried to keep him involved, but they needed to live their own lives, and part of the enchantment of youth is the intensity of youthful friendships, especially those that featured a hint of romance. It was inevitable that Foster, Lenora, Henry and Bernard would tighten their bonds, and that Alex might be left out of the circle. He did not fault them this.

He saw the alternative in his mother, who clung so tightly and irrationally to her past and its loyalties that the very spinning of the earth and the cycle of days with their relentless forward progress became her enemy and wore down her body and mind as she struggled to keep them from pulling her further and further distant from all that she loved.

XIX. Sappers

Lenora told me that Bernard had become a sapper. He had a mind for engineering work and a body that was smaller than average, but strong. He feared the tight spaces of the tunnels and shafts that he and his unit planned and dug slowly, slowly, under the battlefields, across No Man's Land, to the other side, where explosives could be laid under the very feet of the Bosch, transforming a solid, silent plain into a minefield.

Several other men at Swansea were sappers. When they met each other, they always seemed physically surprised, as if they were seeing ghosts. They would be talking to each other in the hallways, exchanging pleasantries or talking sport, and then one would ask, 'What do you do back there?' meaning in the war. The other would say, quietly, "I'm a sapper," and the other, also a sapper, would look with alarm at his companion and slink away down the hall, as if the occurrence of two living sappers together was too much of a temptation of fate.

Even more than life in the trenches, life in the tunnels was so suggestive of the grave that the men adopted a sacredness about their work, laughing heartily their last laugh and breathing deeply their last deep breaths at the openings, then stooping to enter in silence, crawling a hundred yards or several miles along the tunnel's length to begin their careful scraping under the battlefields, so near to the enemy lines that they could sometimes hear the quiet whispers and scrapes of enemy sappers digging their own tunnels inches away.

They would stop and hold their breath and hope, hope, hope that they didn't see the dirt begin to break through from the other side, as no one carried a firearm, and the fighting that would ensue would be a mad jabbing of pick axes and entrenchment tools and knives.

Bernard did not ever stab a German sapper with his pick axe. Once, in March 1915, his party had encountered a German party who had broken through their wall behind their location. He was in the front of the group, and the skirmish that ensued involved only the last man, an Irishman named Murphy. One man died quickly from each side, though the half-screams and gargles of a man drowning underground with punctured lungs haunted Bernard for the rest of his short life. He was appalled at the way the sounds carried through the tunnel but were absorbed by the earth, never reaching any ears above ground. Both parties retreated to remove the bodies and to determine if the tunnels should be re-routed or work should continue as planned. According to the last letter he wrote to Lenora, Bernard's team was to continue as planned.

They helped to excavate the tunnels used to plant massive explosives under Hawthorne Ridge. A tremendous blast had been planned to kick off the Somme Offensive in July, and last minute adjustments could not be made. It took more than a year of sweaty, stifling, tense work, but on July 1, 1916, geography altered, and for a prolonged and awesome moment, initiated by catastrophic explosions timed to go off simultaneously, dirt became sky and peaks were reduced to plains.

So started the year long battle that demanded a sacrifice of millions. Film captured the destruction of the Hawthorne Ridge and the opening attacks, unknowingly a prelude to an engagement that would ultimately end with a whimper, staggering to an arbitrary finish line with the wasted, glassy-eyed gaze of a runner completing a marathon without prior knowledge of the course and its demands.

Bernard did not see the film or witness the culmination of his hard work. He died in June in a tunnel when artillery smashed the earth and collapsed the entrance. No one knew if the men were crushed by the falling tunnel ceiling or if they suffocated or drowned, as artillery often smashed drainage systems, turning fields into lakes and dry tunnels into death chambers. The Colonel decided that it was no matter. There was no need to risk additional life to retrieve the bodies, as they were good as buried anyway.

XX. The Duchess's House

1916 had been a period of immense and heartbreaking activity in France, and 1917 was Belgium's turn. Alex rejoined the same unit upon his return, and spent much of 1917 preparing for and moving to support Col. Flint's stated aim of breaking the near stalemate on the fields of Broodseinde near Passchendaele and the Ypres Salient. To do this, the unit marched many miles through mostly empty villages. They went house to house in Beleuge, a small town near Wavre where the residents worked at cloth mills and grew gardens in small plots of land behind their homes, potatoes and beans, herbs and greens, that would be gathered and sold at a farmer's market on the weekends to the people of Wavre before the Germans invaded. Now the gardens were stripped of their offerings through neglect and foraging. Stores of pickled or root vegetables could be found in isolated cellars that were undetected as the Germans moved swiftly through the area, but the British and Canadian troops that swept after them left little untouched. Alex's unit went through the homes only because they lined the way to another trench system and offered shelter from passing showers.

Rarely did they occupy civilian living quarters for any duration. They went inside the edifices to look for survivors, to scrounge any scraps of food and other supplies such as wool clothing, blankets, and diversionary surprises like dice, cards, paper or pens, and to glimpse domestic life for just a few moments, even a domestic life shattered, empty, and vacant. The sight of bed frames, of colanders hanging from enamel hooks in the window, of gardens and rooftops made them quiet and wistful. It made Alex think of England, and it gave him some satisfaction that civilians suffered as much as they did, and he tried to imagine his own home punctured, sagging, and deflated, and Lenora's.

His men would enter first, usually Mouse followed by Parrish, Lowe, and the rest. Alex would go lastly, hesitantly. He told me his neck hairs would rise and his right hand would grip the handle of his pistol still in its holster. He didn't expect to shoot anyone here, but walking through the homes, moving from the front door to the empty living rooms and into the kitchens always made him tense. Parrish and Lowe would rummage through the buildings as if they had been invited, and other men would sometimes race to comfortable sofas like children playing musical chairs. But Alex's mouth would be dry and his steps slow and deliberate. He rarely took anything from a house, as he rejected this life as much as he longed for it.

One day he came across a house with an occupant. He heard her from three houses down, and he left his men to their exploration of a largely undisturbed home, drawn to the timbre of the voice in this particular residence. He understood, once he had crossed the splintered threshold, that this was the house that had caused him to tense with hostility in all the others. The house was of the tall, narrow variety with a pointed roof, white washed walls, and a gaping crater in the second floor that knocked out 3 of the 5 windows meant to look out onto the unpaved road before it. The room, a bedroom, on the second floor, now exposed to the sky, had rich, bright, yellow walls, giving the house the appearance of a cracked egg ready to spill its contents.

As he walked cautiously through the main room on the first floor toward the kitchen, his boots crushed shards of glass and broken pottery as he travelled toward a woman's enervated voice rising and falling frantically in the kitchen. He could not see her as he neared the entryway, his eyes resting on the large wooden table that stood, like his, in the main room before large back windows overlooking a small yard. He was alone with her, as the others were still enjoying the spoils of the neighboring home and its vegetable cellar, which still had edible cheese and a few dusty bottles of wine.

He stood outside the kitchen entrance, listening to the shrill voice inside and the slamming of pans and cabinet doors. His hands fell to his sides, and his stomach felt heavy. Perspiration formed on his brow and he realized he might faint as the voice in the kitchen became that of his own mother. He had thought of her often since arriving in Belgium. His mind always replayed the moment when she transformed from his young, dependable, devoted 'mum' to a gray lady lost in a relationship with a ghost, for whom her children were an unwelcome distraction with real, present needs, pulling her out of her dream world. Now standing before the kitchen door, preparing to enter and give her the news that would inflict this on her, he seemed to shrink and transform from a soldier who had learned to project some semblance of confidence to a shaking child whose fear, anger, and sadness threatened to overpower his physical form. Now, here, in Belgium, instead of the silence and control that his mother had possessed upon hearing the announcement of her husband's demise, this woman already knew, and she reacted as Alex had always hoped and feared his mother would.

He shuffled toward the doorway on weak legs, tentatively, as dishes and pans were flying through the air and crashing on the far wall. He saw their everyday white porcelain bowls and finest china plates, the ones with blue and yellow flowers and ribbons encircling the central disks, whizz past, smashing into pieces that littered the floor. Shards like eggshells scattered around him, delicate and dangerous. A soup tureen on the stove top was overturned in a loud crash, cabinet doors were swung open and their contents methodically dumped. He could hear his baby sister crying inside that room, and his fear for her safety eventually trumped his fear for his own as he leaned inside the doorway and to the right, toward the sink and his mother. The baby was wrapped in a pink blanket and sat writhing on the countertop, close to the edge, while his mother carried on oblivious to her imminent fall, reaching for any object to destroy in her fury. For an exhausted moment, she stopped to catch her breath, resting her hand on her waist and bending forward like a winded runner. He seized the opportunity to venture forward, keeping his eyes fixed on the soft bundle on the counter and trying not to think about the broken porcelain and glass at his feet, painful and hard to avoid.

His mother lit a cigarette, exhaling a cloud into the air which formed a ghostly, diaphanous shape around her head and her hair, which had come completely undone. She picked the blanket up and threw it over her shoulder, roughly patting the crying child's back. The cries seemed to rise to the pitch of a scream as Alex traversed the distance to his mother, which he always saw as a slow motion journey that took far longer than the seconds it must have taken. His mother held the child out to him at arm's length and cried "Take her and get out!" in a voice ravaged with passion and smoke. He rushed forward and grabbed his sister, caring not about his feet or the blood on the kitchen floor. Holding her like a rugby ball tucked snugly in his arm and against his body, he bolted to the door and then to the fresh air outside, soft air dragging silky rain against his dry lips, leaving his mother to the stale, rancid house and to her grief.

A stone path lead from the house to the road. He dropped to his knees before he got there, as the bundle in his arms seemed far heavier than he expected. He pitched forward to lay the blanket gently down, but his sister was like a large, unwieldy stone and she rolled out from him and onto the wet grass. As he unfolded the blanket, he could see that it was not pink, but white, stained with a washed out red, and mixed with mud. His could see his hands shaking before him, as the layers of blanket peeled away, and his hands seemed to grow, even as the mass inside the layers of cloth seemed to grow, until he was a grown man, and the creature inside the blanket was not a baby but a young girl, likely seven or eight, body broken, dead for a day only or less, as she had not yet begun to decompose but her limbs had grown stiff. He wished that her mother had been with her in her bed when the shells hit. He lifted the body up, on his knees, and pivoted sideways to lay the daughter on the grass, just to the side of the path; her legs and arms were straight, and she lay like a starfish, like someone floating, eyes closed, on the surface of the water. Her cheeks were round but her body was thin, and her hair long and blonde, was soaked dark as if dipped in ink. He didn't want to cover her with the dirty blanket. Walking from the yard, away from the noise of the mother whose rage and pain he knew well, he noticed that the rest of the town stood in utter silence, even the soldiers moved silently around the house, unwilling to go inside. Across the street, an orange cat looked at him and cried once, showing all its teeth, and then disappeared inside the frame of a door that hung from one hinge.

XXI. Attics and Cellars

In the two years that Alex served in Belgium, he never stayed a night in another family's deserted home. That is how he thought of the billets, even though barns, chapels, or other occupied residences were sometimes made available to them. It made him nauseous to sit on another's mattress or worn chair and look at walls stained by rain, blistering paint or peeled paper revealing hints of a woman's personal taste, now laid bare and wasted. He preferred to sleep in the yard if the sky cooperated, or he would seek out one of the many cellars used to store vegetables, wine, or cheeses. The house with the crying cat had such a cellar, where rotten potatoes spilling from broken crates could be pushed aside to make room for a reclining man.

Alex wrote about this day in his journals at length, deeply disturbed by the dead girl and the raving mother. Later that evening, his writings took on a new feature, as he began to draw images of the things he remembered seeing or thought that he saw, when words failed him. In my office, he could look at these images and they would trigger stories that I would transcribe into writings that I would enter into his medical records. I suppose I had no way of knowing if the stories he told were accurate, but this didn't matter! What he believed to be true was as important as what was true! And we seemed to be getting so close...never before had the life of my son seemed so fully recognizable to me...like he was emerging from some nebulous haze. It was not, though, as if he had magically transformed from a boy to a man. No; now, at long last, I could almost picture him as a man and I could sense the kinds of friendships and fears and hopes and principles that formed his life and took him from me, to Australia, to Turkey, a retrospective that no portrait could capture in a single image.

The portrait that I was looking at that day, in my office, was one of Alex's, and it was of a woman with red hair, full lips, and eyes like mirrors. I held his book out to him so that he could see what I saw.

He leaned forward in his chair to look at her a long moment, then he sat back in silence. He leaned his head back against the wall and spoke to the ceiling; his eyes remained closed.

"An old woman in a blue sweater swept a walkway while two middle-aged housewives arranged loose stones into neat piles. Most of the men were gone from places like this. Women with children had long fled. The sounds of explosions in the distance seemed like they must be the low rumbles of thunder, as everything appeared so harmless, quiet and *female*, there. Capt. Whitesell told me to occupy the house where I saw the cat. It was back down the main road about a quarter mile, then to the right. By the time I got there with Mouse and Parrish and Lowe, there were no more sounds from the house across the street. The girl was still there in the front yard, her stained blanket tossing and turning in the breeze like a trodden flag, a bad dream.

The house we stayed in had long maroon curtains waving like a banner in one glass-less window on its second story while the others were stripped naked. There was damage to the roof, the door had been nearly torn off, but otherwise, it appeared sound.

The men were eager to get in and settled. Lowe and Parrish had volunteered to carry extra gear left by wounded soldiers, and they rested on the roadside like massive gray turtles with double packs on their backs while Mouse and I checked out the grounds and peered in the windows.

I called to them when I determined that the house was ready to occupy. Their faces brightened, and Mouse pulled them to their feet.

We entered quietly at first, as if we were intruders in a church. The occasional strong gust made itself felt inside, though the arrangement of interior walls and a central spiral stair created warm pockets. The door closed loudly behind us and our footsteps echoed in the high-ceilinged rooms. We fanned out to explore our lodging and to stake claims to the preferred sleeping spots. I had already eyed a cellar door in the backyard, so this tour was just curiosity and habit, I suppose. There were two great rooms, to the left and right of the central staircase, behind which there was a narrow kitchen. It was safest to sleep on the first floor. The men made themselves at home; Mouse snored on a dusty sofa in the right room while in the left,

Parrish and Lowe had thrown cushions and pillows on the floor as if they were having a slumber party. The walls of both rooms were covered with unusual art work. Paintings of nothing and everything, really…angles and colors that were suggestive of some implicit subject but rendered without realism. They were interesting. I wished Bernard were there to discuss them with me.

Parrish and Lowe went out a back entrance to see if a well provided potable water.

I found myself wondering if any of the paintings depicted the bliss of a warm bath when a woman walked down the central stairs.

She startled me and by the look of alarm that swept her face, I'd say we did the same to her. When it passed, her eyes hardened with hostility at the scene below her, the invasion of her privacy.

'Good day,' I mumbled to her, struck dumb. She was remarkably beautiful either because I hadn't seen a woman like her in a long while or because her pool-deep eyes and angry mouth were framed by stunningly red hair worn loose. She spoke accented English.

'Don't touch my paintings and don't dare come upstairs,' she said in even tones as she passed me without looking at my face. I saw her dark eyes flicker over the rifle flung strung across my back and the dirty gear we'd dropped in a heap in her foyer. She swept into the right room and removed a large blank canvas from a closet under the stair. She could have used help carrying the thing upstairs, but I didn't dare move.

'What's your name, miss?' I ventured, hearing my voice crack like an adolescent, unsure she would acknowledge me again. She managed that frame quite well, gliding up the stair without struggle, her white blouse loose and flowing. She ignored me.

'Right. We'll make ourselves at home, then.' She disappeared into the upstairs hall.

'Thanks for the hospitality!' I waved after her.

Parrish and Lowe returned with two buckets. I headed for the kitchen to see about striking up the stove, forgetting about the woman and thinking only of washing my face and feet.

Darkness fell early; the air moved well enough through the perforated walls to make the humid night bearable. The men were playing cards on the floor, laying across their cushions and pillows and stripped to their underclothes. Our uniforms hung on a makeshift clothesline to air out and dry. I kept my trousers on. I wouldn't have minded joining the boys for a game but, as an officer, it was not expected. My thoughts began to drift upstairs.

She had not come down again, and I was annoyed. She could have been civil and joined us. We were there in her country, after all, acting on her behalf. It would have improved the boys' morale to have the company of such a lovely woman for a few hours. I thought she must be hungry. I wondered what she was painting. No one was paying attention to me, so I ascended the stairs discreetly, with a deep breath."

"Why did you feel the need to go secretly?"

"I don't know…I suppose it seemed wrong. She said not to go upstairs."

"But you went. Why?"

"I don't know…sometimes people say things they don't mean." I had to concede this was true; it has also been my experience that people do things they can't explain that confound them, as if they are actors following a script that they vaguely memorized but then can't produce to consult or to explain their actions. Some colleagues believe that understanding motivation is the key to understanding a person. I always asked Alex 'why, why, why'… 'Why did you enlist?' 'Why did you not tell Lenora you loved her?' 'Why did you go up the stairs?' 'Why did you kill Parrish?' And it was these questions of motivation that seemed to irritate him the most. He seemed to think that the motive did not matter. Only the choice and the outcome. What do motives matter if we kill a man by moving him after an accident if we meant to protect him from further harm? I understood my wife's motives for leaving me, her reason for moving to Australia and for taking our boy with her. I understood Jack's motivation for gaining my attention through success after success. But what of my own motives? Yes, yes, I already conceded that my motivation for taking Alex Liddell's case was partially selfish. But why, why do I readily recognize these less significant motivations but I cannot begin to fathom this most consequential one: why did I ignore my son's efforts? Why did I never tell him: 'You are amazing. I love you. You've done enough'?

"Continue."

"I felt the excitement of going out on a wire party after dark. My heart was racing and my hands shook slightly on the rail, or perhaps the rail shook on its own. It was mostly dark upstairs, but a light from a gas lamp glowed to my right. At the top of the stairs, a shoe flew by my face, almost knocking me backwards. I steadied myself. Anger replaced concern and curiosity, and I stalked into the lighted room.

'What the hell do you think you are doing?' I challenged her.

'I should ask you the same,' she responded, acidly. She sat at a night table, looking into a mirror at her image as she applied a cream to her face. It smelled like lavender and linseed oil. Her back was to me, which was infuriating. There were paintings stacked and displayed around the room in different styles. Some were boringly realistic and others were bizarre. There were scraps of camouflage material lying about, the brightly colored pink and yellow patches that adorned the undersides of aircraft. There were journals and books and a plum-colored couch loaded down with moldy blankets.

'I know it must be an inconvenience to host…' I tried again, but she interrupted.

'An inconvenience to host? It is one thing to have an invading army in my country; it is quite another to have an occupying force in my living room touching my things, taking what you want, feeling entitled to it all. I haven't slept in three weeks! Always on the lookout for more soldiers. Here I am in the highest part of the house and still you have to come here!' Her voice rose to a shriek and then she settled down glumly. 'Go ahead. Take it. Whatever it is you came here for...take it and go.' Her hands gripped the edges of the table tensely.

'I didn't... I mean I just want,' I stammered. There were rumors detailing the way women in Belgium were treated by the German invaders who found them like this, defenseless and alone. Awareness of her vulnerability in this lawless world patrolled by armed men flooded into me and reddened my face. There were no locks, no police, no security at all. We were it. And we looked just like them, the Germans, that is...uniforms, guns, marauding through the land, picking through its contents.

'I'm not like that, we just...' I tried to make her see that we were morally upright, but here I was, standing in her room when she had forbidden it.

I wanted to go to her and touch her hair, but I was afraid her fears would be confirmed. My eyes traveled the room and I picked up a piece of the camouflage fabric instead.

'Why do you have this?' I asked. Her body didn't relax.

'So that you can't see me.' She frowned and began again. 'My husband is an artist. He painted what you see downstairs. Some in here as well. He is quite talented. The government told him he could be exempt from the fighting if he would help them to develop this camouflage. For planes, for people, for objects. He complied...it was an interesting project at first, but it couldn't last. An artist whose work is to make things imperceptible! Creation that's meant to disappear. He couldn't take it for long. He enlisted and has been gone now for eight months. I haven't heard from him since he arrived near Arras, months ago.'

I stepped closer to her as she spoke, drawn to her voice, the timbre of which I hadn't heard in too long. I could see my torso in her oval mirror, her full lips and large, deep eyes. Her eyes were fixed on the reflection as well, but her mind was elsewhere. I could have touched her then, if I had reached out my hand.

'Why do you stay here?' I asked.

'How will he find me if I go?' Her voice had the naïve and weary quality of someone hopelessly lost.

'You paint as well?'

'Women do, you know. Paint. I work for the government, too. Before the Germans came, I painted scenery for the Opera House in Antwerp. Now I paint those," she gestured to a stack of black and white canvases on the floor in the far corner. I moved to them. The images emerged eerily clear to me as I approached them. They were gruesome battle scenes. A naked, limp, pale man impaled with bayonets mimicking the wounds of Christ. Another man in military dress crucified on a crudely assembled cross planted on a nameless field. My mouth gaped and my stomach churned.

'What is this?' I turned back to her in disbelief.

'Atrocities,' she said soberly, rubbing the lotion on her hands. 'They reproduce these images for newspapers and post cards to remind everyone that the Germans are monsters, that the threat is real. To renew the desire to fight on when they fear public resolve might be waning.'

'But they are lies. These aren't photographs. None of this is real.'

'How do you know?' She turned defensive.

'You are making it up! You aren't painting a real scene…you are perpetuating hatred and fear. It's you, it's people like you that are going to make this goddamn war last an eternity. It is your fault that we are all to be consumed.' She paused and her eyes rose to my torso in her mirror again.

'There are monsters here; I do know that. And the funny thing about them is that they all look like you.'

I wanted to throttle and embrace her at the same time. I troubled her; she rubbed her temples and kept her gaze low in the glass.

I wanted her to look at me in the face…she seemed determined not to know me personally, to not see any details that would differentiate me from any other soldier in her paintings. I wanted to engage with this woman who kept me at a distance even when she had revealed her own involvement in keeping me close.

She exhaled slowly. 'Are you one of them? A monster, that is."

'Are you?'

'I wish I knew. I'm nothing I recognize just now.' Her voice was soft and sweet. 'But you want me to believe you are just a human boy, I suppose, who has found himself in the middle of something he didn't expect. Not a soldier, just a boy.'

I stepped closer and crouched beside her. She looked at my face for the first time in the mirror. My arm rested on the back of her chair and I could feel strands of her hair pinned underneath it. She blinked and her eyes welled, as if I were shining bright.

'You look like a ghost,' she said.

'I am not a ghost,' I said into her mirror eyes.

'Maybe you are," she said, "but you just don't know it yet. This place is full of roaming ghosts who think they are men. You're something, anyway. Why did they let you go?'

'Who?'

'The people who love you. How could they send you here?'

'They don't really love me. That's why I came. This has nothing to do with love. Only greed and desire for power.'

'I don't believe you. Everyone is loved.'

'If everyone is loved, why do they act this way? Why do they create so much destruction and pain in the world?'

'So you think we should all just mind our own business and stay out of each other's lives?'

She turned toward me finally and smiled strangely with her lips pressed closed and her head back, regarding me with her inky eyes, as in that picture there. 'Maybe they don't know how much they are loved because no one ever tells them, and they act out, even when they are adults and their toy guns shoot real lead and their soldiers bleed real blood, they act out with the agony of a child whose parents don't understand that providing a good life isn't the same as telling a boy he's more precious than anything in the world.'

I closed my eyes and soaked in the idea of a love filled world. 'How can you speak of love and paint what you paint, to stir up anger and outrage, to justify more death? Love is just an old fashioned idea. It's got no place in this world. This world you're helping to create- the grenades, the shells, the machine guns- is blasting all those old ideas right out of existence. There is no safe haven for old ideas here; your kind has seen to that.'

She flinched and turned her head away.

'Do you mean to tell me," she continued, ignoring my slight, 'that Galileo, Shakespeare, and Mozart don't matter anymore?'

'They are dead men...'

'...whose ideas exist and color our lives still!' She cried adamantly.

'Ideas! Their ideas filled our heads with notions of heroism, of tragedy, of love, of possibility. They've left us as vulnerable as parentless children left completely unprepared to deal with the reality of all this.' With that I dismissed her idealism, but she wasn't ready to concede. I continued: 'You can't have it both ways. You can't carry old ideas into a new world any more than you can bring fish out of the ocean to live on dry ground.'

'Of course, you can! You can put them in a bowl, you can protect... '

'No. You can't control them and confine them. Once you've done this you change their very nature. They are not the same and will never be the same until you realize that they must be released back into the sea.'

'You don't see heroism and tragedy and love and possibility when you look downstairs at your men, at your friends?'

'I see delusions pursued to a nightmarish end. Foolish beliefs that drive parents to push their sons into recruitment offices and generals to push thousands of men into muddy lakes they believe to be battlefields. When it's all over, if it ever ends, someone's ideas will win out, another's will be crushed, and it will all be bullshit. There's the future for you, and there's no love in it.'

'Then why do we do it? Why do you keep doing your duty while I keep doing my duty, at the service of someone else's ideas?'

'I suppose it's because the alternative means admitting that we have traded old ideals for new things. That we care more about what people think of us than whether or not our lives are governed by love. And we are too weak to face this. The ones that use us for their gain, they shame us into believing that here is the only place we can reclaim those ideals. Here we can be heroes; we can find love in its purest form. But we are all just shamed and desperate.' My pronouncement fell from my mouth heavily, wearily, and it seemed as if I could feel gravity and weight more acutely. I was exhausted.

'Desperate for what?'

'I don't know…desperate to find out who we are outside of normal life. Desperate to know how far we'll go for someone and how much someone will endure for our sake.'

'Love and identity, then,' she said, optimistically. 'It's not about shame and desperation at all. It is about love and identity. Two things that are worth all this struggle, I think. If you don't fight for those things here, you'll spend your whole life looking at yourself in mirrors in the morning as you ready for work, catching glimpses of yourself in the faces of your family…you'll spend the rest of your days fighting for your life every step, every drive, every dinner plate. You might as well get it all out in the open, here.'

I put my hand on top of her head and slowly stroked the red hair down to her shoulders.

'You are a fabulous monster,' she said. 'What do you call yourself?'

'Alex. You?'

'Nina.'

I rose to my feet when a loud laugh erupted from the floor below and pressed my lips against her temple, wishing, for a moment that she was waiting for me."

"That wasn't the last you saw of Nina?" I asked him, though I knew the answer.

"No…I saw her on several other occasions, the most intense moments, actually," he nodded his head slightly and pursed his lips as if considering for the first time the shared emotional intensity of the times he recalled seeing her.

"You realize," I prodded him gently, "that Nina could not actually have been at any of the places you describe seeing her after this meeting?" He stared at me then hung his head. I felt a bit like a sadistic schoolmaster tugging a favorite blanket from a school boy who is deemed too old to still need these childish comforts.

"Nina wasn't real, was she, Alex?"

"She was real. She showed me to the cellar." His voice was dried limbs scratching on a window pane.

"You discovered the cellar on your own, when you and Mouse scouted out the property earlier in the day. You told me that you followed the cat to the back yard and saw the door in the ground."

"Yes, I knew it was there, but she lead me to it in the dark and left me there. I remember everything about it. The dampness, the earthy smell of the rotten potatoes, their lumpiness against my lower back."

"Yes, you wrote about this. But you say in your journal that she stayed with you. That your last thoughts before you slept were of… (I squinted at his writing though I knew it well) 'red hair and rottenness. Pulchritude and putrefaction.'" I looked up at him, squinting still as if I were examining a bug on a pin.

"That's not my hand writing," he said, quivering.

"Oh, Alex. It is."

"What do you want from me?'

"I want you to know what happened in your own life! So that you can understand why you are here and how you can leave this place. You do want to leave, don't you? " I don't know what made me say that. The implication was that he was pretending, shirking, and I knew this wasn't so. He thought he was a coward but he was not. Yet here I was, calling him just that.

"She was as real to me as you are." His head was still low, but his eyes flashed upward from beneath the dark brows like angry slashes across his pale face.

"And the mother with the daughter in the blanket, the one that grew in your arms….do you believe they were real?"

"Henry, his hand. Parrish…Foster…was all that real?"

"Yes, Alex. As far as I can determine, that was all real as you described it."

"You want me to believe that Henry ate his hand, that Foster walked without his head, but not that a woman mourned her daughter or that a lady sat in her attic, painting?" His voice was rising and he seemed to almost writhe in the brown chair.

Alex did spend a night in a potato cellar. In the morning, Mouse woke him, lifting the wooden door before first light, exposing the sole occupant to the fresher warm air of late summer. He told Alex, ruefully, that they needed to get moving if they were to make their appointment. They were expected on the line in two days to play their part in what would be called the Third Battle of Ypres. Foster died on the day that Alex spent in Beleuge, in a small skirmish meant to distract the Germans from the advancing force that would constitute the larger offensive.

"I feel everything," he ran his hands through his hair and circled his temples aggressively with his fingers. "What does it matter what's real if it all feels like this? How do I know what really happened and what I've imagined? How do I know that this, here, is real?" His voice was anguished, and I only guessed that this agony was rooted in the pain of his many losses. I didn't know that his agony involved his conviction that he could not pass himself off as well enough to get back to the battlefield, where he desperately wanted to be, even after what happened.

I responded to him the only way I could, with utter inadequacy. I could describe to you my motivations: my efforts to help relieve the pain of his losses, to help him achieve some clarity in his life, to keep him safely with me instead of getting blasted apart in Belgium or France, but what matters motivation? The result is the only thing. I arranged for him to meet with Dr. Hack, the only man who could lengthen Alex's stay beyond the year he had been with us already. He eagerly diagnosed Alex with temporal lobe epilepsy and scheduled him for surgery so that he could get a closer look at his brain. Alex accepted the idea of surgery without pause. He would do whatever it took to get back to his friends. It was the end of October, 1918, and all of his friends, as far as I could account, were dead. He didn't even notice when I brushed the eraser debris from his book, and even though I held the pencil in my hand at the time, I could not really account for the fact that this Nina wore her hair pinned up the way favored by my former wife, but before she did, she wore it in the fashion of a much younger girl.

XXII. Lenora's Perspective on Things

I recognized that Alex was describing his experiences in a fantastical way, through a prism colored by the remarkable story of Alice, but I couldn't isolate the exact moment in which his world merged with hers. It was likely the result of mental exhaustion or some traumatic injury suffered during this time, but certainly not from the moment of enlistment, though his description of that time married with Alice's plunge down the rabbit hole. His recollections were tainted by his affliction, until I realized, wearily, that I could not depend on the accuracy of the account of his own life.

Dr. Hack was not the most respected brain surgeon in Wales, but he was the only brain surgeon that happened to work at Swansea Hospital, which made available most of its medical staff to the convalescent home to serve the war effort. The position of surgeon garnering much respect, he was often consulted for injuries of the mind as well as injuries of the head, and he was eager to apply physical means to eradicate or further understand mental problems, these contributions to research and enhanced reputation being more important to Dr. Hack than the outcome for the patient, it seemed to me.

I disliked Hack's manner with the men, but I needed his signature on paperwork to release patients back to the Army or to extend their treatment. I summoned him to observe a session with Lt. Oster after he had spent more than three weeks at Swansea without a word to anyone. Oster, it was felt, had killed his commanding officer, though no one could prove with certainty that it was Oster's bullet that finished him off, as thousands of bullets were flying in the air at the time, any one of which might have done the job. But to the other officers in the unit, Oster seemed the likely culprit, and he was arrested, questioned, and thrown into a military prison in Paris for his failure to respond to questioning or to defend himself. After several weeks of poor treatment with still no words, a kindly prison administrator saw to it that Oster was transferred to Swansea where he might be made to speak again, thus enabling his trial to go forth and his near certain execution to take place speedily.

Hack was excited about this case, as he was eager to build his prestige in the emerging field of electroshock therapy. While he wouldn't be the one administering the shock, he would have to be consulted for any issues that might affect brain functioning during the process. He sat in a chair pulled in for the occasion of having a visiting doctor in the small office. He regarded Oster with alert eyes and raised brows. Oster's blond hair seemed almost white, and his crowish face seemed much older than his twenty years. He was a mild mannered young man with glowing eyes so dark and damp and luminescent that the blackness seemed like seeping pools spilling forth. He rocked gently when seated, and if he spoke at all, his voice was slow and mumbly. Hack leaned forward in his seat, forearms on his long thighs, and drew a circle on this left palm with the middle finger of his right hand, repeatedly. I asked Lt. Oster gentle questions to demonstrate his inability to answer, as he was among the many patients who often lapsed into long periods of silence.

Dr. Hack seemed visibly agitated watching him; he could hardly remain seated, as a combination of anger at what appeared to be unwillingness to answer mingled with a professional fascination at the apparent inability to answer. I watched in amazement and discomfort as Hack actually licked his lips, as if staring at a buttered lobster steaming on a plate. He shouted: "Speak, can't you!" at the boy loudly for several times to no avail. And then "Were you happy in prison, Lieutenant, away from the battlefields?" with something close to a sneer in his voice. Oster did not reply, though a fat tear rolled down one cheek. His name was added to the list of patients eligible for electric shock treatments.

As I observed his treatment of Oster, I began to grow fearful of my decision to offer Alex to Hack's appraisal as well. But Alex was mentally incompetent to make decisions for himself and his mother was clearly compromised as well. In fact, I had asked his mother to come with Lenora in October to discuss his care, and easily obtained a signature that enabled me to make the kinds of decisions that I was about to make on his behalf. Lenora was harder to convince, but she had no legal claim to him. I had only wanted to win over as many to my line of thinking as possible. I wanted her to see the way forward as I saw it. She didn't, until I showed her Alex's portrait of Nina, and then she reluctantly began to sway.

Presenting Alex as a candidate for medical treatment was the only way I knew to keep him from being sent back to Belgium. His stay at Swansea was already far lengthier than others, even those with visible impairments. I could hide him away no longer without enlisting the aid of someone with Hack's influence and credibility. Hack read Alex's case files with interest, devouring them in one night. I had an appointment to discuss his case the following day. In the time it took for these procedures to be followed, the war came to an unpredictable end. But it was too late. Appointments were made. The treatment was in progress. Less than a week after the war ended, Alex would be sitting under the knife, waiting for his head to be opened like a meat tin.

That was when I called Lenora.

Lenora came to my office and sat in the brown chair willingly, but she spoke with a combination of nervous agitation and exhaustion that made me feel sorry for asking her there. We had spoken briefly many times, and shared letters as well, but now the situation was changed. Alex had been with us for more than a year, but after the Armistice, he had grown somber and silent, giving me plenty of idle hours to sift through his writings. With the war over, I feared for the future of the men still here. They were all in need of continued care, but I was fairly certain that the country would seek to dismantle the places that reminded them of the war wounded in favor of monuments that celebrated the war dead. I had committed Alex to Dr. Hack, as unaware as everyone else that the war was going to come to a surprise ending. Now that there was no need to keep Alex from war service, I felt a sense of urgency to uncover some breakthrough, to save Alex from the knife as well. Lenora's manner was altered, but I had invited her to speak with me, and speak she did:

"He would hate for me to tell his story, but if I didn't give you what I have (she gestured to the stash of letters wrapped in red cord and the two journals that joined the third he had carried on his body), you might not see him the way I do. And the way he is seen is just as important as the way he is. Or was, isn't it? Perception is reality, as they say.

He would already stop me. Reality is the only reality. Perception means nothing. But this is from a boy who lost himself in fantasy and undoubtedly left part of himself there when he came back."

She looked at me and pressed her lips together and squinted, as if to detect if I understood what she meant. I nodded slightly for her to go on.

"He would say, now, that everything he experienced was real and that the fantasy only made the real endurable. Nothing- even in his most fantastic recollections- was a lie.

He would say that it is me, and you, and everyone else who believed or believes that wars are fought for what we are lead to believe they are fought for, that wars are noble, that they are the domain of real men, that what the papers say is true, it is we who live in a fantasy world from which we never return. It is we who are mad.

So I wanted you to understand that he wasn't weak-minded. He wasn't a coward. He was just a boy who had to act like a man who transformed from the love of my young life to a complete stranger."

She had been looking around the room as she spoke, and now her eyes settled on a letter that lay open on my desk. She recognized the lavender paper as being her own. She wrote this to me two weeks ago, and in it she had promised to tell me Alex's story, which is why I asked her to come. She had written:

"It's also the story of my brother and two of our dearest friends: handsome, exciting, smart boys who filled my days with trouble and sports and fun. They disappeared, all of them, into Alex's fantasy world, and so I visit it whenever I can, reading his letters to me, talking to him when I can bear it, trying desperately to keep my memories of them sharp as knives against all the thieves who conspire relentlessly to steal them from me, to substitute kitschy, artificial garbage for the real richness that was our lives together. I sound like him there. His bitterness is mine, too. Yes, I fight to remember, no matter how painful the associated loss, our lives before two centuries collided in a hail of machine gunfire, before tradition withered in a cloud of phosgene, and before Alex's mind transcended all of it with help from a book called Alice in Wonderland."

It was the mention of the book that struck me. And her assumption that the book was responsible for Alex's mental demise and that this was a good thing, a protection of sorts.

"What is it about this book?" I asked her when she sat in front of me.

"I had dismissed him when he had tried to get me to read it, offended by the juvenile nature of the story. I saw it as absurd and unrecognizable. Only later did I realize that the place we sent them all to- all the boys and men we knew- was more unrecognizable and absurd than any literary world could conjure. And the ones who came back faced a country and a people so changed in their absence that they were twice lost.

Like Alice emerging from Wonderland only to open the door to the Looking Glass House, to discover that the pawns on the chessboard were really crying babies writhing on the ground, and that the horror of those moments is something they will never forget."

"Yes, but how did you know that the book ..." I struggled to describe to her what it was that the book did to Alex, but she knew without words.

"When I saw him, after he came back. The first thing he said to me...after many days of silence, his first words to me were directly from that book."

I didn't speak, waiting for her to reveal those first words. She seemed hesitant, as if she were revealing something too private or somehow not protecting him enough.

"He wouldn't talk at all, no matter what I said or asked. On the fourth day I visited and he sat in his chair while I sat on the bed beside him. He leaned forward and put his head in my lap- he hadn't moved to touch me before then- and wrapped his arms around me. He moved his face slowly from side to side in the folds of my skirt and I said 'what is it?' again and 'please tell me.' And after a few moments he said 'I think the mome raths outgrabed me.' He didn't say anything else that day."

I nodded, wondering if he had described in detail his hallucinations to her as he had to me. I wondered if she knew that she was his Red Queen. She certainly knew some things:

"Alex spent much of his time thinking about prescience. About whether artists and novelists are touched by God and give us warnings of our future. He believes that they are, because he lived Alice in Wonderland twenty years after it was written. That's what he thinks. Only he doesn't understand the point of these warnings if no one listens, if we can only understand them in hindsight. Alex is not on good terms with God these days."

"And you? Are you on good terms with Alex?"

"Alex isn't a stranger to me," she exhaled, staring not at me but at the dark wood of my desk. "That part of the story isn't true. I'm afraid of him because he makes me feel all the pain I deserve."

She wasn't my patient, and I did not wish to explore her pain at this time any more than I wished to explore my own over the death of my son. I felt our pain was connected, but I did not reach out to her with kindnesses.

"Were you and Alex ever... a couple?" I knew the answer to this, but I wished to change the subject.

"No. I was with our friend, Roman." She stared still, as if she was trying to see and describe a dream. "Alex was like my younger brother in many ways. It was complicated. It seemed much easier to send them all to France so that I could sort it out. I thought they'd be gone a few months, like a school term."

"But you didn't really send them. The country was in a fever and all able young men enlisted of their own accord."

"I didn't send Roman or my brother, or Bernard, you are right. I certainly didn't stop them, though. But Alex... him, I sent myself."

"You called him the love of your life, but you were dating someone else. And when that one went to the war, you could have had Alex all to yourself, but you sent him away?"

"I told you, it's complicated." She blinked back tears and her eyes settled on my face, steady and cold.

"I would like to help Alex. So anything you tell me would be greatly appreciated." She seemed to consider this for a moment before nodding.

"I'll tell you about the first day I saw him," she said, "and the last."

Part Six

In a Wonderland they lie,

Dreaming as the days go by,

Dreaming as the summers die:

XXIII. Mind the Gap

"Mind the gap," she said over her shoulder to him as the conductor blew the whistle urging passengers to detrain in Blackpool. Instead, he leapt without caution from the train to the platform, stumbling forward and brushing the backs of his friends who had stepped off before him, who now turned to include him in their conversation, accepting without pause that a certain amount of nudging and jostling was a normal part of modern life and even a welcome part of a man's life. No need for apology or excuse.

Alex could sense Lenora's frown aimed at the back of his head, but he was glad to displease her. At twenty, she was his age, but she had treated him as an older sister would for years, offering advice and cautions and criticisms since they had met at age seven. She always knew what was right for him, and she was happy to share the news. Indeed, she assumed the duties of his savior and protector, believing that she was responsible for rescuing him from a life of torment.

He appreciated her. He paid attention to her in a way that others did not. Even when he avoided looking at her, she was keenly aware that his senses were tuned in her direction. He rebelled against her advice even though she knew it warmed him to hear it, to know that she was thinking of him and that she wished for him to continue on, safely by her side, just as they were.

When she first saw him at seven, racing barefoot down the misty lane on a cold morning, collapsing in the grass beneath her window, she recalled how the sodden lawn soaked into his clothes, saturating them. She watched transfixed while he seemed to infuse with color, his pale garments turning dark before her eyes.

She pressed her forehead against the cold pane of her bedroom window and looked down at his white face staring straight up into the gray sky, never detecting the still spy hovering above, beyond the glass. His exhalations came sharp and quick from lungs, as his body tried to compensate for the efforts of his desperate run. His breath bloomed like white gardenias when it escaped its warm confines and met the cold air. She could not clearly make out his face due to the strange whiteness which obscured him, but she was drawn to him.

She instantly dismissed the first notion that came to her, that this boy might be her knight in sodden pajamas, the true love of her life. She had romantic notions but did not believe in love at first sight, and she certainly could not predict the future. There were many boys she had not yet met. She had big plans for herself which would require a boy of a certain physical strength and comportment; one who would certainly not fling himself onto a neighbor's lawn while wearing his bedclothes.

But this boy needed her, she felt. He needed something, surely, beyond a pair of shoes and a set of dry clothes. She would make it her business to be sure he was taken care of.

And though they did not meet on this day, Lenora counted this as the start of their relationship, one marked by equal parts rescue from torment and application of it.

Today was just another day at the beach in August 1914; there would be no torment here, only happy times and good conversation. As she watched their backs, the four of them walking ahead of her away from the train and toward the shoreline, shoulders touching, heads bent toward each other, laughter flowing easily, her frown faded. One of these young men was her brother, one her lover, and one a dear friend. And Alex…her mind struggled to explain their connection to her heart and she set her mouth in firm defiance of reducing their relationship to a label or category. But it was him, Alex, not her brother, lover, or friend, who broke the harmony of their quartet, disrupting the tightly woven line from which she had excluded herself, who forced the pace to slow for her, and who reached out for her elbow so that she could join them.

She did not know, until he wrote to her from Belgium in 1916 that he would remember days like this, days spent on shifting sands in the bright sun with the crash of waves inevitable but harmlessly roaring in the distance like a dormant god who might one day awaken in a roiling, massive surge to wash them all away.

His letters to her revealed that he would recreate these days in his mind during the most excruciatingly boring stretches of time in the trenches, the endless vacuums of waiting, waiting, when even the sun seemed not to move for countless hours. He could almost feel the warm, dry sand conforming to his body, lulling him into pleasant complacency, into a half-awake state, wherein the voices of his friends rose and faded and mixed with the low rumble of the sea. Then her voice, higher pitched, cut through it all and kept him from succumbing fully to sleep. He would open an eye to observe her, but sun-dazzled, his squinting eye could make out only a shadow form perched on the blanket.

On his worst days, when his terrified mind searched frantically for some solace, he would recreate these days, but try as he might, he remembered only how the five of them had come together so briefly, with her at the center, and how, in the shifting sands and the ebbs and flows, things had so quickly fallen apart.

It was on one of these days, a day of advance, when his men rose out of their trenches like goldfish spilling over the sides of a tank filled to overflowing, and flopped like goldfish on the ground, gasping for air, that her voice came to him again. He often heard it singing in his head when he ran across battlefields, leaping over bodies and shell holes and narrow, abandoned trenches. "Mind the gap!" he would hear, as if she were running slightly ahead of him, yelling back a warning. And it was one of these many similar days, when he had heard in conversation about the fate of Henry's unit and then about Henry himself, when he heard the words like a whisper in his ear, "mind the gap", when he realized she wasn't warning him about a tripping hazard; she was telling him how to get out of this mess alive.

But back there, on the beach, feeling the warm sun on her face and linking her arms in theirs, she did not suspect that this would be their last outing together, or that she was willingly throwing them all, like lobsters, out to sea.

XXIV. The Lioness

Roman Foster wanted to be a politician. Alex never saw him more excited than when they sat in on a session of parliament during a school trip in 1913. His hands gripped the back of the chair in front of him and he could scarcely keep seated when the arguments started to fly. Headmaster Stevens smartly seated himself directly behind Foster, and his cane tapped Foster's shoulder periodically, keeping him in check. Foster would turn to Alex and whisper harshly about Home Rule for the Irish, though Alex could tell by his exasperated sighs that Roman knew his friend's blank face revealed his lack of interest in the topic.

Foster succeeded at everything he tried. His athleticism made him a hero on the rugby field. He challenged every instructor at school and even embarrassed a few with his insights and probing questions, but he made no enemies. His pure confidence won over everyone he met. Every girl he sought, he got and forgot. But never a heart was broken. Foster was a friend Alex could not remember being without, yet when it became clear to him that Foster and Lenora were together, Alex determined that something in their friendship had irrevocably altered. He was never sure if he could count on Foster in a pinch, and never revealed his real dreams and desires to him, for fear that Foster would begin to see as desirable that which he valued. He had begun to see Foster's smile as engagingly fake, his handshake too smooth and polished; he always knew what he could get away with.

That day in September 1917, on the ground overlooking Ypres, Foster's men were protected on the flanks by the London Irish. Alex chuckled when he heard this detail, imagining Foster seeking out a rowdy Irishman to debate the timing of the Easter Rising. All just to pass time before the big show, of course. No harm intended. The big show started as planned, as always with a heavy barrage of artillery shells that pulverized the ground, and Alex read about it two weeks later, in a letter from an Irishman who had heard about him from Foster and who saw the explosion that removed his head for himself.

He wrote that the force of the blast rocked Foster's body back a step or two, then, he lurched forward again, several yards, in fact, before he fell. This Irishman had stopped in his tracks when he saw Foster walking around like that, without his head. He believed that stopping as he did saved his life from a mortar that dropped in his path, so felt compelled to write to him, as a way of expressing his thankfulness.

He had already come across Roman Foster's name on a long list of the dead, printed in the newspaper the regular men were not allowed to see. He knew he should never have questioned his loyalty. Death in battle, he explained to me, fixes all character flaws and shames those still alive. Alex had thought himself impervious to this kind of romanticism. But now, he couldn't help but succumb to this powerful belief that the dead were all of them heroes, and it made him cry to know that he was mourning not his friend but a false memory of his friend, and that he was himself abandoning the boy on the bicycle who didn't give up on him then and despite being a bastard at times, lay now, on a field, head disappeared into the mysterious cloud of a shell burst.

Lenora read the paper as well. Sitting at breakfast, alone, while her parents met with a barrister in the city regarding a small inheritance that had come their way due to the war death of a cousin from Sheffield, she saw the name of her friend in the list only after scanning the "L" section and breathing a sigh of relief at her unfamiliarity with any of the names there recorded. Instantly, though, he eyes scanned upward and settled on Foster, Roman, and stayed there for a long, long moment while relief turned into nausea and panic. She had lost all three and there was only one left and no end to the war insight.

She folded the paper hastily as if to swat a fly with it. "I can't stand this any longer!" Her voice rose to a perfect scream as she leapt to her feet and swung the newspaper with a backhand gesture across her body and into the innocent teapot, cups, and assorted crockery that stood silently on the table, defenseless against her onslaught.

As one might expect, they crashed to the ground, spilling their contents, or rocked, upended, on the tabletop until coming to a rest.

Releasing the paper, she gripped the table's edge with both hands and stood, heaving heavy breaths, staring with impotent intensity at the mess she had created and feeling the poignant discomfort of a caged lioness who realizes she is no longer queen of the jungle because her subjects have disappeared, her jungle has been systematically replaced by a landscape she doesn't recognize, and in fact, she may never have been in a jungle at all, which guaranteed the impossibility of a return.

XXV. Art and Insects

Alex and his unit reached the worn, bedraggled ground near Broodseinde in September, 1917. Things were quiet, but would not be for long. As they approached their position, Alex surveyed the area before him, a stretch of insignificance that did not betray any hint of former glory or distinction. Where maps indicated forests, there were no trees. Peaks were flattened; houses were roofless and housed no one at all.

He could hardly imagine what to show the artists when they came, but they were coming to paint the war, recruited in the effort by someone called Mastermind in London, whose job it was not to show the war to the people of England, but to sell it. (His name was Masterman, actually, but I could not convince Alex of this). The artists would come to see the war and paint, it was imagined, anything but what they saw. So they must come to see what not to paint, Capt. Whitesell explained to Alex when he assigned him to chaperone.

Bone and Nash were the artists. (These were their real names, and Alex was encouraged that such connotative names might indicate a willingness to paint with raw authenticity the gruesomeness of life in the trenches. I reminded him that euphemisms like 'accessories' for gas shells revealed that names could not be trusted; perhaps I was thinking of Hack and hoping that names could not be trusted). Bone was older than the other and Scottish, but both had spent some time at the front. They were not home service lackeys who were on a visit to the front. They were accomplished in watercolors and landscapes, so Alex had viewed the land for them, imagining it with the eye of an artist and deciding this landscape was decidedly unlike any ever framed and hung in a museum, but perhaps that very act of containing and displaying it would somehow make it seem controlled, distant, and removed like an exotic creature in a cage, something to be harmlessly observed or just as readily ignored, an idea that did not sit well with him, nor, he found, with the artists.

When Alex expressed his concern to Nash, about the appropriateness of landscapes to convey anything of import to the people of England, Nash pulled his sketchbook out of an oiled canvas satchel and handed it to him for his inspection.

"Don't worry, mate" he said with a quiet urgency, "we are making a whole new world here, and they'll see it all." By 'we' he meant all of them, and by 'they' he meant all of England. Alex took comfort in the artists' loyalties, but he wasn't at all sure how art could exist in concert with war, as he saw in his mind's eye the gleaming battle portraits that adorned great halls and galleries presently.

Nash's eyes seemed to dart and take in everything at once, while Bone, arms crossed firmly across his chest, seemed dour and heavy to Alex, ponderously absorbed, as if he was already constructing his art in his mind and did not need any more exposure to the subject to create an accuracy that would be allowable by Mastermind and the War Propaganda Bureau's standards.

Alex flipped through the drawings with genuine interest, his eyes and face softening at the sight of men melding with their machinery. Others, exhausted, were as drab heaps indistinguishable from the earth on which they slept or died.

"The faces all look the same" Alex observed softly.

"Yes," Nash replied, again softly. "It's a tough trick. Do you show the dehumanization or do you assert the human, specific, face of it all? In the end, these soldiers can be any one of us. We have no names here; I haven't even recorded their names in my notes. They aren't one man or another. It's not a photograph; it's a composite, an idea…"

"A warning," Alex ventured.

"More than that, mate" he almost smiled for the first time. "It's an omen, an albatross, a harbinger, a canary in a fucking coal mine. A whole new world, I'm telling you."

Alex nodded in agreement. Nash was happy to continue: "I mean, how many people here know your name? Only your men. Your unit, that's it. To everyone else, you are just a rank. Hell, I don't even know your name, mate. You're the one they asked to tour us around today. When your name appears on a list of dead or wounded in the papers, only the people who love you will notice it. And how many people is that, really? That really love you? Everyone else who gets that paper will just see the ink, the space the name takes up, the count. But here we are, fighting for all of them, every one. But them, they won't notice our passing with anything but passing interest, a glance." He took a long draw from his cigarette.

"I'm only here for the ones I love, not all of England. She can rot in hell, for all I'm concerned," Alex returned. This was not an idea in development; of this he was sure.

He turned the page of the sketchbook and looked in puzzlement at a sketch of a skyscraper like none he had ever seen, a lean, multi-tiered, angular structure soaring to the sky.

Nash stopped fidgeting long enough to turn the book sideways in Alex's hands.

"That way, mate" he said in the same quiet voice.

The building transformed before his eyes to an image of a soldier from the side, hunched over his machine gun, all straight lines and automation.

"I thought it was a building" Alex said, turning the book in his hands to see if he could catch his first impression again. But once the intended image was realized, there was no seeing the first, mistaken one.

Nash slapped his neck. "Fucking lousy war," he pulled a white bug from behind his ear, squeezing it with disdain. "Lice, maggots... I don't think I've seen more creatures eager to feast on me in one place...except maybe the last time I was home."

"What do you mean?"

"Ah, you know, the propagandists. They're everywhere, can't escape them. I draw men here like they are machines, one with their weapons. But it's them, the one's back home. That's where the machine is, back in England. We're just the gas and the grease that keep it going. Running smoothly. Everyone gainfully employed."

"What if we just stop?" Alex asked.

Nash exhaled sharply through his nose then made his tone more upbeat. "I'm imagining a new bug; let's call him 'Art.' His wings are thinly folded newspaper, his body a coil of film, and his head is a book. He lives in the War Propaganda Bureau offices in London and he feeds on truth."

"What if he doesn't find any?"

"He dies."

"That must happen often," Alex noted.

"It always happens," Nash said, his agitation growing. "To tell you the truth, I feel like they've got my head pulled open like a meat tin. Like they are in there, tinkering with my brain, to try to use my talent without any of my conscience or consciousness. Just the way they've got all of us, really. But this is my art, my name. They can't fucking tell me to paint the war and not paint all this shit."

Alex returned the sketchbook to Nash and saw that tears wet his face.

"You shouldn't do it at all if it makes you so unhappy," he advised.

"It's not that, mate, don't you worry. It's not the art. I'll take care of the art." Bone had returned to the connector trench that would take them back to the rear, and Nash turned to follow.

"Problems with my side. My ribs. I fell and broke a few, apparently. Seems I'm going to miss all this." His voice cracked, and as he departed, he added: "I'll make sure this bug bites England in the ass and doesn't let go."

And he was true to his word.

Alex thought about Nash and the physical and mental toll that his struggle to be true to his art in the face of pressure was extracting. He thought about Nina and her conflicted motives and her openness, his mother and her attempts to ignore truth and what had become of her life as a result, and Lenora, who ruled most of all by ignorance and received notions. He thought of his father, of course, and how he would never know his father's truth, what he had wanted for his family, what he had wanted to impart to his son, what he intended to communicate in his paintings. He could see if he closed his eyes, the brown eyes and the open mind. He would never know for certain if his father felt that he, too, had been tinkered with or if he had found, in soldiering or in fathering or in the practice of his art, something that made him feel transcendent, like something beautiful and powerful emerging from a shell or a cocoon.

He had a few moments, then, that felt almost like peace, like warm water relaxing his entire body, as he came close to understanding that all of these people who believed themselves to be in conflict with others were more lethally in conflict with themselves, and that they, all of them, everyday, fought for their lives, alone. But that they could, if they didn't give up, find something like victory.

Then he remembered that internal war and actual war were two different things. Shells were incoming, and the warmth turned to weariness and receded as quickly as it had come.

XXVI. A Mad Tea Party

Night was the only time that any of them dared to look out on the battlefield stretching before them, beckoning and quiet like a stretch of newly fallen snow that a child can't wait to corrupt with his footprints. It was not snow that glittered across the fields this night, though. Rather, Alex could sense, even in the dark, that the ground before him was transforming into a glittering sea, as smashed drainage pipes and the naturally low level of Belgian soil conspired to betray their imminent efforts to advance and attack. It was as if the earth itself had said "Enough! Enough of this violence! If you can't figure out how to stop fighting, I'll take away your battlefield and we'll see what you do then!" Every crater welled as if the earth was trying desperately to heal its festering wounds. The mud was so coagulated here that even the machines, the landships which seemed so impressive and impregnable, made no progress, leaving the attainment of objectives entirely up to the men. Alex knew that the orders to advance could not be executed, and he, finally unwilling to be executed because of someone else's decisions, determined that something must be done.

He turned from his post, pushed past Lowe and Capt. Whitesell, and entered, stumbling, into the winding, narrow connector trench that would lead him, eventually to Col. Flint and his Adjutant, Maj. Knight. He was compelled to inform them of the conditions on the ground, as he suspected that no one else was doing so, afraid of upsetting the Colonel or perhaps afraid of appearing unwilling or weak. The Captains, he suspected, were painting white roses red and portraying the conditions on the ground in a way that was at best overly optimistic and at worst, completely false. Surely the Colonel, miles away and nearly underground, could not see what he saw.

He stooped and ducked habitually, though there was no firing. The shallowness of the trench, reaching only to his elbows, and the singularity of his movements, made him feel like a goliath, an easy target, and hazardously exposed.

The connector trench traveled through a changing landscape, winding away from the front through a former wood that now resembled an archery field with arrows sticking out of the ground, hopelessly off target. Not one piece of wood seemed the width of a tree and certainly none reached a tree's height. The light of early morning illuminated these shards now, and as he passed them he was reminded of books he had read about Africa, of spears that lined the pathways of warrior kings and of spears that warned enemies of danger ahead, planted in the ground and waving impaled heads and hearts.

Staggering forward, he was drawn to the sound of voices and the distinctive clattering of porcelain, and soon he was upon a tea party in the dirt. The connector trench spilled, at last, into a spacious dugout, not unlike a basement, with narrow channels snaking off in three directions from three of the four walls. He felt, standing there for a moment and catching his breath, like a piece of food must feel as it squeezed through the esophagus and then spilled into the cavernous stomach of a great beast. The sense of roominess would soon be replaced by a sickening, acidic quality.

Before him sat the Colonel, his Adjutant, and a lowly soldier who had likely delivered the latest order and been entreated to join the other two for a spot of tea on a warped barn door used as a table top with no legs. The door rested, instead, on two wooden crates used to carry Mills bomb components. The entire party perched on helmets around the table and prepared to drink from the Colonel's own tea set, unbelievably white on the outside though tea stained inside for want of proper washing facilities. The poor soldier, exhausted from his deliveries and bored with present company, could barely keep his eyes open and indeed slumped forward on to the table top, upsetting his cup.

The Colonel, a tightly wound man of classic features and little sense save an elevated sense of his own wisdom and standing in the eyes of his men, was quick to scold him: "Good God, man! Hold yourself together. A shot of tea is just what you need to get back to being some use to your unit and you somehow manage to upset the lot. Are you a shirker?" His neck and head seemed to snake toward him at this danger-laden inquiry.

"No, sir!" he yelped, pathetically, holding himself erect with rigid arms pressed firmly against the tabletop.

The Colonel whispered loudly to his Adjutant, who seemed to view himself as something akin to a swashbuckling pirate in his flair and jaunty carriage, and who had seen little enough of battle to not yet have his illusion destroyed.

"We could court martial him right here" Knight offered with an arch of eyebrows that indicated a sly desire for this kind of diversion. "Won't be the first shirker shot dead, and certainly won't be the last" he added without pretense of whispering.

The soldier sat gloomily still staring at the overturned cup. The tea had spilled toward the Colonel and was now beginning to drip off the end of the table and onto his folded legs.

"That's enough. Everyone moves two turns counterclockwise!" he commanded. As it was, it would have been easier and ended in the same result if everyone had moved just one spot clockwise, but the Colonel was not one to envision or prescribe the courses of action that caused the least amount of trouble for others.

All stood and obediently moved as if playing musical chairs. The Adjutant now stared at the overturned cup before him, the soldier's legs got wet, and the Colonel, known without affection among the men as just another empty-headed brass hatter, sat before the Adjutant's perfectly settled and sweetened cup of tea.

"Gentlemen," Alex sensed his opportunity to speak.

"Who are you calling a gentleman, Lieutenant?" goaded the Adjutant, with an attempt at humor that sounded to Alex like a threat.

"Sir, if I may, I wish to counsel you briefly on the planned attack on ___ "

"What do you know of it? Have you been spying? Bribing messengers for information?" the Adjutant continued, working himself into an excited state while the Colonel merely eyed Alex suspiciously as he sipped.

"No, no...the men have been talking, sir" Alex stammered an explanation.

"Oh the men are talking about an attack on Ypres and you assume that we'd attack at the salient despite the enemy's far superior numbers, his superior position, the immense challenges presented by the weather, the sheer exhaustion all around, and the doubtful strategic advantage of what could possibly be gained by such an advance? Have you actually thought for a second about the likelihood of this rumor, or do you simply believe everything you hear, Lieutenant?" The Major smiled with disdain.

Alex did not respond, recognizing the rhetorical quality of this question and the military style of the conversation which was, in fact, to silence one of two participants so that only one view emerged.

The Colonel jumped in for no reason in particular, as the conversation was clearly over.

"We will attack at the Ypres salient. If the good people at home want us back by Christmas, we can't very well achieve that objective by sitting in the dirt drinking tea, can we, Lieutenant?"

Alex was too confused to speak sensibly. "But..." he uttered. He wanted to say "Who cares about Christmas!" But he didn't.

"Is that all you came to say, Lieutenant, 'But'... 'well'?" the Major stared up at him with annoyance. Alex hadn't said "well" at all, if he could remember correctly.

"Speaking of wells," chimed in the soldier, relieved that talk of shirking had past and someone else was the target of abuse.

"I was patrolling through Nancy three days ago and I came across this well. Looked like a mound of rock, really with a red wooden structure on top with the rope attached and a handle. It was behind a farmhouse that was in perfect condition- untouched by bombs or fire, which was so remarkable and was the reason we were drawn to it in the first place. Anyway there was a woman, with long, blonde hair like rope, lying against the mound, face against the rocks, not moving, just barely talking. She was making this funny sound, 'mon, mon, mon,' over and over again, and I swear she looked just like a ghost, no expression on her face, no color at all. Like she would disappear in a second. She looked right at us, but it was like she didn't see anything at all. Talked to her husband, who was missing a leg. Turns out she had put her 2 babies into the well like a bomb shelter. It was dry, and the rumors were that bombing would destroy the village. But as it turned out, the bombing was light due to the weather. It rained for 3 days straight. She ran out to the well during that first day of rain, but it was already too late. Filled up with water. So every morning since, she brings cheese out to the well in case her kids float up to tell her how hungry they are.

The cheese was on the ground by her feet. Hadn't had cheese in weeks, myself, so picked some off the grass and ate it. Good, soft. Could have spread it on crackers." He smiled at the memory.

"You, there!" The Colonel pointed at Alex as if he had not heard the soldier's story. "You could certainly use a haircut and a shave."

"A haircut? He ate cheese meant for dead children and all you can say is that I need a shave in order to be home by Christmas?" Alex's mouth was dry and his legs trembled.

The Colonel's cup rattled as he slammed it down on the white saucer; more dark liquid dripped onto the soldier's leg.

"Look here, Lieutenant," the Adjutant intervened, relishing the opportunity. "You should think about what you say before you say it."

"I mean what I say," Alex uttered in careful, controlled tones, "and I say what I mean. This battle plan is going to get a lot of good men killed for no good reason. The battlefield is a swamp, a lake…"

"What do you know of reason, son?" the brass hatter challenged him, pulling his coat straight and eyeing Alex as if he would devour him. "You're not a professional soldier. You're a volunteer or a conscript," he snarled this last word with disgust. "These plans come from higher headquarters, from professional soldiers who have dedicated their lives to the art of war."

"There is no art here," Alex countered, suddenly headweary and footsore from his journey. "Only science, physics, chemistry, engineering, biology," he could hear his voice growing smaller as if he were shrinking.

"And you must think you know more than Generals with years of experience. Then, Lieutenant, perhaps we should allow you to draft the plan of attack. But we don't have time for that. There is a war on, in case you haven't noticed, and if it's to be done by Christmas, we have to execute the plans we have been given!"

The soldier's ears pricked up at the word "execute," but seeing that it was not he who was the subject of abuse, he quickly resumed his seated stupor.

"What time is that attack to launch, sir" the Adjutant asked with eagerness.

"Let's synchronize our watches" the Colonel lifted his arm and pulled back his sleeve.

"Ah, mine's stopped working" the Adjutant listened for ticking.

"Mine's clogged with mud. It's stuck on ten," yawned the soldier.

"Maybe that's why you are so tired" suggested the Adjutant, helpfully.

"Blast! Mine is missing the minute hand and the hour is stuck on four. Tea time!" The Colonel turned to his cup with renewed vigor.

"It's 6:45!" Alex shouted exasperated. He turned without ceremony, without bidding good day, and reentered the trench closest to him. This time the fit was just right, and he didn't have to stoop or pitch forward. The walls were close, the coverage ideal. He wondered if he had been reduced in size or if he had been replaced by his boyhood self. He settled on the notion that it didn't matter who he was, and he remembered the earlier feeling he had as he moved through the trench, the sensation that he had been swallowed by a monster.

XXVII. Schoolboy Soldiers

He squeezed through the trench, his stomach heavy, because he knew that they were all lost and that he would not be able to save his men any more than he could save himself from the madness of the situation. He walked for what seemed like hours, climbing out of the trench where it was smashed without concern over whether he was making himself a target for snipers. The day was strangely quiet and stranger still, when he climbed out of the trench for the fifth or seventh time, he saw to one side a grove of what he could only describe as trees. Having not seen trees in quite some time, he naturally abandoned the trench to examine this cluster of tall, jagged, leafless forms that he only classified as trees because they had roots that grabbed at the earth like knobby, grotesque, determined fingers.

Even stranger still, as he began to walk through the trees cautiously, as one would walk through a graveyard or a museum exhibition, he realized that he was not alone. He approached two figures with trepidation, moving quietly and with exaggerated slowness, as a hunter who spots a deer in a nearby clearing might. The two bodies, small like those of children, were sitting, slumped against two thin trunks, legs sprawled out in front of them, either in sleep or in death.

They seemed to Alex, for just a moment, to be Parrish and Lowe miniaturized, their childhood selves transported to Belgium to join their adult selves, or to rescue them, perhaps, or to magnify their eventual, inevitable loss to anyone who would notice these forlorn, out-of-place kids.

Alex was torn between a desire to protect them and an urge to wake them so they could run off as if they were schoolchildren evading an unpleasant series of classes. His thoughts were interrupted when they simultaneously sprang to attention upon hearing his approach. Instead of nervous exclamations of military protocol ("Good morning, sir!"), they spoke to him with the casual confidence of old veterans or street toughs.

"Didja think we was dead?" asked one in a way that sounded rhetorical.

"Maybe you should speak 'stead uv sneakin' up on two blokes catchin' a few winks 'fore the big show" the same boy spoke, but the second one nodded his agreement and frowned at Alex.

Alex glanced around in a wide sweep. He saw no other soldiers in the woods, and though there certainly was to be a big show, as the first boy, Pvt. D. James Ellis alluded, Alex could not be entirely sure that these two were not attempting to desert before kickoff.

"What are you doing out here alone? Where is your unit?" He heard himself asking in a voice that seemed to come from someone else. His own voice resounded in his head with other questions: why aren't you in school? Where are your parents?

"I could ask you the same thing," the other boy, Pvt. Robert Dumbarton stepped forward aggressively.

"Which of you is senior man?" Alex's concern was giving way to irritation.

"Well if you mean by rank, we're the same. Joined same day, lieutenant" said D. "If you mean by age, then I've nearly a month on this young private" he jostled his friend with his shoulder.

The two looked like twins, and Alex found himself looking at one face then the other then back again, sweat breaking out on his brow. He knew he should detain them both and march them straight back to the Adjutant for court martial.

"How old are you both, then?" He delayed his action with conversation.

"Seventeen, just turned" said Dumbarton, boastfully.

"You shouldn't be here," Alex returned, but none were sure if he meant in the woods alone, or in Belgium in oversized uniforms stuffed into oversized boots and carrying rifles that were nearly as long as they were tall.

Ellis broke from his tough, defensive stance first. "Tell ya the troof, sir; this here ain't quite what I signed up for."

Dumbarton shot him a look meant to quiet him but picked up for his faltering friend.

"We's Accrington PALS, East Lancs," he explained, waiting to see Alex's reaction. He could feel the disgust rising in this throat and the lines of his face tightening in anger. Dumbarton, believing the anger was meant for them, was compelled to speak further to delay Alex's next words, which he was sure would be an announcement of their arrest.

"A recruitin team came to school and tells us we'd get out a year early and stay with our chums if we all joined together. Said we'd be like a football team, you know, like the West Hammers."

"Well, they didn't exactly lie," chimed in Ellis. "Just didn't tell us that we wouldn't likely be footballin on this team of ours. But we are togever…that's something!" He added brightly, looking at his friend, who embraced him quickly, never changing his scowling face.

Ellis continued: "I'll never forget this recruitin sergeant, he seemed like an old man, nearly 30! Always smiling. Turns out he was on home service. Club foot made him drag his feet; like a walrus he looked, I tell you, long mustache, and feet bent and draggin like flippers. Never stepped one bloody flipper on the continent, though, I'll tell ya straight. Anyway, 'ere comes this sergeant and an old Colonel, Carpenter was his name, looked like Kitchener's twin, like a grandfather who slips you money when your mum's not looking. There were posters tellin everybody in town these two would be at the school on such and such day. And sure enough that morning, our mums brushed our hair and scrubbed our faces for us like we was going to take first holy communion or somethin. Kids that don't even go to the school were sent out in their best to hear what these men had to say about the bloody war and the glory. And our mum's wanted us to make a good impression! I wish they'd kept us home, hidden away!"

Dumbarton gave him a sharp pat on the back so that he could continue his tale: "Them older boys, they knew the drill. They stayed away that day like they was ditching exams. But old Capper, that's what we called him, he didn't mind. There was enough of us young ones for him. He was like the Pied bloody-Piper leadin us out of Hamlet."

"No, mate, it was Hamburg."

"Bloody hell, who cares? He lead us here and they ate us for lunch down at Lens, they did, like they were servin us on a platter. Sixty thousand gone for zero yards gained, that's a score for you," Dumbarton's toughness dissolved into anger and accusation, and his eyes looked searchingly at Alex for some explanation of this betrayal. Ellis saved him:

"But Capper, he got his, him and gold braids and ribbons. But they don't learn, do they? Same trick at the Somme. Twenty minutes in, more than two hundred PALs gone, all from the good ol' AC. They won't print that score in the papers, will they? But they won't get me and they won't get him." They embraced again and held it for a long moment. Too long, for Ellis, as the embrace quickly turned into a headlock and a tussle, with both boys rolling about on the ground at Alex's feet.

"Get up will you!" Alex commanded. The pulled each other up, uniforms askew. Alex heard material rip.

"Look what you did!" Dumbarton cursed. "Bloody…this was brand new!" he twisted his head to examine his ripped collar.

"New, he says. You got that off a dead bloke!" Ellis complained.

"It's new to me, man! Now it's ruined!" His voice rose to a scream. Ellis removed a green wool scarf from around his neck and began to wrap it around his friend, covering the offending torn collar.

"All better now," he said. "There! You's protected from uniform violations and from losing your head alike," he said with seriousness, adding as he glanced at Alex: "Losing your head's the worst that can happen to a bloke in the thick of things, you know."

Alex was already stepping away from them, "It is bad mate, but it's not the worst thing."

They both blinked in irritation before raising their rifles toward him. They were not aimed at him, but nearly displayed to him, so that he would notice that they had two weapons and he had but one.

"Think it's time you pissed off, Lieutenant. If you think we are going back, you're mad."

He didn't think they were going back and he was sure that he wasn't going to insist on it. Winds suddenly rushed through the leafless branches and stumps of trees, whipping the scarf across Dumbarton's face and carrying with it the sounds of explosions that reminded Alex that he had obligations elsewhere.

XXVIII. The Red Queen and the Final Party

They would be involved, Alex's men, in one of the most insignificant and tragic of the later battles of the war. Unlike a runner who sees the finish line and finds unsuspected reserves to reinvigorate and propel him through a strong, fast finish, these men would face a debacle as their bodies and spirits, completely depleted, flailed and jerked and collapsed in the mud and metal in the area around Ypres.

But before they could attack, they had to wait out ear-splitting, core-shaking artillery barrages and then another wire party.

There had been blasting and shelling and explosions for endless days to take care of the defenses, but the Germans had been quite secure in this area for more than three years. Even the bombs that Flint loved so much could not be entirely relied upon, so Alex, Mouse, Parrish, Lowe, and a handful of young privates eager to prove their fearlessness wordlessly crawled into the dark to finish the job that thousands of pounds of explosives had started.

The field was sodden, engorged, and bursting with filthy water. Shell craters as big as basements filled with mud, death chambers masked by a smooth sheet of black water. There were duckboards laid across much of the battlefield by engineers and regular soldiers working at night to combat the rising water levels. Alex assumed that if he followed the duckboards he would make it to the normal location of the wire emplacements eventually without slipping off and disappearing into the glimmering pools of mud that lined them. The party set off at a good pace, eager to be done with it. They did not know that Alex had tried to intervene on their behalf, and so they did not hold any particular disappointments in their hearts at his failure. They were silent as usual, and followed one behind the other so that Alex could almost forget they were there with him and forget his reason for being there at all.

After crawling for longer than he expected, Alex raised his head and shoulders in an attempt to survey his progress. To his surprise, he was not 10 feet from his entry point, having taken a seemingly straight path that, in actuality snaked and twisted and bent and returned him nearly exactly to his start. Lowering his head again, Alex set out once more, determined to pay attention to direction, as perhaps his mind had wandered in the previous attempt.

After what felt like an hour of slogging across muddy, splintering planks, he again lifted his head and shoulders to check their progress. Instead of seeing coiled silver wire ahead of him in the dark, he saw something unexpected on the horizon, about 100 yards distant. Standing boldly outside of the cover of the trench and just before what he expected to be the German line, was a woman in a bright scarlet, billowing dress with long sleeves the hem of which dragged slowly across the dirt. The contrast of this red glowing column against the black sky was transfixing.

It emboldened Alex to rise up himself and stumble across the open ground toward her.

As quickly as he moved, and he did break into a run eventually, she never seemed to get closer, though clearly she was facing him and moving her legs and arms as if travelling toward him.

Exhausted from his frustrating efforts, Alex paused enough to catch his breath and assess the situation. In a flash of clarity he realized that if he wanted to get where he wanted to go, he must do the opposite of what would be sensible to a rational creature. His first step in the right direction was coming up out of the trench. Surely no rational creature would do this. Next, he abruptly turned away from the red figure and nearly crashed into her, as she stood only inches away. Her boots made her nearly his height, and so his nose nearly brushed against her cold, porcelain skin and his chapped, dry lips fairly planted themselves on her wet, painted ones. But he recovered himself and stepped back slightly.

"Lenora, what are you doing here?" His voice had the ragged quality of one not used to speaking. He was not surprised to see her, only curious about the timing of her appearance.

Folding her right arm around his left, Lenora guided Alex out of the mud and back to the nearest duckboard.

"Here," she told him when their feet were securely planted. It seemed to him that the sky lightened and all of Belgium stretched out under his feet, sodden plains and trench lines obscuring verdant fields, rows of splintered wood standing in for tall pine forests.

"You keep getting lost, but look how simple it is." She swept her left arm before them in a grand gesture, and indeed it seemed to him that the intersecting trench lines and rows of broken trees snaking randomly across the earth formed a steady, predictable grid, as fixed as the lines of a chessboard, super-imposed across the whole world.

He looked at her in wonder: "It's all a game then?"

She only smiled and tilted her head slightly at his observation.

"And I'm just a pawn," he continued bitterly.

She grabbed his hand in hers, untangling their arms but still holding him fast. "You wanted to be a pawn, didn't you?" Her smile was different now as she looked directly, frankly at his face. "You volunteered. You believed what everyone believed, even when you should have known better."

He stared wordlessly at her. She was always a tease, but her accusations, this time, were grave.

"You wanted me to be the pawn. You!" he complained weakly.

She just smiled a sweet smile that took on the curve of something more sinister. "Silly boy," she said. "You have no idea what I want, do you?" There was a pause as she considered him with a cocked head and cruel smirk; then she brightened, his protector again.

"You have a long way to go to get anywhere, but I'll tell you your next move," she said.

He didn't remember how it started, but he found himself running as fast as he could, still holding her hand. It struck him that he was always running when it came to Lenora. Always running to catch up to her or to get away from her or to do her bidding. In reality, he would hardly move or move only subtly in reaction to or against her, so as not to draw attention to himself or her influence. But inside, his heart would always be racing. Now, though, they ran together, hard. The tracks of mud, rotten duckboards, and lakes of slime slowed him down and more than once they leapt over obstacles, but she didn't slow down, shouting "Faster!Faster! Go! Go!" Until he thought his heart would explode. The rifle banged painfully against his leg and as he paused to adjust the sling, he found himself alone again. Standing above ground across from a battlefield, he could hear whistling all around him. It took him only a moment to realize that the sound was not coming from her lips, and that in half a second he would have to move.

His men didn't know what it was that made him suddenly rise and run across the field, but the reason didn't matter. He exposed the party and drew a storm of flesh ripping steel upon them. It was nearly miraculous that only Lowe was hit.

XXIX. Parrish and Lowe

Parrish would not leave Lowe, even when the unit was ordered to advance in the face of withering machine gun fire. Parrish stayed where he was, half-submerged in the lake-like crater into which Lowe had slipped and disappeared forever. Parrish had grasped Lowe's arms just above the elbows when it was clear that Lowe could not get up and when automatic fire made it impossible for Parrish to get up as well. His gripped slipped away as the hours, until at last he had only Lowe's fingertips in his fist. He had fought to keep eye contact with his dear friend, to shout encouragements and to hear last wishes. But Lowe could barely speak; his eyes squinted and grew in alarm when he realized the mud of the rain-filled crater was sucking him in like the sticky, hungry mouth of a mythical beast. The water level rose in the continuous rain and the earth itself seeped water from smashed drainage, forming a deadly pool for men too damaged to extricate themselves. Pelting rain drops puckered the surface of the pool so that Parrish was reminded of a Japanese garden where his mother had used to take him for walks when he was a boy. The garden's ponds were filled with hungry koi who, when fed, would open their great round, sucking mouths in an insistent frenzy of gulps, until the surface of the pond was nothing but a grotesque field of surging, sucking tubes. Parrish talked to him of home, and cursed him again for working on the docks without being a strong swimmer. Didn't he know how stupid and dangerous that was?

Over the long night, after his legs had been destroyed by rifle fire, Lowe had lain in the crater where Parrish had dragged and carried him for cover. While the rest of the wiring party had been able to run for the trench, those two alone had remained in the land where no man should have remained, and there the land itself doomed them both, slowly drowning Lowe, and forcing Parrish to disobey an order to advance with his unit the following morning when he awoke to find his friend entirely submerged. He cursed sleep, the Germans, and Lowe himself as he splashed the water in anguished remorse. He could not find his body in the mud. Every scoop of slimy earth he pulled out of the place where Lowe must have been was instantly replaced by brown water and more earth, frustrating all his efforts, until his tears mixed with the rain. Using both hands, he dug with even more effort, but it was no match for the hungry ground.

All night, Parrish had watched his friend grow smaller and smaller as the water rose and the mud sucked him in. It was so dark that Parrish didn't see when the water reached his eyes, when he would have already been drowned. Parrish's eyes, closed by anguish and exhaustion, opened to the sound of a whistle blowing from his trenches, heralding the unit's advance. The whistle was still sounding its long, sharp note when the popping and whizzing of machine and rifle fire from the German lines drowned out the sound. Parrish didn't have to look to see his own men spilling out of the trench and slipping off the duckboards into the water. He knew this would be the picture. He had already seen it too many times. Now, his eyes were transfixed by a sight even more disturbing: a smooth, tense lake where his friend had been. Moaning like a wounded animal, Parrish slogged through the crater, back and forth, yanking his feet with all his might when the greedy hole tried to grab him as well, covering every inch of its diameter, dragging his arms through the opaque liquid, but there was no sign of his friend. The mud had swallowed him entirely, and there was no evidence he had existed at all, except for the pathetic moans of Parrish, whom Alex saw but could not hear, as the sounds of battle raged on the crater pocked field.

Once things quieted, Parrish eventually found his way to the unit. They were easy to find, as their ill-advised advance had failed and nightfall found them occupying the exact same trenches as the previous day, having gained no ground but significant living space in the trench, as there were far fewer bodies to accommodate.

But, Alex knew, Parrish had missed the advance (and retreat). In the face of rumored French desertions further down the line, and subsequent fear that their own troops might elect to abandon their posts en masse, the British command felt the need to take a firm line against dissent and other behavior which threatened morale and good discipline. Thus, when Parrish jumped morosely back into his place in the trench, he was promptly arrested.

XXX. A Trial and Alex's Evidence

Alex could not recall the first time he saw a man killed nor could he tell for certain the moment he had killed for the first time. Shots were fired indiscriminately without aim or murderous intent. He knew for certain, though, that he had killed at least three men: one was a German, and the others were Lowe and his friend, Parrish.

Alex knew he had arrived at the courts martial when he recognized the courtroom-like setting arranged in the trench to mimic the description of such locations in books, as no one there assembled had any experience as prosecution, defense, judge, or jury.

The warped-door table was cleared of all its tea-time accoutrements save Col. Flint's own cup, and the Colonel himself sat at the narrow end of the table with Maj. Knight, his Adjutant, crowded both together on one chair. Presumably these were the judge and his Adjutant, as the Colonel wore a large wig under his military headgear, and Maj. Knight looked like his Adjutant still.

To the side, fourteen men from the unit were grouped together in two even rows, one standing and one kneeling before the other. He didn't know for how long they had been assembled, but they were busy writing notes to occupy themselves, and when Alex looked over their tablets, to see what he had missed, he saw that they were mostly drawing sketches, compiling lists of favored mixed drinks, or writing letters home, letters which would first go to Alex.

When the trial properly began, the fourteen barely gave a glance from what occupied them, as the events of the day were entirely forgone.

Indeed, the start of the trial was marked by the Colonel's call to order, followed by the Adjutant's loud recitation of General Order # 585, which, they all already knew, rendered the accused guilty until proven innocent. Allowing the gravity of this challenge a moment to sink in, Col. Flint commanded: "Adjutant, read the charge."

Parrish stepped forward from where he quietly stood, flanked by two guards who still admired his experience and calm under fire.

"The accused, Cpl. Liam H. Parrish, on October 7, 1917, was absent from his appointed place of duty and deliberately ignored a direct order to advance, endangering the lives of all those most dependent on him and indeed, contributing to the deaths of many. He is thus charged with dereliction of duty, abandonment of his post, disrespect to his commanding officer, cowardice, and murder."

Through it all, Parrish stood not glumly, but silently, staring at nothing and no one until Alex was called forward, and then, for a few moments, he stared at Alex without malice, and almost apologetically.

"Lt. Liddell, first witness!" Maj. Knight cried out, though the space was so confined there was no need for crying out.

Alex had no prior notification that he would be called upon to testify, although as Parrish's lieutenant, he certainly should have. At any rate, he was surprised and angry for being put on the spot and suspected that his words were about to be used for purposes that were not his own.

Col. Flint asked him crisply, "Lt. Liddell, is Cpl. Parrish in your unit?"

"He is, sir."

"Was your unit commanded to advance on the morning of October 7?"

"It was, sir."

"Of course it was; I commanded it." He returned with some annoyance. Alex was not sure to whom he was speaking, as Col. Flint had a tendency to shift his gaze from one face to another as he spoke. His face grimaced as it scanned the jurymen. He continued his questioning:

"Did your unit, in fact, advance as commanded, Lieutenant?"

"Well," he considered this carefully, as the unit had advanced as commanded, but also retreated, contrary to the order. Parrish had also both advanced and retreated, just not with the rest.

"Speak up!" Flint leaned forward, an eyebrow raised, fist slamming the table. Several of the jurors dropped their pencils or folded their papers at this unexpected outburst.

"Sir," Alex cleared his throat, unwilling to be confined to a simple yes or no answer; the truth was not a matter of absolutes. "Sir, the corporal retreated with us; so in order to have retreated, he must have advanced."

Col. Flint nearly bit his tea cup and Maj. Knight reddened. Alex swooned as he recalled the oscillating movements of his unit in those last weeks, the ebbs and flows of a tide lapping at a shoreline ineffectually. And yet, though their position had not changed, though they had not achieved objectives, though the Germans held, lives were somehow irretrievably lost.

"Lieutenant," Col. Flint addressed him gravely, "did or did not Cpl. Parrish advance with your unit as commanded." Parrish looked away from Alex.

"He did not, sir. But his actions caused no harm to the unit and added not one to our total losses, unlike those who gave the order in the first place..." He could hardly believe they were not stopping him. He stopped himself, taken aback by the silence around him. Instead of addressing this accusation, Flint merely continued as if he had heard only the first three words.

"Lieutenant, do you have any evidence to prove Cpl. Parrish's loyalty to this unit? Anything that shows, perhaps, that he did not intend to ignore a command and shirk his duties?" Flint raised his eyebrows and smiled a toothy grin in pleasant anticipation, as a shark must before a feast. Alex was at a loss.

"That letter there, perhaps." Flint gestured, and the Adjutant approached him and removed several loose pieces of paper from his coat pocket before Alex even registered to what he was referring.

Unit letters that he was meant to censor, none by or to Parrish, who was illiterate, and a few pages of his own script were now in the hands of the Adjutant. Most were already riddled with black lines, some hardly legible as a result.

Flint to Parrish: "Are any of these your letters, Cpl?"

Parrish: "I wouldn't know, sir."

Flint: "Do you recognize your handwriting?"

Parrish: "No sir, I don't."

Flint: "Well, if you don't recognize your own writing, how am I expected to know which are yours and which are not? They may as well all be yours!"

Knight: "Ah! Here, for your consideration..." He held up a letter more black than not and squinted hard to make sense of it, though Alex suspected that he saw even less this way. Nonetheless, he continued: "though I and you are half a life asunder....yes, yes, here: I shall not heed the raving blast."

He read more to himself, mumbling a few words, skipping to other letters, and reading more, as if they were all authored by the same man, one continuous diatribe. Flint's gaze now traveled slowly, from a close scrutiny of Parrish's face, to a self-satisfied examination of Alex's.

The Major read again: "He sent them word I had not gone, / (We know it to be true):/ If she should push the matter on, / What would become of you?"

And still more: "She gave me a good character/ But said I could not swim......If I or she should chance to be/Involved in this affair, / He trusts to you to set them free, / Exactly as we were.....Don't let him know she liked him best, / For this must ever be/ A secret, kept from all the rest, / Between yourself and me."

The Major rested all the letters on the table and settled his gaze on Alex.

Flint: "Clearly he meant to malinger around a pool of water while the rest of the unit…"

Alex: "Ridiculous!"

Flint: "You're right, actually. We have no obligation to prove the corporal's guilt, rather quite the reverse. These letters mean nothing! Guilty as charged."

Alex: "Sir!" He grasped the table with his hands, causing the judge and his Adjutant to both leap to their feet, grabbing their end lest it all capsize.

Flint scowled, "The time for words is over, Lieutenant."

All were looking at him now, and Alex later recalled the distinct feeling that he was a morsel of bread and that they were all sea gulls, rising in a mob, about to descend upon him.

Parrish was found guilty on all counts and sentenced to enter No Man's Land at nightfall to advance alone, without his rifle, until such time as the rising sun revealed his presence to German snipers. During the night, Alex heard distant sobs, but they were not from Parrish, who had expressed no emotions at all since returning to the trench without his friend. No, the sobs were his own, and the bullet that put an end to Parrish's wanderings was his as well. He didn't have to wait till daybreak, as his eyes were well trained for seeing in the dark; he only waited for the time he knew it would take for Parrish to find the shell crater and take his position beside it.

After firing, he sat, crouching in his hole, hunched over like a man three times his age. He tried then, in the quiet dark, to recall his child-life, before his father died, when he knew the pleasures of simple joys and the stings of simple sorrows.

XXXI. The King of Nothing

After Parrish and Lowe died, Alex took to brazen acts. He would climb out of the trench and saunter brazenly across the battlefield instead of crawling on his stomach at night to cut wires, insisting that no one come along. He would sit on the parapet and eat his breakfast, a time when both sides observed an unofficial truce and withheld firing. Still, no one fully trusted this truce, so Alex sat on the parapet alone and looked out over his kingdom of desolation. He was not taunting death; rather, he knew that death would come eventually, and he refused to live his remaining days as some animal, crouching in a rat-infested hole, never feeling sunlight on his back.

He could sense, without being told, as an animal might, that a storm was about to be unleashed. He knew that something was about to happen, and that it would be bigger than anything he had seen previously. Colonel Flint was unmoved by any entreaty and unfazed by logic or sensory perception. Another Christmas was around the corner and the bombs were ready.

That morning, as he ate his biscuits and cheese on the parapet, he wasn't alone. He saw, across from him some fifty yards, what appeared to be three mud mounds carved into thrones. Abandoning his food, he picked up his rifle and walked ahead, licking his fingers and taking his seat in the middle chair, flanked by two piled high with mud like dripping wax; bits of bone and teeth were embedded in the high arches of the seat backs. On his left sat Nina, and to the right was Lenora.

Nina's eyes were moist and her manner agitated. Lenora, in floor length red velvet with a high neck and long sleeves, seemed supremely bored of the bleak scene before her, her composure punctuated by bursts of unexpected ferocity.

"Here comes one! Get him, will you?"

Alex was startled to see a single German soldier emerge from the semi-darkness of early morning, climbing out of a trench some five hundred yards distant.

The hairs on Alex's neck raised and his arms tingled as he jumped out of his seat, took three paces forward, and held his bayoneted rifle before him. He had faced this threat before, but never with Lenora and Nina so close at hand. With their presence, the act of battle transformed from nihilistic self-preservation to desperate protection of loved ones in immediate danger. This was a new concept for him and it made him shift his feet, his mouth dried, and he instantly sensed how the families in these occupied lands felt every day, hoping to shield their children from starvation or worse.

He readied himself to attack; he saw that the German, too, had fixed his bayonet and that he was slowly closing the distance between them.

"Go now! What's the matter with you? Georg Schaettner awaits your meeting!" Lenora prodded aggressively.

"What?" He turned to her with his face only, his body frozen in anticipation of struggle.

"Georg Schaettner," she spat dismissively, rolling her eyes at him. "Bookkeeper from Lindt, father of two-girls. Hannah and Maria." She admired her finger nails.

He sputtered, "Why are you telling me this?" Nina shifted her eyes uncomfortably from Lenora to Alex.

"He's closer. Kill him." Lenora deadpanned.

"She's right. He is right there," Nina urged with pain in her voice.

"I can't kill him! Not if you are going to introduce him to me!"

"Well there's glory for you!" Lenora threw up her hands in disgust.

"I don't know what the hell you mean by glory" he said through clenched teeth.

"Of course you don't; until I tell you." She said with haughty displeasure.

A shot rang out from an unseen place behind the mud thrones and Georg Schaettner, father of two from Lindt, crumpled to the ground wordlessly.

Nina shook her head, covering her eyes. Lenora shifted impatiently in her seat and pointed across No Man's Land again. "It doesn't much matter, does it? Here comes another."

Alex looked incredulously at the trench line before him and, as promised, another shape rose and, after a few minutes of forward progress revealed itself to be a man.

"Yes," Lenora spoke with authority, "that one is Lucas Wiesel, 23- like you, Alex! Shame. Get him, won't you?"

"No, I certainly won't. Stop this!" He had his Lee Enfield on his shoulder, hands supporting the barrel, which pointed directly across the field, but he could not bear to look at the man walking toward him.

"What does it matter, knowing their names?" Lenora asked with honest confusion. "You know they all *have* names, whether you know them or not, yes?"

Nina sensed an opening: "If I took away your name, Alex, would you cease to exist? If I called you by a number or a rank, would you be any less the boy I know you to be? Would you transform into something else entirely? Would you disappear? What would remain of you if I took away your name?"

Lenora returned to the conversation brightly: "Take this blade," she gestured to his bayonet, "and run him through (you know you are going to do it, you might as well think about it), what will remain?"

Alex was still flustered, "I don't deny I'll do it, I just…"

"Just, just just," she mimicked. "Is this about fairness? This is not a place for logic, my dear. In its place I offer you some poetry:

                Fury said to
                  a mouse, That
                    he met in the
                      house, "Let
                          us both go
                            to law: I
                             will prose-
                              cute you.-
                             Come, I'll
                              take no den-
                             ial: We
                               must have
                                the trial:
                              For really
                             this morn-
                              ing I've
                           nothing
                         to do.."
                    Said the
                      mouse to
                        the cur,
                         "Such a
                            trial dear
                              sir, with
                                no jury
                                 or judge,
                                  would
                                   be wast-
                                  ing our
                                    breath."
                        "I'll be
                          judge,
                      I'll be
                  jury,"
                  said
                    cun-
                      ning

old
Fury:
"I'll
try
the
whole
cause,
and
con-
demn
you to
death."

She recited the words with increasing speed and delight until Alex felt sickened.

"I think you must have made some mistakes," Nina leaned forward, criticizing Lenora mildly. "That's not how I remember it."

"Your memory hardly works right," Lenora countered. "What good is a memory if it only works backwards? Now him," she returned the conversation to Alex, "he doesn't remember a thing about it, as he did not pay close attention at school, did you my dear?"

Nina again: "His mind was busy with other things, more important things."

Lenora: "If he'd paid closer attention, he would have known all this would happen, because school trains your memory to work backward and forward, you know."

Nina: "He's not here, in this situation, because he didn't know what would happen…he of all people knew. He didn't come thinking it would be different. Perhaps he thought he could lessen the pain for his friends if he shared their burden." All the while she patted his hand sympathetically.

"Lessen, lesson," Lenora said testily, "well if he wished to lessen their pain, it clearly did not work, which underscores my point that he retained no knowledge, even, of how to subtract properly."

"What are you talking about!" Alex was getting to a point where he really felt as if he couldn't take another minute of feeling perplexed and overwhelmed.

Lenora's mood shifted to anger: "Let's get back to it! A lesson, then, in lessening. Alex, Lt. Liddell" she corrected herself to amplify the formality of the lesson. "If you run him through," she nodded in the direction of the slowly approaching man, "what remains?"

"I know!" said Nina, "His remains, of course."

"Yes, well, only temporarily," this from Lenora.

Alex denied them: "His memory would remain, in the minds of those who knew him."

Lenora looked upon him with condescending pity: "But who knows anyone, really? Even you, the memories you have of your friends are false memories, only the ideas and images you want to keep, the rest is discarded. The memories we have of you will only be what we choose them to be, false, a compilation, a dream.

"Nothing remains, then?" he asked, but it sounded to him like an acknowledgment.

"Except the remains, of course, temporarily." Lenora.

Nina added quietly, "And what will remain of you, Alex, when you kill him? Is something taken away, or something gained that can never be taken away?"

He wanted, like a child, to collapse onto the ground and find himself transported magically from this place to the warmth and comfort of his own bed, under his own blankets. The knowledge that this would not happen was enough to make his mind run desperate for relief.

"I don't know, I don't know," he mumbled to Nina, but he was already moving forward with determination. He could hear their voices behind him, one shouting 'if' statements over the other in an effort to make their riddle more meaningful:

"If you take the trees out of the wood, what remains? If you take the boy out of the bank, if you take the father out of his life, if you take the men from England, if you take the laws from the land, the logic from our minds, the truth from art…"

Lucas Wiesel had closed within 100 yards.

"If you take the name from the soldier, what remains?" Lenora continued, undisturbed.

"Everything!" Nina insisted.

"That's right! All the responsibility, the obligations, the justice, the dreams, the morality, and the love- it all stays! That's what's bothering this one." She jerked her thumb toward Alex. "He wants to believe that if you take away his name, nothing remains. No family to mourn, no pain to be felt." She shrieked with laughter.

Alex's irritation suffused with anger. Lucas Wiesel stepped cautiously. Even in the mud-covered uniform and the oversized helmet, Alex could distinguish features of this man, blond hair, light eyes closely spaced, a bony nose, hollow cheeks, wide lips. He approached unrelentingly to within ten feet. Alex's breathing grew heavy and his grip on the rifle stock tightened. He lunged forward and pierced Lucas's chest, through the wool coat, through the flesh. Something produced resistance, likely a rib, but he shifted his footing slightly and slid forward, finding easy and soft access to the body's core and beyond.

Lucas exhaled sharply and wheezed out his last breath like a punctured balloon, a long and pathetic exhalation that tapered to a whisper. Alex's rigidity and the rifle position kept the man on his feet, just a few inches from Alex so that he could smell his breath and sweat, and the dirt present on everyone and everything. His eyes were upturned and fixed, denying Alex access to their secrets.

Lucas's hands, gloved save the fingertips, released his rifle and reached helplessly to the vorpal blade and then to his throat, as if loosening the wool collar would ease his discomfort. Squinting at his pain, Alex could hear the burbling of life ebbing, and he swore the hollow face transformed for a moment into the fleshier, ruddier countenance of

Lowe, gasping for air and burying his face into Parrish's hair, for filter, escape, or one last desperate connection before the gas settled.

Slowly, Alex guided Lucas Wiesel to the ground, kneeling over the body as it came to its final resting place on the sticky earth, staring up at the lightening sky. It had begun to spit rain. He could hear Nina's soft sobs, but Lenora was still prattling in unchanged tones riddles with no answers. Nina rose from her seat, mud marring the pristine whiteness of her long night gown. Her hands were dirty, too, he noticed, as she extended her arm down to him and curled her hand around his chin. Her fingers smelled like earth and he leaned all his weight, still kneeling, against her legs. She stood firm as a tree.

Lenora still cackled on her mud throne. "If you take the trees from the wood, what remains? Everything and nothing! The ground remembers how to re-grow the forest…it just forgets to wonder why." She swept her arms before her in a grand gesture, surveying the rugged ground littered with men, material, metal, discarded; shards of wood appeared to puncture the earth and steam rose from the trenches as if the whole place was deflating and on the verge of withering into nothingness.

"Nothing beside remains!" Lenora was pleased with herself. "Nothing worth anything remains here beside us, and there is nothing beside us except remains. Come, come, sit!" She patted the empty seat beside her. "Take your seat. You, my love, are the King of Nothing. Beside remains, of course."

Before Alex could rise, a low rumble arrested his attention. It was barely perceptible at first, but within moments it grew into an unmistakable roar. Nina tightened her hold of Alex's chin and pulled him forward firmly into her skirt. Off balance, he wrapped his arms around her legs to steady himself.

"Here it comes!" Lenora yelled, frowning at the physical contact between her companions. They could barely hear her amid the rising wind and deafening noise.

"Take care of yourself," Nina's yell was like a whisper in his ear. Alex looked in the direction of the opposite trench. Dark shadows seemed to spill out of it, all along its length, and rush forward.

"Something's going to happen!" She warned.

The noise was deafening. Airplanes roared over head, blotting out any light left and peppering the ground around him, which came alive in response, sputtering dirt, water, and gore.

"I can't take this any longer" his anguished voice went unheard by anyone. As he pulled himself to his feet, Nina disappeared and only the red figure was before him. He closed the distance in one second and had his hands, dirtier than Nina's, around her red velvet neck. She looked at him with terror for only a moment; then she went limp as a doll, her eyes frozen. Her body offered no resistance and seemed, in fact, to shrink.

"Sir, enough! That one's done for. Run for cover!" Alex heard the anxious yelling above the noise of the oncoming attack wave at nearly the same time that he felt Mouse's strong hand on his shoulder, breaking his concentration on the figure he was choking on the ground, a soldier of such short stature that he could only be a boy, the welling wound adorning his neck severe enough to not require additional effort to end the life spilling forth.

He knew he had killed the German with the bony nose on the ground a few meters away, but he couldn't say if he had killed this boy. Then again, he shrugged as he followed Mouse back toward the trench, it didn't really matter to the dead who did the killing, did it? One soldier was as good as any other.

He decided then that nothing, in fact, did remain of his life that mattered. That his life and all the ways he had struggled to differentiate himself from everyone else in his town, and all the individualities that made him who he was, all of those things existed, but they did not matter.

That began the barrage that lasted for three weeks. At some point, Alex had enough of the noise and the relentless blasts that dropped unpredictably around him like lethal rain. He climbed out of the trench and ran as far and as long as he could. He knew he was deserting but he did not fear court martial. He only regretted leaving Mouse, but the others were already gone, he knew. There was no one left to disappoint. Every muscle and tendon and nerve and bone of his body seemed united in the grand effort not to escape his end, which he knew was inevitable but to modify the means. He knew he was about to die, but he wanted to choose the place, and he wanted them to find his body intact. He did not want to disappear into death and become another myth. He didn't want to be exploded, and he did not want to be buried in a trench.

He ran as hard as he could until he reached the flimsy cellar door. Yanking it open, he collapsed inside, onto the lumpy ground that had once provided him privacy and quiet. She was there, too, waiting for him.

XXXII. The Potato Cellar

A shaft of morning light slipped between the slats of the cellar door like a bayonet blade cutting a swathe of color across Nina's form.

"Nina," Alex murmured sleepily, gazing at her sandy, golden hair against his thigh. "I thought your hair was red."

Her face turned to his and her ink-dark eyes were flesh colored and fused. Her mouth opened in a sad smile and her voice gurgled harshly: "Open your eyes!"

"Sir! Lt. Liddell. Wake up, sir! Are you with us?"

Mouse's boots braced on the mud soft as candle wax, as he leaned into the trench and shook Alex violently by the wet lapel. He bent over the dazed man sitting below him and surveyed the grim scene in the communications trench 450 yards behind the front line trench he had abandoned. Alex's eyes were open and the light nearly blinded him. His ear drums were blasted and voices were unrecognizably altered, adding to his confusion. His hands reached out to steady himself on the shifting pile beneath him. The soft lumps became mush beneath his hands.

Mouse persisted softly in his accented English: "Sir, do you need a medic? You've got something on the side of your head, there."

Absently, Alex touched his ear and felt sticky blood. He lifted his other hand out of the gore beneath him, offering the slimy, wormy mass in his fist to the only man left who had been with him since that first night. "Mind the gap," he cautioned his wireman with a laugh.

A brown eyeball glistened by his boot, and he fished it out of the muck eagerly with his bloody fingers. He held it up for Mouse's inspection. "Eyes don't get much more open than that, do they, mate?" He asked. Alex squinted hard at the eye, while Mouse squinted hard at Alex. He was already gesturing for assistance when he heard his lieutenant ask the eye, "Do you see everything, or nothing? Is this a dream or is it real? Is it your dream or mine?" Alex heard the words in his head, spoken with the slow deliberateness of those shouted underwater to a swimming companion. Mouse disappeared from his limited view. In moments, arms underhooked his and strained to haul him out of the trench. He could still hear his own words falling on ears that chose not to listen: "Who am I, then? Tell me that first, and then, if I like being that person, I'll come up; if not, I'll stay down here till I'm somebody else."

"It'll be alright, Alex. Take it easy. We'll get you some help."

Take it easy!

He lay on his back as men bustled around him. It seemed like another lifetime ago that he had seen the sky so dominant in his field of view. Stretched on the ground, the calamity that had overtaken all those things that lived and grew on the earth seemed strangely insignificant under the calm, unchanged whiteness of the sky. Nothing on earth, not mountains, trees, or men was unaltered. Shifting his head slightly to the right, he could distinguish the remnants of a tree pointing upward, like a giant bony appendage reaching from its earth covered grave to accuse the skies of inflicting this torment. He squinted. Bodiless legs dangled from a single branch.

He shifted his eyes back to the sky, smooth and white like the dividers that had encased the beds of the dying at the field hospital. He wondered if there was a God hovered above them and if he saw everything or nothing.

Part Seven

Ever drifting down the stream –

Lingering in the golden gleam-

Life, what is it but a dream?

XXXIII. Waking

At 0630 on November 11, 1918, Alex ate dry toast and tea at a table with Lt. Oster. Although no one ever saw them speak, they enjoyed each other's company well enough. Oster sought Alex out when in the yard or at mealtime or late in the evenings when most men were alone with their ghosts. Alex suspected that he must remind him of someone. At any rate, Oster was no bother to anyone.

At 0730 on November 11, 1918, Alex met with me again. His surgery was upcoming, and though he had on most occasions been a willing and talkative patient in our sessions together, I sensed a growing irritation. He was fearful that the nature of the operation and its expected recovery time would threaten his return to the front. He had grown tired of the delay in his restoration to full duty and suspected that I was detaining him against his will and against regulations. But with the surgery imminent, with others involved, he had begun to see this progression of events as inevitable. He didn't regard these meetings with disdain or defensiveness any longer. He certainly didn't regard them as hope for some elusive cure. That irritated me, I confess, and it was the subject of our conversation that morning as Alex sat in that earth-brown chair. I was a way to pass his time; in his journals he described me as being earnest and generally inoffensive. He wrote that I believed I was doing my duty to the war effort by administering to the needs of the soldiers. I did so, he went on, with the persistence and determination of a twenty-year-old sapper slowly digging a dark tunnel beneath the surface to explode the enemy. I did so, he imagined, as if I had something to prove.

That day I said what I could: "Alex, I must say that I am pleased with your progress, even if you yourself don't believe that any has been made."

"Progress presupposes a goal, Doctor," Alex responded dryly, as if they were playing chess and Alex had moved his pawn into its predictable place.

"But there is a goal," I insisted, leaning forward in my chair and tapping my notebook excitedly with a marbled pen.

"An end to these means, a method to this madness?" Alex offered, with little enthusiasm, gesturing to the yellow walls, the paper cluttered desk, the voice-haunted hallway.

"No, no. I mean a goal for you. And for every man who finds himself within these walls."

"And what is that goal, Doctor? To make us well enough to return to the front? Well-enough in the brain that we can stand in a neck-deep trench and wait patiently for a bomb or a bullet to destroy the body? Here's something for you to jot down in your book, Doctor, with all due respect: a man doesn't need to be right in the brain to soldier. You'd be doing us all a favor to leave us quite loony."

I bit my lower lip and removed my glasses. I did not wish to anger this boy, but any emotion was an entry wound for further exploration, however painful.

"Alex," I cleared my throat after a rough start, "I'm not here to make you well enough to soldier. I want you to be well enough to function as a man in the world. The war can't last forever, you must acknowledge. Things are looking up. Soon you will return to your home and will find a job, take a wife, care for a home and a family… stop thinking about fighting. You've done enough."

He found my disillusion heartbreaking, I learned later, and we looked for a long moment at each other, full of pity that neither of us could fully grasp. Alex wrote that he had been transfixed for a moment by my watery blue-grey eyes, but he looked away because he could not bear to see in them a reflection of this world still as myth-ridden as Avalon. Rising to Alex's tongue were words to lay bare my illusions, but he was too tired. Perhaps it was the lugubrious effects of the heavy red hospital robe and the flannel pajama pants, as he was not yet medicated. Nonetheless, he was sapped of all argumentative energy and wanted nothing more than to crawl into bed and wake up underground.

He placated me: "Yes, you are right, Doctor. Things are looking up." He flashed a curt smile and rose, moving to the heavy door. With his hand on the knob, he turned to me as an afterthought and asked, "I may go, yes?" I was surprised at his question, as I had again found myself staring after him as if seeing a ghost. His words startled me from my dream. I blinked and distractedly waved him away with a "Yes, of course." That was the last time I saw him as he was.

At half past nine on November 11, 1918, Alex longed to walk on the lawn and breathe fresh air, but clouds had moved in and a steady rain began to fall. Dejected, he returned to his room and fell on the bed. He slept a dreamless sleep.

At 1100 on November 11, 1918, the war ended.

Alex reawakened at half past two. There was a racket in the hallway, and he thought for a moment that he might have slept till the New Year. He rose and poked his head into the corridor. Nurses were dancing and hugging the cooks. He smelled the sickening sweetness of thick icing. Doctors removed their coats, loosened their ties, and drank directly from champagne-colored bottles. Soldiers stood idly in their doorways. Alex caught Oster's eye for one long moment as he took in the spectacle. His eyes were dark and heavy lidded. He retreated into the solace of his room and shut the door behind him.

Routines were ignored. Alex wandered to the dining room for early supper at four. The kitchen was deserted; soldiers in robes grumbled and milled about the round tables. Soon, he knew, the kitchen would be invaded and soup would be assembled and warmed, but he was not hungry enough to participate. The rain had stopped, so he went outside at last and walked to the far edge of the sodden lawn in his slippers. The sprawling grass ended at a steep drop-off overlooking the sea. Despite the cold November air and the wetness, he sat and listened.

He heard the booms of guns fired in jubilation and thought, for a startled moment that he had been transported in his sleep to Belgium, or that the Germans had invaded at long last. He saw the explosion of red and blue fireworks above him and sensed in his periphery that they were behind the hospital building as well. Everywhere celebration.

Booms and cracks. A low buzz of talking, singing, congratulations grew.

He reached into his robe pocket and removed a creased photograph. Lenora took this picture of them after Bernard and Foster had joined up. Bernard was in uniform already, hat removed. The others wore trousers and rolled up sleeves in the late summer heat. They sat in the field by Tenley Park where they would sometimes walk or hide from their parents in the high grass. Foster and Henry looked at the camera. Foster's legs were outstretched and he smiled with easy humor. Henry's arms were wrapped about his knees and his mouth opened as he informed Lenora about proper camera operation. Alex sat in profile, turned away from Foster and Henry, engaged in conversation with Bernard, ignoring Lenora. Bernard swam in an oversized wool coat. He had just postponed his entry into an engineering college in Switzerland for one year and was telling Alex about the situation. The day was sunny. Henry squinted; Bernard sweated. Above their heads Alex scrawled in black wax pencil the news of their fates as he learned them: Foster- killed, 1917. Henry- killed, 1915. Bernard-missing, 1916.

It was night. Behind him the hospital glowed with light in the darkness and the sea and what lay beyond retreated into the smudge black mist. Nurses whose shifts were long over stayed to dance and drink. His friends were out there, irretrievable, in the disappeared place that he could no longer reach. There was no chance he would find them now. Time was up. He had tumbled back through the wardrobe door, climbed out of the rabbit hole. And that place, too real to be imagined, and all those souls, still mired in its mudsucking grasp, were lost to him forever.

He was alone. The war was over.

XXXIV. The King in Repose

Lenora was staying in a hotel in Swansea, and she came to the hospital two days after the armistice. I had not seen Alex, but all the patients remaining in the hospital seemed strangely affected. Many had stopped talking, absorbed by the shock of the news and the struggle to comprehend what it meant to be veteran in the post-war era. How would they rejoin their lives? Would they even recognize their lives when they saw them?

Her dress was gray and sedate, but her lapels were decorated with tiny Union Jacks and her hair sported red and blue ribbons, making her look rather silly, I recalled when she passed my office. Her face shined with the delight of a nation. That cheer had not penetrated Swansea, but she did her best to bestow upon us her pleasure, striding down the glossy hallways with the confidence of a victorious queen.

Alex sat in his bedside chair, the photo resting in his lap, on the red folds of his robe. Lenora's eyes glanced down to it as she entered then looked away.

"Well!" she sang as she bustled about the room, throwing open the heavy cotton curtains. "It's over! Can you believe it? You'll finally be home for good. The nightmare is over."

Her smile was fixed and she nervously moved about the small space, fussing with his poorly made bed. His hand shot out and grabbed her arm, puncturing her good mood like a pin. She collapsed at his feet and her eyes searched the photograph in his lap.

"Alex, what is it? Please tell me. Talk to me, I beg you."

For the first time he could remember, he looked straight into her clear eyes, young and untroubled, desperate to find something in them to which he could connect. He wanted to tell her about Parrish and Lowe and all the rest. He didn't want to torture or accuse her; he just wanted to reach out to someone he once trusted, to see if together they could find their humanity again. His mouth opened but no sound escaped.

He closed his mouth and shook his head. Tears filled his eyes and dripped down onto the photograph. He wiped it against his chest and held it there, sobbing. Lenora's arms wrapped around his waist, her head rested on his thigh, and she cried with him. Once more she tried to draw him out: "Please, talk to me."

She thought of all their happy silences, reading together in her sitting room or on the hillside, floating together in the sea when sometimes their fingertips would touch. These silences seemed satisfyingly full, as if they were sharing a rich conversation that no one else could hear. Now, she wished she had not been a coward and that she could remember the sound of his voice because of the memory of a million words between them. But that day he did not know and could not invent the words to make her understand what the end of the war meant to him, and they sat together, a thousand miles apart, in silence.

She told me, later, that even though she saw him each of the next five days, he spoke not a word to her or to anyone else as far as she could tell, keeping it all inside before his head was cut open and his brain exposed in all its tangled, brilliant glory.

I might have argued more strongly against the surgery. I did object. I told Hack as he was washing his hands in preparation, "He's my patient, you know."

He returned, "Yes, then you invited me to take over his treatment and I accepted. He's mine and I'm afraid you can't have him back."

"He's not an experiment! I won't have you practicing your new medicines on him."

"I've had plenty of practice, Doctor. I've even had my own practice in Cardiff. So you'll be pleased to know that no one is better suited for this occasion." He shook his hands dry and left the preparation room for surgery. The door swung closed in my face.

I could see the operating table from the windowed observation room. Lenora stayed in his room, not wishing to see the surgery itself, nor was there any of his family represented. A crowd had assembled in the observation room, eager doctors and researchers gawking at the show just beyond the glass. Alex was in there, of course, his eyes open, lying on a thin, draped mattress. A nurse in white had shaved his head and was painting a deep amber disinfectant solution from just above his eyes all around his scalp. He bent his arm at the elbow, lifting his right forearm as if attempting to gain the notice of a teacher at school. The nurse bent over him and his mouth moved. I couldn't hear him at first and leaned forward with everyone else till we all heard his voice with escalating volume: "I...I....I" and nothing else. The nurse looked uncertain.

Hack, with the bravado of a magician's assistant lifted a thin metal ring for all to see and then placed it over Alex's head. Alex closed his eyes, looking like a fallen king.

XXXV. The Return of the King or Which Dreamed It?

It wasn't until February that Alex was deemed recovered enough from his surgery to be released from Swansea. He made the journey home largely by train. I accompanied him to London as I had a desire to reopen my pre-war practice in the bustling city, and I had an appointment to view some potential office spaces. He was eager to see his sister and mother again, but fearful that his home and his street would bring upsetting memories of his lost friends. I was afraid of this, too. But he was eager to see Lenora again as a man and not as a patient in a convalescent hospital, and not as a soldier, even though he was all these things.

His house did make him feel strange, like an overgrown being trapped in the space formerly occupied by a little boy. Little had changed physically, but so much had changed in him that the familiar felt foreign. His mother, forced to adapt to making her way through the world without him, had pulled herself together with strings that were thin and tenuous at best, threatening to snap at any moment despite her otherwise pleasant appearance. His sister had changed more than anything else, as years in the life of a child are so different from the years of an adult. She had seemed to him just a child when he had left, but now her legs were long and thin and she wore the face of a young woman.

That first day back, he mostly relaxed and took in the details of his surroundings, checking the reality against the memory of his memory. He had remembered the wallpaper with a certain degree of fade, and he was surprised to find it not so shabby. Then he couldn't be sure if his mother had had it replaced in his absence. His first day was filled with this kind of quiet. The next day was different. He wrote about it in detail and though it was inevitable, I winced at the anger and pain that he suffered that day; I had hoped that he would have anticipated this, that he would have planned for this eventuality and would have protected himself from the pain.

"Lenora is coming at ten," Mum announced. "Or did she say twelve? No, ten, yes, ten." This was a warning meant to prod me into getting properly dressed and presentable. I didn't look up from the papers and instead reached for my tea.

"Why don't you get properly dressed, Alex? Lenora is coming at ten," a command sweetly delivered by someone who had grown surprisingly adept at walking around land mines. I snapped the useless pages of the news-less paper together and rose from the table feeling all of ten years old.

"Of course, Mum."

Oh, to be ten years old again! No, at ten I was fatherless, struggling to care for a bereft woman and keep this house from being taken. No, to be seven again, just turned. Yes, that was the magic number.

In my room, which had not changed at all in the intervening years, I pulled respectable clothes from a mahogany closet. Before I put on the fresh wool socks, I held them to my nose and inhaled deeply. Never again would I take clean socks for granted. More care went into the pulling on of the socks than went to the rest of my dressing routine. Finished, I stood to peer at my face in the oval reflective glass over the chest of drawers. It was the same face as always- a little too gaunt through the cheeks, but decently formed- but, of course, it was nearly impossible for me to connect this image with the reality of life as I'd lived it. I was a soldier still, hiding from some unseen enemy in the body and clothes of a middle-class British boy. Perhaps my friends were hiding, too. Waiting for the right moment to expose themselves. Would I recognize them when I saw them again? I remembered Henry chewing on his hand. No, he wasn't hiding. But maybe Bernard?

"Alex! Lenora is here!" Mum called from the bottom of the stairs. I didn't respond with words, leaving my image in the glass and lumbering down the stairs carpeted with a worn, black runner emblazoned with fading tea roses. The women were talking softly, the voices, but not their words, reaching me before I entered the room. Lenora sat at the table dressed in a red and white striped shirt that was nearly masculine. Mum poured tea. They stopped when I entered and both looked at me as if I were an actor just taking the stage. They grew simultaneously silent and turned toward me, which made me want to bolt. I thought for a moment that a shell must have blown a hole in my head the way they were staring. No, that was Foster.

"Lenora," I began with a thick voice. I cleared my throat and started again, but she stopped me with a rush out of her chair and an "Alex!" and her arms around my chest. There was something desperate about her holding me like this, I thought, perfumed and beautiful. Her skirt was deep ruby red, the color of so many unspeakable things, and her lips were the same color. I took her face in my hands and kissed her directly. I knew I was being imprudent, but my mind was on David Thomas begging to hear one more time the silly, urgent wishes of his love. She didn't pull away. I opened my eyes and released her. Her eyes were lowered and she leaned on the table behind her.

"I have something to tell you," she said in a low voice. "I am engaged."

Mother set down Lenora's cup and reached to fill mine.

"No, mum. That'll do," I heard himself telling her. "I'm quite through."

I left the house abruptly, setting off for god knows where, ridiculously underdressed and swimming with emotion. She did not follow. I walked the entire day, ignoring hunger, strange looks, and cooler temperatures than I was dressed for. I walked and welcomed the cold air rushing into my lungs, flooding into me and pushing aside the heaviness and darkness that seemed to fill me. It was a painful, physical purging. I found myself running, mouth opened wide, breathing the fresh air of the hills as I ran to the fields where we had played. I ran until I felt the air had hollowed out a space in me. I didn't feel vacant or empty. I just felt lighter.

That night, I had a dream.

London, looming over my hometown with all of its weight and stale grandeur. Instead of the characteristics that make it unique and charming to visitors, it appears to me as an anonymous city bereft of those faces and memories that once made it familiar. Across London Bridge the spires and towers that spoke so movingly to a collective past now stand hulking, ominously silent and still, the paragons of urbanity profanely deflecting the pain of the war in a steadfast, imperceptible march toward the future.

Who would inhabit this brave new world? On a bank I stand, feet grounded in rugby matches and the romantic potential of a day at the beach with Lenora. There, in the city, Lenora waits now. For me or for her new husband? She was transported from the past to the future by sheer will over the sterile bridge that spared her the cold starkness of what runs in between. The war.

I step onto the bridge and begin to cross over. It takes years. Every step is a whizzing round. My heart pounds in my chest like an artillery barrage. Footsteps fall around me in unison like so many quick-marches. Gray faces pass me, abandoning the city to return to the far shore, dressed in identically filthy wool uniforms. Gray faces missed, loved, long dead. I see one I recognize. Bernard passes with a deep nod and a blue face. His hand extends and he places a heavy stone in mine. Then he is gone. Parrish and Lowe. Two more stones. I push them deep into my own wool trench pockets because they keep coming. I want to say 'I love you! I'm sorry! But what could I have done? How could you not know?' We never had to prove anything to each other…how did we come to this? Henry with a lopsided grin and a mangled hand. Foster now, lurching by with a pat on my shoulder. David Thomas, died of wounds, a folded letter in his breast pocket and an I-told-you-so smirk. I am reeling.

Grasping the sides of the bridge, I stretch my face into the cold morning air and lean out over the dark water. Sunrise. Stand-to. Grim routines. Incoming. I hear Lenora's urgent whisper "Come." Turning to the city, I see no welcoming face, no beckoning gesture. Yellow-sweatered arms wrap around me from behind and squeeze me tightly. The weight of a small woman presses against me. A thin cheek caresses my back. "Alex." My mother's voice is a comfort and a terror. I feel her leaning against me and she grows from her small self into a taller one with longer arms and a flowery smell. Lenora.

I'm coming, I say silently to my old friends. If I didn't want to jump, she would tell me to do it and I would do it. But I do want to jump, and I do it, without saying goodbye, leaving her as they left me: abruptly, rawly.

The icy water brings it all back to me. The inescapable cold misery. Lungs filling with foreign fluid. It is the only place where I can belong, where I feel what they felt in those final moments. Through water-filled eyes I see my mother and Lenora together, both in yellow, arms linked, at the end of the bridge, looking down at me. They link arms, tighten their sweaters about themselves, turn to the city, and step firmly into the eroding wind."

Alex had described this dream to me before. He had it often, or a variant involving the ocean. It was his only actual dream of the war.

Lenora came by again the next day. Their first meeting outside his house was lunch at a popular restaurant in the center of town. It sat on a corner, with huge plate glass windows overlooking the business section and its considerable foot traffic. It was a former bakery that had turned into a breakfast and lunch restaurant when people stopped routinely eating pastries during the war out of a sense that small deprivations were nationalistic. It was the kind of place that I had told her to take him, but whenever they were approached by a well-wisher who remembered Alex, he would take the opportunity to tell them the story of Parrish and Lowe or the two boys in the woods. She loved to hear him talk as much as she had loved to read stories and talk to him about them before. After his absence and all his long days and nights of silence, after yesterday, she wanted him to open up to her, to let her in and to confide in her.

Other people didn't know what to think of a story that seemed to have the elements of a fairy tale but the ominous undertones of a warning when they expected only a polite greeting and the normal civilities. They would stand by the table, some still shaking Alex's hand and smiling in greeting, listening politely until they realized what they were hearing. Lenora amazed that their faces didn't register anything amiss for several long moments. It was as if they were hardly listening at all. At the end of the story, and Alex would thankfully keep it brief, they would remove their hand, letting it hang limply in the air, turn to Lenora for some explanation, get none, and walk away from the table with a vacant 'Yes, well…'.

"Alex, do you have to?" She would ask, after they had gone, and he would not answer, feeling suddenly self-conscious.

"If only you had been there with me," is all he would say, wiping his mouth with a napkin or taking a drink of water that drained half the oversized glass. She longed to take him out of this place, away from the shadow of the city, to the beach. Across the table from her, he seemed so far away. He would go with her, she knew. Anywhere she asked.

"Tell me another story, then. Take me there. Don't tell them, tell me, only me." She said this matter of factly, with the tone of a teacher challenging a student, a tone she knew he would respond to.

And so he talked and she listened and asked questions and let him speak uninterrupted when she sensed he simply must get something out all in one rush, and she let silences fall where they must. They left the restaurant when lunch service had ended and walked the streets of the city. It was cool, and she wrapped her arms tightly around herself, burying her hands in the cuffs of her jacket. Robby, she thought for a moment, would put his coat over her shoulders, a gesture of chivalry that actually provided little relief. Alex walked on, his hands in his pockets or waving in the air around him in an effort to amplify the power of his words. He had thought there was nothing to be gained from speaking to Lenora about many of things he spoke to her about that day. He thought, in fact, that he would not be able to find the words to give people and events justice. He thought, at times, that his inadequacy betrayed the memory, and he told her this too.

That was to be their last full day together. She would be leaving to go to London in the morning, where she would spend some time with Robby's family, and then wed in late spring.

That night he dreamed again of the bridge. In this version, his friends did not give him stones to weigh him down. They only gave him sad smiles and shook his hand. When he jumped, he did not sink, he floated, and even when he dove down into the depths of the river, he found nothing to anchor himself there and he kept coming to the surface. His last image of this dream was seeing himself as if from a great height, as if from Lenora's view on the bridge, looking down on his body floating on its back in the water, white and shining, and like a starfish, suspended.

In the morning, he woke to the sound of a high-pitched tapping. He was sweating from his dream and his hair was wet as he lay in his bed, searching the ceiling for some explanation as to where he was and what was that sound. When it came again, it drew his face toward the window, and then he saw the source, as two small white pebbles hit the glass in quick succession.

He rose and went to the window, looking down at the grass and seeing her there, looking up at him hopefully. She was dressed in a long cotton nightgown, light blue and easy, and refreshing to him, her hair loose. The hem dipped into the early dew adorning the grass, and her white boots shined from the wetness. He still wore the pants he had on the day prior, and he pulled out a shirt, slipped into shoes, forgetting the socks, ran into the bathroom to splash water on his face and rinse his mouth, then he was downstairs and outside in the biting, barely-lit morning.

She was smiling, but her forehead was wrinkled. He remembered then that she was leaving the town today for the city. She wanted him to take her. He got his coat, said not a word to his mother or sister, and walked silently with her to her house at the end of the road, where she took his hand instead of leaving him in the foyer to wait, and pulled him, gently with her to her room, up the stairs and passed Henry's room. Though the door was closed, she anticipated him, and looking back, she moved her hand from his hand to his chin, keeping him focused on her and their silent move through the sleeping house. In her room, she gestured with her hand to the bed, and he sat on it, for the first time in his life. He did not care about the color of the blanket, the paint on the walls, the size or manner of the furnishings. He looked only at her body as she swiftly removed her clothes and donned new ones with little self-consciousness. She was never entirely naked before him; when her nightgown was removed, she wore beneath it a tight white lace chemise that she did not remove. Still, he had never seen her in less, not even at the shore, and he wished she would stay just like that for longer, but she was in a hurry. She slowed when she could, pulling her lavender cotton stockings up, feeling her face redden as she bent over to smooth the gathered material over her ankle and up past her knees. He did not move. Adding to the lace which clung to her angular, athletic frame, she added a mint green blouse with pearl buttons, and a dark green felt skirt that fell straight to her ankles and skimmed the top of cream colored boots. He looked at every detail of her clothes as they covered her body, then he looked at her back when she sat at the vanity and fixed her hair and ran her hands on her cheeks. She glanced at him in the mirror for long moments, at his body filling the space in her mirror as if the room around them was no longer. His hands were relaxed, at his sides, and when she stood up at last, ready, he sat still looking at her felt skirt in front of him, at the waistband where her shirt tucked in, at the gapping fabric between the two lowest shirt buttons that gave him the smallest glimpse of the chemise underneath. He lifted his hands to her waist and held her in front of him firmly, feeling the bones that made her most enticing curve, feeling the softness of the felt and her under his fingers. He leaned forward and rested his forehead against her, against the waistband, pulling her off balance. She steadied herself and placed her hands on the back of his head, feeling his growing, damp hair slide through her fingers as she stroked his neck. He breathed in deeply and concentrated hard on remembering her nearness. She wanted him to pull her down with him on the bed, and of course he wanted this too, but he did not. She stepped back and he rose.

"My bag is downstairs by the door," she whispered. "You don't mind driving? Just to the underground. Then we can take the tube the rest of the way."

He nodded, and when he followed her down the hallway to the stairs, his eyes did not veer from the three buttons that bound her skirt together at the small of her back. While they drove toward the city, he concentrated on the road, as he had not been in a car in more than a year, and the route was not familiar. He could sense that she regarded him from the passenger's seat as carefully as he had her earlier in her room. They did not speak about anything that mattered. The sky was lightening and people, mostly men in dark suits and bowlers, were streaming down their steps and crowding the sidewalks and the roads as the hour grew later and they neared the city.

They boarded the subway at the start of the underground line of the Metropolitan Rail. Alex made no objections to accompanying Lenora all the way to her new home, though the thought of being underground made him visibly nervous. His mouth parched as they descended the stairs toward the ticket station. Lenora noticed that he stepped closer to her. This was his first ride on an underground train, and only now, as they bought their tickets, did it occur to her that he might not like it. The townhome she shared with Robby was at the end of the line, near the London Bridge terminus, then a short walk, and then he would have to return alone.

The car they boarded was packed full of morning commuters, and they stood nearly as close together as they had in her room. Her back was toward him, her face to the door, watching the signs in the station go by until it there was just a gray blur outside the window, then darkness. He stared hard at the back of her head, just below his eye-level, searching for some indication of a transformation in her that would save them both from what had happened to them and what was coming. For the first time he just looked straight at her and saw her for what she was, all her human frailty apparent in the gentle slope of the back of her head, the hollow where her spine joined her skull, at the fading brightness of her brown hair and the subtle differences in shade from strand to strand. At pieces that were broken and uncontrolled, at the effort put into learning and executing the French twist. He stared hard at the collar of her coat and at the woven, multi-color threads that from a distance or to the disinterested eye appeared a uniform periwinkle, but to him swam with dark and light blues, purples, and roses. The coat smelled new and she had worn it for him. The unlined wool irritated her neck and her skin bloomed red where it rubbed.

He stared so intently at all of the humanness at the back of her head that he felt he could see right through to her face, so that he saw her smile before she turned her head and it appeared before him.

He stood so close she could smell his skin and see the sweat over his lip and on his forehead as the train followed its track down, down through the tunnel. His legs were apart and braced, and she could sense the tenseness that charged through his body, keeping it rigid. The fingers of his left hand only grazed the overhead railing for balance in a show of control and nonchalance, but the sweat betrayed his nerves. She couldn't understand all the reasons why, but she knew he was struggling to hold himself together for her, and so she withheld all the glib remarks and toying criticisms that once might have risen to her lips and struggled herself to do something she had never done for him. She stared, with no distractions or obstructions, into his clear blue eyes that saw everything, and she kept her gaze level and steady and refused to look away.

As it had for thousands of trips, the train charged out of the darkness of the underground and met the overland tracks in a near seamless exchange. For the passengers engulfed in sizzling white light, the transition was not as easy. The light of an overcast day seemed intensely bright to those grown accustomed to dimness and artificial illumination. Their eyes would adapt, soon enough, without conscious thought or application of effort.

"This is the end of the line," she said as they lurched to a stop. The doors groaned open and bodies around them rose on cue and funneled through the narrow space.

"Mind the gap," he said to her without irony and almost soundlessly. She stepped forward and peered over the edge of the subway car at the dark gray space between her and the platform. The ring she removed from her finger disappeared just as quietly as his voice into the void when she dropped it.

"If we stay, the train will go back in a few moments. Let's stay," she said, though it sounded like a question. He hadn't moved from his spot, and she returned to him while around her everyone moved on.

I don't know what happened to Alex and Lenora once the car doors closed and the train headed back out of the station, the way it had come, any more than I know what happened to my boy, Jack. Any more than Alex knew with certainty what happened to any of those he had loved who had been lost in the war. Speaking with him for the time that I did showed me how little I knew of anything, really, until I began to doubt that I even remembered our meetings or the details of his convalescence accurately. I would look through the piles of papers I'd assembled to sort it out, but after a while, they became disorganized and separated, and I would fill in the gaps until I wasn't even sure if I was recalling the details of Alex's life or imagining Jack's. I remembered telling Alex, before his surgery, "You've done enough", but his face when I said that looked so much like my boy's that this had to have been a dream.

I must stop myself here and confess that I am telling a fairy tale or writing a fiction. A projection, really, of a future that did not happen and could not have happened. No one stays on the train; no one turns away from the wedding and the secure life. None of us actors ever really depart from the script. Lenora did marry Robby. I know because I treat her now, one of those middle-aged women who can't work out why they are so tired and unhappy and dissatisfied with their lives. When Alex was released from Swansea, I escorted him because he could not walk on his own legs. The surgery had gone bad, and he never walked again, nor did he speak. I took him by train to a station in London where he was met by his mother and uncle. It was the least I could do for him.

Lenora had told him of her engagement to a barrister from London named Robby when he had visited for his respite after being shot in the shoulder. Foster was still alive. The dreams Alex had about plunging off the bridge he wrote about while he was in Swansea, awaking nearly every night as wet as if he had jumped into the Thames, or into the shell crater to help Parrish pull out his friend Lowe.

Lenora last visited Alex on August 4, 1919, the fifth anniversary of the start of the war, but when he looked at her vacantly, she was certain he could not recognize her, and she thought it might be best. She hoped he had forgotten everything, but his little sister, Lizzie, who'd become a young woman while no one looked on, crouched by his chair, head tilted toward him, as if she were listening to him tell a story, and when Lenora had entered the room, she hadn't liked the look she received from the girl.

I've told you too much already. Revealed too much of myself. But this is the modern way—we've gone from a time not long ago when we revealed next to nothing of ourselves to this: a time when we reveal everything, willingly, happily, but nothing of substance. It hardly matters, this strategy we adopt of getting along in our lives…the end is always the same despite our sense of superiority to our past selves. Even the most shocking and heartfelt revelations fade before our eyes like the grin of the Cheshire cat, disembodied and diaphanous, leaving no lasting impression. Look at me, I haven't even told you my name, and his, of course, was a play on the name of a real girl who was transformed into a character. And if you ask me for that information, if you even ask, 'did you, after all, construct some meaningful recollection of your son's life?' I will smile vaguely, shuffling through my papers, pretending I hadn't heard the question.

But I still think about him whenever I travel to a new city, whether it's London or Paris or Berlin or New York. I marvel at the mammoth buildings glinting like teeth in the blinding sun and the tunnels pulling people en masse to their workspaces and I think despondently of battlefields and beaches and progress. Sometimes, when I ride an underground train, I'll watch the vacant-eyed men, veterans, no doubt, of that first great war of the century, blending with the disinterested older ones and the blank faced younger ones, and I will imagine the hundreds of conversations going on in their heads, what this one wishes he had said to his wife, what that one believes he should tell his boss, and what this one must say to himself to get through the day. Nothing rises to the surface; the only sounds are of the train click clacking over the track rhythmically.

When we get to a stop, I'll watch them depart the cars in a crush, seeping to the doors and through the station gates, where they separate wordlessly into human currents drifting without purpose or passion toward routine destinations that fulfill their unsworn social contracts, thinking only of today and never of yesterday. And when they arrive at their destinations, I know that they scarce give a thought to how they got there and, when tomorrow arrives, they will greet it, always, with alarm.

Author's note: This book relies heavily upon images, themes, and ideas present in Lewis Carroll's *Alice's Adventures in Wonderland and Through the Looking-Glass* and at times uses words and phrases directly from these writings. It's the central conceit of the story: filling in the details of a life with a familiar storyline, making sense of the unimaginable by relying on fictions!

The edition used most frequently in the creation of this book is the 2004 Everyman paperback edition with an introduction by Penelope Lively.

All poems and illustrations in *Nothing Beside Remains* are from this book and from the website *Lenny's Alice in Wonderland Site*, found at http:// www.alice-in-wonderland.net/alice2a.html which features a vast collection of illustrations by John Tenniel, not all of which appear in the Everyman 2004 edition.

Paul Fussell's *The Great War and Modern Memory* was the catalyst for *NBR*. Read it for a fascinating look at the images, themes, and ideas that emerge in the writing of men (and some women) involved in WWI and how their recorded experiences echo the trials, troubles, and transformations of Alice.